A FRENCH INHERITANCE

JENNIFER BOHNET

Boldwood

First published in Great Britain in 2025 by Boldwood Books Ltd.

Copyright © Jennifer Bohnet, 2025

Cover Design by Debbie Clement

Cover Images: Shutterstock

A CIP catalogue record for this book is available from the British Library.

Paperback ISBN 978-1-83678-087-8

Large Print ISBN 978-1-83678-088-5

Hardback ISBN 978-1-83678-086-1

Trade Paperback ISBN 978-1-80635-306-4

Ebook ISBN 978-1-83678-089-2

Kindle ISBN 978-1-83678-090-8

Audio CD ISBN 978-1-83678-081-6

MP3 CD ISBN 978-1-83678-082-3

Digital audio download ISBN 978-1-83678-083-0

This book is printed on certified sustainable paper. Boldwood Books is dedicated to putting sustainability at the heart of our business. For more information please visit https://www. boldwoodbooks.com/about-us/sustainability/

Boldwood Books Ltd, 23 Bowerdean Street, London, SW6 3TN

www.boldwoodbooks.com

'Love is like a tree, it grows of its own accord,
    It puts down deep roots into our whole being.'

— VICTOR HUGO

1

FIVE YEARS AGO

Elliot Belgrave stood in the middle of the farmyard that apparently formed the heart of his older brother's newest business venture in the countryside behind Cannes in the South of France and shook his head.

'Adam, you can't be serious about turning this into a desirable expensive property complex,' he said before turning to look again at the various buildings that were littered around.

He assumed they had all been outbuildings of the original fifty-hectare farm, but now they were basically ruins. Some had roofs, some were open to the elements. Windows were broken, doors missing and broken terracotta roof tiles were strewn everywhere.

All were covered in foliage, mainly ivy, making it impossible to judge how bad a condition they were truly in. The stable block situated a little way from the main complex looked to be in a similarly distressed condition. The old farmhouse itself, standing at the head of the farm driveway overlooking the desolation, had survived the last two decades in a better condition. Its roof was still intact and all its doors and windows were in place unbroken but with only flakes left of the olive green paint that had once covered the doors, window frames and shutters.

Elliot turned to his sister-in-law. 'Lucy, I know it's too late, you've already bought the farm, but can't you talk him out of this madcap scheme? Put the place back on the market? I know he's an experienced builder and good at it, but he's never tackled a project as big as this before.'

Lucy smiled and shook her head. 'I tried. Believe me, I tried. But in the end I agree with Adam. To rescue this sad place, to bring it to life again would be a good thing to do. So together this is what we will do.' She pointed at the farmhouse. 'The house itself had been lived in until about a year ago when the old couple who owned the estate died. Parts of it date from the early eighteen hundreds, but thankfully it isn't listed and Adam has promised me we'll do the essentials in there first – update the kitchen, put a modern bathroom in, and sort out a bedroom for us and one the girls can use when they visit, to make life easier before we start to rebuild everything else. In the meantime, we are camping out in two of the rooms. I've put you in what will be the girls' room on a camp bed.'

'How do the girls feel about this place? Have they seen it yet?'

'They've seen the estate agent's brochure so know there's a lot of work to do, but they haven't visited yet,' Lucy said. 'I think, like me, they've simply accepted it as Adam's midlife crisis project.' She smiled at Elliot.

'Is that how you feel about it?' he asked quietly.

'No, for me it's more empty-nest syndrome and something for us to tackle together. Besides, who doesn't like the thought of living on the French Riviera?'

'Can you afford to do it though? It's going to cost a hell of a lot of euros.'

Adam sighed. 'Come on, bro, give me some credit for planning stuff and making sure there's enough money in the pot. As well as these buildings, there are three or four more cottages spread throughout the land. The plan is to have at least a couple of them renovated within the first three years and rent them out and then that will slowly finance the rest of the project. If the worst happens and money becomes too tight, we can sell them on individually. Re-establishing the vineyard, renovating and renting some of these outbuildings to local artisans' – he gestured at the ruins clustered around the driveway where they were standing – 'is also in the plan to bring an income in.'

'Establishing a *pépinière* is in the plans too,' Lucy added. 'People like buying trees, shrubs and down here decorative olive trees for their villas.'

'We've also got a secret project in the pipeline which we can't talk about yet – something that's quite new in the South of France.' Adam smiled and tapped the side of his nose.

'So secret you can't tell me?' Elliot asked.

'You'll be the first to know when it's sorted, I promise. Be a couple of years before we can do that, I suspect.'

'And we're going to do YouTube videos showcasing how we're doing things,' Lucy interrupted. 'If we can get enough people interested in following our progress week by week, that will bring in some money.'

'You make it sound so feasible, so easy, but...' Elliot shook his head again.

Adam put his arm around his wife's shoulders. 'You know how much we both love this part of France and want to live here and now seems to be the right moment to do something like this. The girls are off living their own lives now they've finished uni. Neither of us want to spend the rest of our lives regretting not stepping out of our comfort zone and doing something different.'

'But you could lose everything.' Elliot said.

'But we could end up with something so much more. Think of this place as our pension fund. Fifteen years down the line and this complex will be worth a lot more than it is today.'

'And it could just as easily be totally worthless and you've lumbered yourself with a huge debt. Let's face it, most of these buildings look like they are ready to crash down to the ground.' Elliot waved his arm at the ruins. 'I'm sorry if I sound pessimistic here. I'm just trying to be realistic – you're taking such a huge gamble.'

Adam gave his brother an exasperated look. 'I get that it's not something you and Robyn would ever consider, but Lucy and I will make it work. We're a good team. So if you could find it in your heart to wish us well even though you do not share our passion for the place or see our vision, that would be good. If I could persuade you to pick up a hammer and knock down a few walls whilst you're here, that would be even better.'

Elliot smothered a sigh. The phrase 'we're a good team' had cut through his thoughts. Married for twenty-five years, Adam and Lucy had a great marriage. Whereas he and Robyn... Elliot gave himself a mental shake, now was not the time to allow his thoughts to run wild down that particular route, before smiling at Adam and Lucy.

'Okay, I'll push all my worries over this place to one side and wish you both good luck – or should I say *bonne chance*? I'll even come and give you a hand when I can. Starting now. Where's that hammer?'

Elliot didn't add that he'd welcome the chance to vent his anger and frustration on something. It might help him to become calmer before he talked to them and asked their advice about the state of his marriage, which he planned to do over a glass of wine later.

2

PRESENT DAY

The incongruity of two major life events happening on the same day didn't immediately register with Briony. When an American company had taken over Raise Your Hand Auctions a few weeks ago and serious talk about redundancies had become a coffee-break topic, she'd had something else on her mind. Her impending divorce. She'd sat through the necessary legal meetings with the new bosses, looked at the redundancy figure she was entitled to, put the date of her final day at work in the diary and tried to think hopefully about the future which would begin once her divorce was finalised. Who would have guessed that her decree absolute would have landed in her life on the same day as her final day at work?

Briony and her best friend at work, Maeve from accounts, walked out of the building for the last time, holding their few belongings. As the doors with their over-the-top Fort Knox-security-type system slammed behind her, Briony flinched. Shut out forever.

'Commiseration coffee?' Maeve said, nodding in the direction of the café where they habitually got their lunch sandwiches.

Briony nodded and followed Maeve across the road and into the café.

The two of them sipped their coffees, both deep in their own thoughts.

'A decent reference, but six months' pay isn't going to go far,' Maeve said resignedly.

'You're a good accountant, you ran the accounts department brilliantly. I know you'll be snapped up once word gets around that you're available,' Briony said.

Maeve shrugged. 'Hope so. Both kids are off to college soon and you know how much that costs parents these days.'

Briony did know, but only because it had been a major concern of Maeve's for weeks now. Perhaps it was a small mercy now that she was divorced and as much as she had longed for a family, babies had never been on the agenda for Marcus. She gave Maeve a sympathetic smile before taking a last sip of her coffee and replacing the mug on the table.

'They say things happen in threes, don't they? I did wonder what the third disaster was going to be for me after Granny Giselle dying and my divorce. Turned out to be redundancy. And guess what arrived earlier this morning? My decree absolute.'

'Well that's good, isn't it?'

'Yes. I should be celebrating, but...' Briony shrugged.

'Oh Briony.' Maeve reached out a hand and touched Briony's briefly. 'I know the last few months have been hard for you, but you are better off without Marcus in the long term. Your gran was in her eighties, and you say she'd had a good life. As for this redundancy, look on it as giving you total freedom. You're free now to have a completely new beginning in both your love life and your career. You are free to do your own thing. I wish I could say the same, but there are too many responsibilities still to walk away from. Maybe once the girls finish college.'

Briony looked at her curiously. 'You're happy with Brian and the girls though, aren't you? You wouldn't change your marriage or your family life, would you?'

Maeve shook her head. 'Of course not. I wouldn't want to be without either of them. But I would like to think that one day I can do something different. Ever had a holiday on a narrowboat?'

'No,' Briony said, surprised at the change of subject.

'We took the girls a couple of years ago. It was wonderful. Gliding along the canal, all the wildlife, the birds, so peaceful and yet invigorating. I'd love to live like that, exploring places, meeting new people,' Maeve sighed. 'Like I said when the girls leave home, maybe I can persuade Brian to sell up and buy a canal boat.' She smiled at Briony and shrugged. 'Dreams, eh?'

Briony nodded in agreement but found herself inwardly wondering where her own dreams had gone over the last few years.

'Are you going to start job hunting straight away?' Maeve asked. 'I am.'

'Definitely. But Mum and I are supposed to be going to France to sort Granny Giselle's things out. Mum has had a letter from the French notaire and he needs a rendez-vous with her. And we also have to decide whether we want anything from the cottage before putting it on the market.'

'Your mum doesn't fancy keeping it as a holiday

home? Or even living in it full-time? Lots of people would love the opportunity to live in the South of France.'

Briony shook her head. 'She hasn't suggested it. I'd miss her if she did that, so selfishly I hope that doesn't happen. Although I suppose I could go for holidays.'

After they'd finished their coffees, they hugged each other goodbye, promised to keep in touch and Maeve set off for the bus stop whilst Briony walked slowly back to her new, meant-to-be-temporary place, deep in thought.

She'd expected that her seven-year tenure as team manager would keep her safe from redundancy. In the eight years she'd been with the auction house as well as managing her team, she'd also gained the grand-sounding title, Deputy Sales Manager. In reality, she'd organised everything for the general auctions the company held both in Bristol and the surrounding area. This was the year she'd hoped the word deputy would be lost, that she'd be awarded a pay rise and she would become the Sales Manager when Todd retired at the end of the year. The plans she'd started to think about for the rest of her life when the divorce was finalised hadn't factored in the practical necessity of finding a new job.

Briony arrived back at her current flat deep in thought. She'd taken the six-month shorthold rental lease on a furnished one-bedroom flat in a new build not far from work as a stopgap when she and Marcus had separated. Four months down the line, she still didn't think of it as a home. It was just a place to eat, sleep and go to work from. Once the divorce was done and dusted, she'd planned to get on the property ladder with a two-bedroom flat in Clifton Village with a view of the Suspension Bridge. Property brochures were piled on the bedside table. Bedtime reading that had been sending her to sleep with a happy smile dreaming of her future home. Had today scuppered her plan? It would definitely delay it – no job equalled no mortgage.

Marcus had bought the flat they'd lived in just before they were married and over the eight years they were together, she'd paid half of the mortgage. When it all fell apart, Marcus had told her bluntly that he had every intention of staying there. His fury when the divorce lawyers had worked out the sum she was entitled to in her divorce settlement was unsuppressed. Petty revenge meant that he'd got rid of the expensive state-of-the-art coffee machine that she'd treated herself to for her birthday one year before she'd had a chance to collect it.

Inside the flat, Briony placed her things on the kitchen table next to her laptop. She took out of her bag the envelope containing the decree absolute, that she'd pounced on so happily this morning telling herself, 'My new life begins today' and placed it on top of the debris from her working life. Because now that new life couldn't start.

Briony pulled out a kitchen chair and sat at the table. She needed to get organised and at least make a plan to try to kick-start job hunting and put some sort of money-saving strategy in place. She also needed to start to figure out something to do for the rest of her life. Or, at the very least, the next few months, getting back on an even keel. Of course, making appointments to view the flats she'd been eying on Rightmove wasn't going to happen now. Instead she would be scrolling through LinkedIn and other job pages on the internet.

While she waited for the laptop to boot up, she took the mobile out of her bag and called her mum. Jeannie Aubert answered almost immediately.

'Everything okay? You don't normally ring from work.'

'Last day today. I'm now officially unemployed.'

'I know you were really happy there,' Jeannie said. 'Still, looking on the bright side, you're free to have a complete change if you want to. Do something different – follow your dream. You haven't had a proper holiday for a couple of years, now you can.'

'I suppose so,' Briony said. 'But I do need to start job hunting straight away. I doubt that I'm going to find a job quickly.'

'What with your divorce and now redundancy, you deserve a break; take time to reflect, not rush into another job.'

'I had all sorts of plans for life after Marcus when the divorce was finished – new clothes, weekends in London and Paris, exploring the Louvre, seeing lots of live theatre and concerts...' Briony tailed off.

'And now you have unlimited time to do all those things,' Jeannie said. 'Starting with our visit to France. We can stay for as long as you like now.'

'But all my plans need money,' Briony let out a frustrated sigh. 'Money that I won't have if I don't have a regular income, so finding another job has to be my priority before I can even think about those plans again.'

'But you have your redundancy money,' Jeannie said. 'And what about your emergency "rainy day" fund you've been squirrelling money away in for years?'

'Oh, I can't touch that. It's my security for the future. If I blow it on holidays and clothes and enjoying myself, it won't be there for any rainy days that do happen.' Briony shook her head. 'No, I'll have to put everything on hold until I've found another job.'

There was silence for several long seconds and Briony began to wonder if the call had been disconnected when Jeannie said quietly, 'Briony, don't you think your rainy day has arrived? Losing your adored granny, a heart-breaking divorce and now redundancy, I'd call those three things a veritable rainstorm. Give yourself a break. Follow your dreams. Use your rainy-day money. Live a little.' There was a silence for several seconds. 'Right, I'm taking an executive decision on your behalf. I'm off to book our flights to France for one day next week. And then I'll ring Lucy at the farm to ask her if she has the time to air the cottage a little.'

Even as she went to protest that it was too soon, Briony realised her mum had already finished the call. Ruefully rubbing her hand across her face and accepting her mother's impetuous decision, she wandered into the sitting room and stood staring thoughtfully out at the small garden with its shrubs and benches the developers had optimistically provided as a 'community garden'. Briony had yet to set foot down there, but she could see an elderly couple sitting on one of the benches having a sandwich, enjoying the sunshine and making the most of the open space. If she didn't get a job quickly, maybe she'd have lunch down there sometimes when they got back from France.

Was this redundancy truly a rainy day in her life, like everyone seemed to regard it? In her mind, rainy days consisted of accidents that threw one into catastrophic circumstances. Being made redundant did feel like a catastrophe to her but not totally catastrophic, if that even made sense, because she knew she had enough money to survive. But if she spent the money and then couldn't get a job within, say, six months, then that would be a real catastrophe.

Her rainy-day savings were healthy, despite Marcus trying to persuade her over the years to invest in something other than Isas and bank accounts with their low interest. She'd only ever mentioned her Premium Bonds to him once, when he'd decried the zero interest they paid unless your number came up. She'd never told him when several of her numbers had come up over the years. Not with huge amounts – fifty pounds here and there, two hundred a couple of times, money she'd reinvested instantly in more bonds. He'd been keen enough to take some of them off her though when the lawyers fought over divorce assets. But realistically she knew she had enough savings to fall back on for a few months.

Thinking about her mum pointing out she was free to have a complete change if she wanted, free to follow her dream, was fine, except for one thing. Briony couldn't remember when she'd last had a desire to do something different. Definitely not in the last few years she'd been married to Marcus.

She'd enjoyed her job in the auction house where no day was alike and she met so many different people in the course of organising the sales. And she'd absorbed so much information about a wide variety of things. She was no expert, but she appreciated and knew how to recognise good workmanship when she saw it. Marcus had kept urging her to take exams, become a fully fledged auctioneer or a specialist in something, anything – porcelain, silver or even wine. 'Do you good to expand your horizons.' When she'd told him she was happy as she was, he'd muttered something about her being 'risk aversive' and stormed away from the conversation. In a light-bulb moment, she realised his comment had been true. She didn't take risks in any aspect of her life. She needed security – the security of a job, the security of money in the bank, the security of a loving marriage – except none of it had quite worked out like it was supposed to, had it?

The first of twelve loud dongs from a nearby church clock made Briony jump. Midday. Not normally home at this time, it unexpectedly reminded her of the clock tower in Granny Giselle's small village in the South of France. At this time of day, it was the signal to stop whatever you were doing and make for the village square to either enjoy a simple aperitif with friends before going home for lunch, or staying to savour the plat de jour with them in the local restaurant.

Briony smiled sadly as she remembered how Granny Giselle had often spoken affectionately of the village and her local friends there. The last eighteen months living in the UK with Jeannie, her daughter-in-law, had been necessary because of her health. Both Jeannie and Briony had done their best to give her a good happy life for her final years, but everyone knew how much Giselle missed her homeland and the dog she'd had to rehome when her health had started to fail.

To think, one day next week she and her mum would be able to join the locals in the village and enjoy a plat de jour, although undoubtedly it would feel strange to be there without Giselle. Everybody would definitely raise a glass to her.

Briony turned away from the window. A week's holiday in France would be good for both her and her mum. But before they went, she'd start to put out some feelers amongst her contacts in the auction business, because word would have surely got out about her redundancy. She knew she had a good reputation with lots of auctioneers – maybe someone would be able to offer her something. Then, when she got back, refreshed and raring to go, she would give all her attention to finding herself a brilliant new job. One that would enable her to buy her dream flat.

* * *

Jeannie Aubert put the phone down after the conversation with her daughter and ran her hand through her hair distractedly. The last few months had been a difficult time. The death of Giselle Aubert, her mother-in-law, whilst expected, had been hard for both Briony and herself. Briony had lost a beloved grandmother and Jeannie had mourned, and was still mourning, the loss of a woman she had loved liked the mother she'd lost at an early age.

From the day Jeromé had taken her home to meet his maman, she and Giselle had taken to each other and, down the years, the relationship had become even more special to both women. Briony became the centre of both their lives after Jeromé died seven years ago, leaving them as a small family unit of three, with no other relatives.

The upcoming visit to France to sort out and settle Giselle's affairs, although emotionally sad, would also be the ideal time to tell Briony the truth about her grandmother's will. Staying in a place she adored and had always loved visiting would give Briony the time and the space to come to terms with everything that had happened in the last year and the chance to plan her new future.

Poor Briony, so much had gone wrong in her life recently, Jeannie knew that she regarded this redundancy as the final straw. But, if Briony did but realise it, the timing was perfect.

And then there was her own news she needed to talk to Briony about and Jeannie couldn't help but wonder about her reaction to learning something that she, Jeannie, had been hugging to herself for a few weeks now. News that could affect both their lives.

Jeannie could only hope that things in France would work out the right way for everyone concerned and that Briony would welcome her own news when she told her.

3

ONE WEEK LATER

It was ironic really that the two letters the *La Poste facteur* had handed him that morning had arrived in the same post. One with an English stamp; the other with a French one. One with good news; one with something he had no interest in.

The English letter was from a TV company asking him to take part in a programme about veterinary practices in the UK. Elliot stared dumbfounded at the words he was reading. Were they crazy? After all he'd been through when he'd been thrown into the bear pit that was tabloid sensational investigative journalism these days, there was no way he was getting involved with anything that thrust him back into the public's gaze. Screwing up the letter and the envelope, he threw them into the log basket. He wasn't even going to deign to give them an answer. His silence would surely be telling enough.

Elliot took a deep breath and opened the French envelope. He took out the letter he'd been waiting for, with a smile on his face. After spending the last three months on an intensive French course, he'd passed the government's exam and had the confirmation that he was fluent in French and could now use his Royal College of Veterinary Surgeons qualifications and practice as a vet in France. His enforced sabbatical had come to an end. Finally, he was able to get back to the only job he had ever wanted to do. He'd already put out feelers and the overworked veterinarian clinic in the nearby small town of Pégomas had promised they would welcome his working presence in the local area as soon as he was legally cleared to work. He couldn't wait to tell them, and Adam and Lucy, the good news.

When everything in his life had started falling apart in the last year, Adam and Lucy had welcomed him to the farm, insisting that their home was his for as long as he wanted. Without them on his side, he knew he would have continued in the downward spiral that Robyn had thrust him into. He owed them both big time.

Glancing out of his cottage window, he saw Adam and Lucy, with Django, their Australian sheepdog, sitting between them, talking to the scaffolder removing the scaffolding from the old stable block, now renovated to contain two more self-contained gîtes. Elliot knew how much Adam had been looking forward to that milestone being reached.

His big brother and his wife had certainly pulled out all the stops with this building project. In the last five years, three of the smaller individual outbuildings had been rebuilt and turned into artisan workshops. Two of them were now occupied – a potter in one and a leather worker in the other. Adam was hopeful that the third one would soon be rented out to a local artist. Two cottages, including the one Elliot now lived in, had been renovated, with Lucy doing the interior design and furnishings of them both. The other cottage, which Lucy had run as a gîte for the first time last summer, had proved to be very popular and Elliot knew she was hoping for the same success this year. There was still a lot of building work to be done – the three or four cottages scattered on land further away from the farmhouse – as well as lots of land, including the small vineyard, that needed attention, but the rush to get the business off the ground had eased somewhat.

The *pépinière* Adam had been keen to establish was up and running in the field alongside the driveway with its easy access. Plants, shrubs and olive trees, with terracotta pots and garden statues also on display, were already bringing customers to the farm.

Elliot glanced down at Luna, his Weimaraner dog, who was patiently curled up in her basket, watching him for any indication that a walk might be on the cards. Now five years old, she'd needed a new home a year or two ago and Adam and Lucy had offered to take her in. Whilst Luna had been no trouble in that short time and seemed happy, she became a different dog when Elliot arrived. She was besotted with him for some reason and became his shadow and within days it was clear she regarded him as her master. Which Elliot was more than happy to accept, as were Adam and Lucy.

'Shall we go and tell them the good news?' he said now, opening the door. Luna was instantly at his side and together they made their way towards the stable block.

The last of the scaffolding had been loaded and Adam shook the hands of both the driver and the scaffolder before the lorry drove out of the farmyard.

'You look happy,' Lucy said. 'Not that you don't

normally these days, but...' She gave Elliot an apologetic look.

'I am extra happy today,' Elliot said. 'I've finally got the legal go-ahead to practise in France. *Mon Francaise c'est très bien.*'

'Oh, that is great news,' Adam said. 'Well done. We shall look to you now as our in-house language expert to help us translate all our many pages of French bureaucracy that arrive.'

'Supper tonight with us to celebrate?' Lucy said.

'Love to.'

'Right now I've got to go and open up Owls Nest Cottage. Jeannie rang to say she and her daughter are coming over to sort it out now that Giselle is no longer with us. I guess that means the cottage will be going on the market. Shame. I miss Giselle. Even though she was just minutes away via the field track, and two kilometres by road, she was our nearest neighbour.' Lucy looked at Elliot, 'You never met Giselle, did you?'

Elliot shook his head. 'No. She'd left before I arrived. I don't think it was personal.'

Lucy laughed. 'Lovely lady. Her daughter-in-law Jeannie seems lovely too. I'll catch up with you two later.'

Elliot turned to Adam. 'Luna and I are going for a walk. Any chance of you and Django joining us?'

'I was going to take the quad bike and go down to see Bruno in the vineyard. Do me good to walk instead.'

Together, the brothers began to make their way up through the farmyard, passing the farmhouse, now boasting a new front door and refreshed paint-work. Adam opened the large five-barred gate that shut the imaginatively named Top Field off from the back of the farmyard. Once in the gently sloping field, they followed the hedge along for several metres before reaching another large gate which opened into the eight-hectare field with its rows of vines.

'That's a lot of vines. Is it going as planned in the overall scheme of things?' Elliot asked, looking at the vines stretching right across the field to the bordering hedge.

'It's the most uncontrollable part of the whole project,' Adam sighed as he too looked across at the vines. 'It's going to take a lot of work between now and September if we're going to have a chance of making even a litre of wine. The original vines had been sorely neglected before we bought the place and the harvest for the last four years has been pitiful. The late summer storms last year didn't help either.'

'If you do get a harvest, how will you deal with it? I've never seen any signs of winemaking equipment on the farm.'

'Sold off years ago. Wouldn't be up to modern winemaking standards anyway,' Adam said. 'Initially, we're using the local co-op to deal with the harvest and actually producing the wine for us. I'm holding back on establishing our own winery on the farm in case the vines never recover sufficiently as wine-making equipment is horrendously expensive. I'm hopeful the new vines – Grenache Noir and Cinsault – we planted and grafted the year after we moved in will bear fruit this year. On a good note, we do have a large cave under the house that will be perfect for storing any wine that we do make.'

'Is Bruno hopeful for a good harvest this year?' Elliot knew that Adam had to rely on his vigneron's expertise.

'Won't commit one way or the other,' Adam said. '"Wine growing is in the lap of the gods" is one of his favourite sayings.'

'Let's hope God is on your side this summer then,' Elliot said. 'I'm going to walk down to the lake. See you at supper later, if not before.'

Strolling after Luna as she raced through the adjoining field of spring grass towards the boundary hedge, Elliot smiled happily to himself. Today's letter meant he could finally start to get his life back on track after all the unexpected changes life had forced on him in the last twelve months. The Robyn disaster, giving up his job in the UK, moving to France and renting one of the renovated cottages on Adam and Lucy's farm, were all things he'd never anticipated happening in his life.

As always, Luna stopped by the final boundary hedge and sniffed the air before returning to sit at Elliot's side as he stopped to take in his surroundings. Standing looking out over the French countryside bathed in sunshine under a perfect blue sky, he reflected that not all the changes had been bad. Moving to France and having Luna adopt him were two of the best. He was happier than he had been in almost a decade, especially now that he had his chosen future in front of him again.

He'd phone Julian at the veterinary clinic when he got back to the cottage, tell him the good news and hopefully start work next week.

Elliot bent down to stroke Luna's head before straightening up. 'Come on, Luna, let's get back. I've got an important phone call to make.'

4

Briony held her breath in anticipation as the plane began its descent onto the runway at Nice airport, glad that Jeannie had the window seat. That way, she could avoid looking out of the window as the sea got closer and closer. In her heart, she knew it was safe, pilots landed plane after plane here every day of the year, but she'd never get used to how narrow the runway looked from the air, or how close it was to the sea.

As the wheels touched down smoothly onto the tarmac and the aircraft slowed and taxied along the runway, Briony exhaled with relief.

Jeannie looked at her, amused. 'That landing still get to you? I love it.'

'I love flying, but this landing always scares me,' Briony admitted.

It took them longer to get through customs than Briony remembered it taking in the past. 'Still setting up the visa thing we now need in addition to our passport,' Jeannie said crossly as they finally made their way to the luggage collection point. 'So much red tape these days. Still, we need the security, I suppose.'

They both waited for their luggage to show up on the conveyor belt before walking through customs and out into the Arrivals Hall and making for the car-hire building to collect car keys.

'How lovely of them to upgrade us to a Renault 5 all electric,' Jeannie said, smiling. 'Can't wait to drive it. Come on. Let's go find it. The man said we can't miss it.'

The blue sky and the warmth from the afternoon sun as they exited the building hit them both. Briony stopped pushing the luggage trolley and took off her jacket. 'Forgotten how warm it is down here even this early in March. Right, let's find that vehicle.'

'The man was right,' Briony said, laughing a few moments later when they found the car. Bright yellow, it stood out in the rental car park filled with black and grey vehicles, like the first bright daffodil of spring.

'Ooh, I'm looking forward to driving this,' Jeannie said. 'Unless you want first go? We're both named drivers.'

'It's fine. You've had more recent experience than me driving on the wrong side,' Briony answered, relieved that she didn't have to drive a strange car immediately into the busy traffic that she knew existed outside the airport. Something which didn't seem to bother her mum at all.

Humming happily to herself and ignoring the autoroute signs, Jeannie made for the *bord de mer* and they were soon bowling along surrounded by traffic in the direction of Cannes.

'After Cannes, we'll take the scenic route up into the back country,' Jeannie said. 'Oh, it feels so good to be back down here.'

Briony glanced at her mum. 'You're looking forward to this holiday, aren't you?'

Jeannie nodded. 'I've always loved it down here. I'm sorry that Giselle is no longer with us and I know Owls Nest is going to feel strange without her there but...' She shrugged. 'It's good to be back.'

'Have you thought about keeping the cottage as a holiday home?'

'No, of course not. Besides, it's out of the question. Things are complicated.' There was a certain tightness in her mother's voice that made Briony look at her.

'Why is it out of the question? What's complicated? You're on your own. Dad's been gone for seven years. You can please yourself where you live. You could even move down here permanently if you wanted to.'

'It's not as simple as that, so much bureaucracy these days after Brexit,' Jeannie said. 'And right now it's not up for discussion. Another ten minutes and we should be turning up into the back country. Shall we have some music?' And with that, Jeannie touched the screen in front of her and Riviera Radio was playing.

Sitting there watching the Mediterranean on the left-hand side glistening in the sunshine, Briony wondered why her mum had suddenly become so uptight about keeping and using the cottage as a holiday or even as a permanent home. There had to be something she wasn't saying.

After leaving the *bord de mer* on the other side of Cannes and following the signs for Mougins, they were soon on the quieter country roads leading to Giselle's old village. The old farmhouse, built nearly two hundred years ago from local sandstone, with its red tiled roof, its shutters painted an olive green and its front door shaded by an ancient wisteria in spring and early summer was three hundred metres or so from the village. Set back from the road, there was a short driveway edged with pretty plumbago shrubs and one or two palm trees. An outbuilding on the end had been converted into a garage and Jeannie pulled up in front of it. She turned off the ignition and applied the handbrake on.

'That was fun,' she announced. 'I'm going to enjoy this car whilst we are here.'

'I'd forgotten how traditional the cottage looks,' Briony said as they got out of the car. 'I love the long shape of a traditional Provençal farmhouse.'

Jeannie held out the front door key. 'Open up and let's get our things in. I'm gasping for a cup of tea.'

Briony pushed the key in the lock and turned it. As the door opened to show the hall with its terracotta tiled floor, the old-fashioned polished coat stand with its mirror and seat, the wooden staircase with its curved steps at the bottom, she swallowed hard to stop the urge to call out 'Granny Giselle, I'm here.'

The house felt strange and empty, as if it were silently waiting to be brought back to life. Quickly, she walked through to the kitchen. On the table was a wicker basket filled with a loaf of rustic bread, some home-made palmier biscuits, tea bags, coffee, tomatoes, lettuce, a jar of olives, a packet of crisps and some local almonds. A handwritten note was propped up against the basket.

Milk, eggs, cheese, ham and a bottle of rosé are in the fridge. Do come up to the farm for coffee in the morning – about ten o'clock? No worries if you've already got plans. Lucy.

'That's so kind of Lucy,' Jeannie said, coming into the kitchen. 'She's been keeping an eye on the place since Giselle came to us. I'm looking forward to seeing how Adam has got on with dragging the farm into the twenty-first century. He took on a mammoth task.'

Briony moved across to the tap and let the cold water run for a moment before filling the kettle.

Jeannie unlocked the French doors and stepped out onto the terrace. 'Shall we drink our tea out here – it's certainly warm enough. Can't believe it's only just the second week of March.'

Five minutes later, after the two of them had pulled the terrace table and chairs out of the shed they'd been stored in, Briony made the tea, plated up the palmier biscuits and carried everything outside.

'I'd forgotten how quiet it is here,' Briony said, looking out over the garden towards the bordering fields and countryside, where she could see a lake shimmering in the sunshine.

'It's a real little oasis of peace,' Jeannie said. 'Lovely to be able to see the lake in the distance again. Adam must have had some of the trees re- moved. I know he told Giselle he planned to do some management of the woods so that she'd be able to see the lake again. She told him he'd better be careful not to destroy any trees the birds nested in.' Jeannie sighed.

'Sounds like Granny.'

'She often talked about Adam and Lucy and their plans, sad that she'd not seen many of them come to fruition before she came to live with me. One thing that did make her happy was the fact that they took on Luna.'

'That was good of them,' Briony said. 'D'you think the owls still use that hollow in the old oak tree? The one that lost a branch in a storm.' She looked towards the bottom of the garden where there were several large trees including a large mimosa and the old oak that had been struck by lightning several decades ago. 'I remember listening to them calling on several occasions when we all came for the summer holidays. Seeing a tawny owl fly across the garden late one evening was special.'

'I would hope they are still around,' Jeannie said. 'The cottage has been called Owls Nest forever, so the owls must have been here for a long time.'

'Maybe we'll hear them tonight,' Briony said. 'Do you want to go out to eat in the village this evening? Or shall we use some of the food Lucy has left us?'

'Let's eat in tonight,' Jeannie answered. 'It's been a long day. There will be plenty of time to reconnect with people and to eat in the village restaurant. I suspect the local grapevine will already have announced our presence, so people are sure to want to talk to us and offer their condolences about Granny.'

'Okay. Ham and cheese salad tonight, washed down with a glass or two of rosé out here in the garden.' Briony stood up. 'I'm going to unpack, have a shower and then go for a walk, suss out the lake.'

'You can go through the field. You remember where the gate in the hedge is?'

Briony nodded as she gathered up the mugs and plates before taking them into the kitchen.

Jeannie watched Briony disappear indoors before letting worry over a certain matter take over her thoughts. Now she was here in the cottage, she was beginning to rethink the plan she'd made. The plan that had seemed a good idea now felt stupid – wrong even. It wasn't going to be any easier here, like she'd hoped, than it would have been back home. She hadn't even mentioned the appointment she'd made with the notaire for a couple of days' time. She knew the questions would start immediately after she mentioned that. Maybe she could just say the notaire needed some papers signed and let him break the news.

No, it was her responsibility to tell Briony herself, like Giselle had wanted. But she knew whenever, whoever, told her the true situation, Briony was sure to be upset on Jeannie's behalf and would probably be overwhelmed at first by the decisions she had to face making. Jeannie could only hope and pray that she would make what she and Giselle both considered to be the right one. When the dust had settled, she also had to find the right moment to broach the other subject that was playing on her mind.

5

With a vague memory that the path to and around the lake had often been muddy in the past, Briony pulled on a pair of her old wellingtons that she'd left at the cottage years ago before setting off on her walk. The gate in the hedge at the bottom of the garden was stiff from non-use, but after the second or third try, Briony managed to push it open. She made sure the gate closed firmly behind her, hoping it would be easier to open on her way back. Walking carefully along the track that stretched the length of the field, thirty-year-old memories of running along here with the grandchildren of the old couple in the big house surfaced in her mind. She didn't remember the vineyard that surrounded the field on three sides being so big and well tended, though.

Approaching the lake, she could see where Adam had cleared saplings and shrubs from around the edge of the water and also taken down some trees to open up the surrounding area. There was a small rowing boat tied to a jetty sticking out into the lake that Briony didn't remember ever being there. Imagine the fun she could have had as a child, learning to row and rowing the boat out to the middle of the lake and staying there, drifting in the silence. If she'd ever learnt to row she'd do that right now, but sadly she'd never learnt. She did remember swimming in the lake one hot summer, though. The water would definitely be too cold for that on this visit. Besides, she hadn't brought a swimming costume.

Adam, the new owner, had clearly thought about the wildlife – the trees had been cut up and left in a couple of piles, providing shelter for hedgehogs and other creatures. Bird boxes had been fixed to a few of the beech and oak trees and Briony smiled as she saw a blue tit flying back and forth with nest-building material. The whole area was a mini nature reserve.

A bench had been placed near a weeping willow tree and Briony happily sat down and surveyed the scene before her. Her mum was going to adore this when she saw it.

Jeannie had been really happy on the flight over, driving the car here super excited, but after that short conversation about keeping the cottage for holidays or even living in permanently, she'd been uptight, less joyful. Now they were here, was she worried about emptying the cottage of Granny Giselle's things? There had clearly been so much she'd been unable to take to England with her. It wasn't going to be easy, Briony knew that, these things never were. But doing it together would hopefully make it less painful for her mum. Perhaps she'd try to get her to talk about it before they started. Get her to open up a bit.

Briony jumped with shock as a large silvery grey dog suddenly appeared from nowhere and head-butted her legs.

'Luna?' she gasped, stroking the dog's head. 'Where have you sprung from?' Briony looked up just as the man reached the bench.

'I'm so sorry. Glad you were sitting down, she might have had you over otherwise. She doesn't normally rush at strangers like that. Luna, come here.'

The dog reluctantly left Briony and stood at the man's side, her eyes watching Briony's every move.

'Maybe she recognised me? You must be Adam,' Briony said, standing up and holding out her hand. 'It's lovely to meet you. I'm Briony, Giselle's granddaughter. Thank you for keeping an eye on the cottage and big thanks for looking after Luna. She's clearly very happy with you.' Briony smiled.

'I'm Elliot, Adam's brother,' Elliot said, shaking her hand and letting it go quickly.

'Oh, sorry, my mistake. I knew Adam had taken Luna in and assumed you were he as I have yet to meet him...' Her voice trailed away. 'But Luna obviously likes you too.'

'She's my dog now, not Adam's,' Elliot said slowly and deliberately. 'For some reason, when I arrived she became my shadow. We're inseparable these days,' he added with a self-conscious half shrug. 'She comes everywhere with me.'

'A case of love me, love my dog?' Briony joked, her smile fading as she saw the look on Elliot's face. 'That's good. Um, I hope Adam won't mind me being here – technically, I suppose I'm trespassing. It's a lovely spot he's created. Totally different to when I played here thirty years ago. The new jetty is a lovely addition.' Embarrassed, she could feel herself jabbering away in an effort to change the subject.

'I'm pretty certain Adam will expect you and your

mother to enjoy the lake whilst you are here,' Elliot said. 'I'd better get back. Nice to meet you, Briony. We'll probably bump into each other again whilst you're here – I'll make sure Luna behaves next time.'

Briony watched as Elliot turned and strolled away, Luna trotting at his side. Once they were out of sight, she began to walk back the way she'd come. The dog clearly adored him and Elliot had definitely been making sure that she realised he was now the owner of Luna. Was he worried that she or her mother would want to have the dog after all this time? He'd certainly taken off quickly once he'd got his message over. Didn't hang around to make small talk with her. Maybe her 'love me, love my dog' comment had upset him? Next time she saw him, she would attempt to reassure him that they wouldn't dream of trying to claim Luna as theirs. Their lives in England were incompatible with having a dog. Hopefully putting that into words would be enough to banish any lasting doubts he might be harbouring and even bring a smile to his face.

Back at the cottage, she found Jeannie on the terrace reading a paperback, a glass of rosé on the table in front of her. 'Sorry, I couldn't resist opening the bottle. It's lovely, cold and delicious. How was your walk?'

'I'll just get a glass of rosé and tell you,' Briony said. 'Shall I organise some food as well?'

'Pour your wine and come and sit down. We'll get supper together in a bit. It's still early.'

'*Santé*,' Briony said, returning with a glass of rosé a few moments later. 'It's lovely being back here but so strange without Granny here. It's hard.'

'Yes, it is hard. But don't you feel that her very essence, her spirit if you will, still lingers here? She loved this cottage so much. I keep expecting to see her in the kitchen every time I walk in,' Jeannie said quietly. 'I have so many memories of her teaching me how to prepare and cook meals like a true French wife.'

'She was a brilliant hostess too. Loved having friends come for lunch – and stay for supper.' Briony smiled. 'You must walk down to the lake soon. It's been turned into a beautiful oasis. There's a rowing boat tied to a small jetty too – wish I could row. There's a bench there in a perfect position to sit and watch the birds. The next time I walk down, I must remember to take my phone and take some photos.'

'Have you brought your Nikon as well?' Jeannie asked.

Briony shook her head. 'I've got out of the habit of using the camera. My iPhone takes such good pictures.' Briony took a drink of her wine. 'Guess who came bounding up to me down there? Luna. I think she actually remembered me, even though she hasn't seen me for a few years. She's grown into a lovely dog.'

'You've met Adam then?'

'No. His brother Elliot was walking her. He made it quite clear that Luna is his dog now; apparently they are inseparable.' She glanced at her mother. 'Did you meet him when you came to see Granny before she moved over to be with us? He seemed nice enough but a bit...' she hesitated. 'Not unfriendly but reserved.'

Jeannie shook her head. 'Adam did mention a brother on one occasion, but our visits never coincided. Maybe we'll see him tomorrow morning when we go up for coffee.'

Later, as the two of them ate their ham and cheese salad supper before having an early night, Briony found her thoughts returning to Elliot. There had been a certain uneasy air about him when they were talking. Her unexpected presence down by the lake had made him uncomfortable for some reason. Was he shy? Or was it just Luna's reaction to her that had unsettled him? Either way, Briony hoped that the next time they met it wouldn't feel so awkward.

6

Briony left the bedroom curtains open and the window ajar when she went to bed that first night, hoping to hear an owl or two. She didn't hear any owls, but woke in the morning to the sound of the dawn chorus. She lay there listening, wishing she could attribute more of the songs to the individual birds. There was definitely a blackbird in there and a chaffinch.

Apart from the birdsong, it was quiet. No traffic noise. No neighbours. No police sirens in the distance. So different from Bristol, where, depending on the atmospherics, there was nearly always some sort of low background traffic hum.

Briony lay on her back looking at the faded solar

system her dad had stuck to the ceiling many years ago. The room's wallpaper had been changed over the years, but the ceiling had remained untouched. She remembered her excitement watching her dad stick all the stars, the moon and the planets in their places and had asked for the same for her bedroom ceiling at home. But for some reason that had never happened.

As the birdsong died away and it grew lighter as the sun rose, Briony threw off the duvet and made for the bathroom, thinking about the day ahead. Coffee with Lucy up at the farm this morning, possibly lunch in the village after buying some food supplies and then maybe Jeannie would want to start sorting things out. That's what they were here for after all, so a busy day to look forward to.

When she walked into the kitchen, her mum was already there, coffee made and fresh croissants on the table.

'This looks good,' Briony said, pulling out a chair.

'I was up early and walked into the village,' Jeannie explained. 'The boulangerie is now run by a young generation of the DuBois family – still as good though,' and she poured Briony a coffee.

'You planning on walking into the village every morning?'

Jeannie smiled. 'Probably not. Today I need to talk to you and I wanted to clear my head with a walk first.'

'Is something wrong?' Briony glanced at her mother, concerned.

'No. I simply have to explain something. And to tell you about Granny Giselle's last wishes. It's something that I should have talked about after I received the notaire's letter, but Granny Giselle had asked me to wait until we were over here. I think she felt that being in the cottage would bring back good memories and inspire you to really think about your future.'

Briony waited as her mother pulled a croissant apart before taking a sip or two of coffee.

'I agreed to wait because I naively thought it would be easier to do once we were here. Turns out to be just as difficult as it would have been back home.'

Jeannie took a deep breath.

'There are two things I need to tell you. First, the bit that is straightforward and which I knew already but you probably did not realise. French inheritance law is uncomplicated in one major way only: property goes from parents to their children. In Granny Giselle's case, sadly her only son, your dad, died before her, and there are no other relatives who have a claim.' Jeannie paused and looked at Briony. 'The truth is you have inherited Owls Nest from Granny Giselle, not me. Giselle couldn't leave it to me, even though I was her daughter-in-law. You are her closest direct descendant, therefore, legally, the cottage passes to you.'

Jeannie picked up her cup and drank her coffee before pushing the empty cup away.

'The second thing I have to tell you is, Granny told me exactly what she would like, and what she hoped, you would do, when she was gone.' Jeannie exhaled a breath slowly. 'Before we discuss her wishes – how do you feel knowing that the cottage is now yours?' She smiled questioningly at Briony.

'Stunned,' Briony said. 'I'd always assumed Granny would leave it to you, and then in the future you'd probably leave it to me...' Her voice trailed away.

Jeannie nodded her understanding.

'But why didn't Granny talk to me before she died? Tell me herself whatever it is she's told you.'

'She was going to talk to you the weekend you came home and told us about the divorce; then it didn't seem the right time. She was so cross about the way Marcus treated you.'

'Granny was never his greatest fan, was she? And, to be fair, she turned out to be right.' Briony took a deep breath. 'So what does she hope I do about the cottage?'

'A few things. She hoped you wouldn't sell it – although, of course, you are free to do that if you wish. She wanted you to live in it, although Granny did realise that your current job would initially prevent that – but now there is no job.' Jeannie gave her daughter an ironic look before carrying on. 'If you decide you can't move here permanently, she wanted you to at least come to stay. Use it like the holiday home you suggested to me.'

Jeannie paused.

'She also had another idea. This one makes me feel particularly awkward putting it into words as it concerns me, and I completely understand if you don't want this to happen and say an outright no to it.' Jeannie bit her bottom lip anxiously. 'If you can't live in it, rather than sell it, Giselle said she would like you to let me move over and take care of the place.'

Silence followed her words as Briony stared at her mother.

'Is that something you would like to do?' she asked finally.

Jeannie nodded. 'I'd sell up in the UK, apply for a resident's visa and move into Owls Nest and be very happy. Look after it for you, maintain it, do the garden – anything that was necessary, so it wouldn't be a burden on you. And, of course, you could come whenever you wanted.' Jeannie pushed her chair back and, standing up, took the coffee mugs over to the sink. 'Giselle might have made the suggestions I have just told you about, but they are not a legal re-quirement of her will. You can do what you like with the cottage – although Giselle did hope you wouldn't put it up for sale immediately – if ever. I do know that Giselle truly believed living here in France would be a good life for you. And I know that is what she hoped you would decide to do. So promise me that you will at least think about it.'

7

'I promise I won't make a habit of leaving Luna with you,' Elliot said as Lucy handed him a bacon sandwich. 'It's just this first day I'm supposed to be shadowing Julian and I'm not sure where exactly this shadowing is going to take me. Might be all day in the clinic, might be out and about, and I don't want to have to leave Luna in the car for hours.'

'It's not a problem,' Lucy said. 'You forget this kitchen was her home before you turned up, and Django loves having her here. Jeannie and Briony are coming for coffee this morning and I know Jeannie at least will love seeing Luna. I haven't met Briony yet.'

'Luna has already greeted and been greeted by Briony with open arms down by the lake.'

'What's she like?'

'She seems... nice. A sensible sort. But not too sensible.'

Lucy glanced at her brother-in-law sharply. 'I take that "sensible" to mean she wasn't tottering about on high heels down by the lake?' Lucy had never forgotten the one and only time Robyn had visited the farm with Elliot, dressed like a fashion plate, right down to her Louboutin heels.

'Blue wellington boots with rainbows on them.' Elliot remembered, suppressing a smile. He'd seen the boots while Briony was petting and talking to Luna. Practical but fun.

Lucy looked at him thoughtfully. 'Jeannie mentioned that her daughter had just gone through a bitter divorce and was depressed. Maybe you—'

Elliot swiftly swallowed the last of the bacon sandwich and turned to leave. 'Thanks again, I'll see you later. Luna, be good.'

'Good Luck,' Lucy called out as he disappeared.

Elliot had known without the words being spoken where Lucy was going with her comment. Lately, she seemed to be making it her mission in life to find him a new, better, wife than the one he'd divorced. Useless to protest that, a) he didn't want another wife, and b) he had no intention of ever getting close to a woman again.

Opening the door of his Toyota Outlander, he double-checked that his emergency medical kit that he routinely carried was in place before he turned the engine on. At the same time, he switched the thoughts in his head off and his brain into work mode. It was such a relief to be getting back to do the job he lived for. When he was in work persona, he was the respected vet he'd worked so hard to become, a safe outward version of who he truly wanted to be. Rather than the man who'd lost everything at the hands of a scheming woman.

* * *

Lucy stood leaning against the bar of the big cooking range, drinking from a large mug of tea and watching Adam devour the pile of toast that she'd made. Breakfast and supper were the two times of day when they could both be sure of having time to talk and discuss things.

'Elliot get off all right?' Adam asked between slices. 'Big day for him.'

'One he's been looking forward to for some time,' Lucy said. 'His biggest worry was leaving

Luna behind, but he knows she's happy with us – and Django likes the company.' She laughed, looking across to where both dogs were curled up in the extra-large dog basket together. She took her phone out of her pocket and took a couple of pictures of the dogs. 'I need to start to put a new video together today and tomorrow – are you doing anything I can film today? Haven't really got a lot of footage since the major renovations finished. I thought I'd showcase the gîte cottage and possibly Bruno down in the vineyard, although I know he's not keen.'

Their YouTube channel had been a hit with viewers from almost day one and had become a useful source of income for them over the years and their subscribers had now reached almost half a million. Lucy was afraid, though, that their viewers would drift away if she didn't continue to put out interesting content.

'How about a quick walk around our not-so-secret project now that it's finally underway and there's actually something to show?' Adam suggested.

'Good idea. We need to get the word out, even though we're still a few years away before we have anything to sell.' Lucy gave Adam a speculative look. 'You happy to go on camera and explain what and why we've invested in this particular product? Rather than me doing a voiceover as I walk.'

Adam pulled a face. 'You know how much I hate being on camera, but I suspect for this I need to explain our reasons. Can't do today. Tomorrow morning?'

Lucy nodded.

'The stables are looking good too now the renovations are complete. Going to need your magic touch on the decor – maybe do a couple of shots of the bare rooms before you start explaining the plans you have?'

'I'll do that,' Lucy said. 'But I think the videos are slowly becoming more about our lifestyle in France now all the banging and hammering is slowing down. Are you happy with that?'

'Think so. Wouldn't want them to be too invasive, though,' Adam said. 'I know people love to see behind the scenes, but we do need to keep some privacy. And don't forget we've still got the cottages further down on the farm to renovate, so there will be more building work going on this summer.'

Lucy nodded. 'It was easier when all the major rebuilding work was happening – there was so much of it to show people! Think I'll cut back to a thirty-minute video once a week this summer, rather than two a week like I've been doing. I should be able to film enough interesting content for that.'

Adam stood up. 'Right. Talking about those cottages, I need to get down there and assess what building materials we need and how much of everything to make a start on one of them. Be good to get it underway this summer.'

'I'll walk the dogs and then make a couple of cakes – one for the freezer and one for Jeannie and Briony this morning.' Lucy reached up and gave Adam a kiss. 'See you later.'

Her mobile pinged as Adam left.

'Hi Debs. How's things?'

'Great. Mum, just checking if you want us to bring anything over Easter? I know it's a few weeks away, but I'm trying to get organised.'

Lucy laughed. 'Be a first if you manage that. But thanks, can't think of anything. You've given Dad your flight details yet?'

'Yeah. Think we land about four o'clock. See you soon. Love you. Bye.'

'Bye,' Lucy echoed, but the call had ended and she gave a small chuckle. Debs loved her phone for sending emails and texts and keeping up with social media, but she had a real phobia of actually making phone calls. She always raced through them at top speed.

Lucy gave an inward sigh. She hadn't even had a chance to ask how Hannah was. Never mind. Easter wasn't that far away when they would both be home for a few days.

* * *

Briony and Jeannie decided to walk up to the farm via the track through the fields rather than drive round by road to have coffee with Lucy. The walk up to and through into the Top Field proceeded in silence. Opening and closing the various gates Briony could sense that Jeannie wanted to say something and deliberately kept walking a couple of metres in front of her. As they opened the final gate into the farmyard, Briony glanced at her mum.

'Can we please not mention the bombshell you dropped at breakfast? I've got to get my head around it before I start talking about it to strangers.'

'Of course,' Jeannie agreed. 'You've got a lot to think about. We can talk about it again later.'

They saw Lucy waiting for them.

'Jeannie, how lovely to see you again,' Lucy said, hugging her. 'I was so, so sorry to hear about Giselle.'

She turned to Briony. 'Welcome, Briony, nice to finally meet you. Giselle talked about you so much, I feel I know you already. Come on into the kitchen. I've made a coffee and walnut cake to go with our coffee.'

As the three of them walked into the kitchen, both Luna and Django got out of the basket and came to greet them, with Luna making a beeline for Briony before suddenly stopping, sniffing the air and charging quickly across to Jeannie.

'Remember me as well, do you?' Jeannie said, bending down to stroke her before straightening up. 'Adam not joining us for coffee?'

'He'll probably pop in to say hello whilst you're here,' Lucy said, crossing over to the coffee machine and pressing buttons. 'He's down at the cottages working out what materials he needs to order first for the next rebuild he's getting ready to start.'

'He's done wonders with this place, in such a short time,' Jeannie said. 'I know Giselle thought you'd both taken on too much, but I think she seriously underestimated Adam's abilities.'

'Most people thought we were crazy,' Lucy laughed. 'But we were determined and, thankfully, it seems to be working out. Elliot arriving unexpectedly a year ago and pitching in to help has been good too.

He's started his new job today though – that's why Luna is here.'

'What does he do?' Briony asked.

'He's a vet. A brilliant one, actually. Was on course to have his own practice in the UK until things went wrong in his life – the story of which is not mine to tell,' Lucy said, smiling at Briony. 'Anyway, the French accepted his RCVS qualifications months ago with one proviso. He needed to be fluent in French to be allowed to practise here, so he's spent the last three months doing an intensive French course, which he has now passed.' Lucy stopped talking and picked up a knife and started to cut the cake into generous slices. 'So if you want help with your French while you're here, Elliot's your man.'

'Having grown up with a French father and grandmother, I'm a rather rusty bilinguist,' Briony said, smiling.

'Gosh, you've got a head-start. Right, coffee is ready, milk for everyone?'

'Just black for me,' Briony said. 'No sugar. Thank you.'

'Giselle said you were an auctioneer,' Lucy said, looking at Briony. 'That sounds a fun job.'

Briony shook her head. 'I wasn't strictly an auctioneer, I organised auctions for a large auction company. But yes, it was a fun job. Sadly I've just been made redundant.'

'Oh, I'm sorry to hear that, it's always a blow.'

'You never know, sometimes these things prove to be a blessing in disguise,' Jeannie said quietly. 'This cake is delicious. Giselle used to make a similar one.'

'It's Giselle's recipe,' Lucy said, smiling at her.

Briony tuned out as her mother and Lucy started to talk about Giselle, her recipes and how much she was missed in the village. Her head was still buzzing from the earlier conversation with her mother, the almost casual way she had broken the news. Giselle might have wanted her to move to France and live in the cottage, but it was a ridiculous idea. Her life was in England. There was no way she could move here permanently or even keep the cottage as a holiday home, however much that idea might appeal. She didn't have the resources. And how could her mother possibly think redundancy could prove to be a blessing in disguise?

As for her mother wanting to sell up and move over – was that a ploy cooked up by her mother and grandmother to try to keep the cottage in the family in the hope that she, Briony, would one day realise she wanted to make her home in France? The likelihood of that happening in the near future was remote, to say the least, despite the fact she could tell Jeannie was sincere when she said it was something she longed to do.

Briony sighed. She knew it would mark the end of an era, which was sad, but she couldn't see any way around the problem other than selling the cottage. People like her simply didn't own cottages in France and, in reality, it would be nothing but a financial drain to own property in a country you didn't reside in.

'Briony,' Jeannie's soft voice broke into her thoughts. 'Lucy was asking if you'd like to have a wander around and see the improvements they've made.'

'Sorry, I was miles away. Thinking about Granny,' Briony apologised with a smile. 'Yes, that would be lovely,' and she dragged her thoughts back to the present moment.

Ten minutes later, coffee and cake finished, the three of them made their way out into the farmyard and down towards the artisan workshops and the *pépinière*.

The stable door to the leather workshop was open and Lucy quickly introduced them to Calvin, who was busy stitching a saddle.

'Holly, the potter, is usually here, but she's a

single mum and her little girl isn't well at the moment,' Lucy said, gesturing at the middle workshop. 'We were hoping to have a local artist using the remaining one, but she rang yesterday to tell Adam that she's had to go back to the UK for the foreseeable future. I'm sure somebody will turn up wanting to use it this summer.'

As they had a quick look at all the plants on offer in the *pépinière*, Jeannie wondered silently about buying an agapanthus or two. The blue ones in terracotta pots would look stunning on the cottage terrace. She hurriedly pushed the thought away. Far too soon to be having thoughts like that when everything was up in the air and Briony hadn't had time to come to the decision she prayed she would.

8

Walking back to the cottage after saying goodbye to Lucy and Adam, Jeannie suggested they drove to the nearest *supermarché* and stocked up on some food.

'Good idea,' Briony said. 'I'll drive this time, shall I? We should also think about charging the car. Hopefully the *supermarché* will have a charging station.'

Driving into the *supermarché* car park, Briony spotted the electric charging section with several vacant spaces. Once they'd figured out how to do it and plugged the car in, they grabbed a trolley and went shopping.

Half an hour later as they joined the queue at the checkout, Jeannie laughed as she looked at the contents of their trolley, which included a bottle of champagne and several bottles of rosé and red wine, as well as essential food items. 'You don't think we've overdone the wine?'

'Definitely not,' Briony said. 'We're on holiday.'

Back at the cottage putting the shopping away, Jeannie said. 'I know we've now stocked up with food, but I quite fancy lunch in the village today.' She glanced at her watch, before looking at Briony hopefully. 'One thirty. I think we've still got time before they close.'

Briony shrugged. 'Just so long as you're ready for the locals descending on us.'

'The villagers are old friends and have always welcomed us,' Jeannie said. 'Giselle was very popular.'

'Come on then. A quick walk will do us good.'

* * *

There was one pavement table available when they arrived at the village restaurant with its striped canopy pulled out over the table and chairs. Briony and Jeannie went to sit there but stopped, seeing the 'réservé' sign.

'Maybe there's a free table inside,' Briony said.

'Jeannie, *asseyez-vous*, the table is for you and your daughter.' Odette, the patron of the café, bustled over as they hesitated. 'We saw you coming on the road. Welcome back.' She kissed Jeannie on both cheeks, muttering condolences in her ear over the loss of Giselle, before turning to Briony and kissing her.

'*Merci*,' Jeannie smiled.

'We talk later. For now, I fetch your plat de jour – *beef en daube Provençal.*'

Jeannie pulled out a chair and sat down with a happy sigh. 'It's good to be back, despite Giselle no longer being here.' A quick look around at the other customers to see if she knew any of them, and there he was, sitting alone at a table on the far side of the restaurant. Her heart skipped a beat. It had been so long since she'd last seen him in the flesh so to speak, she'd almost forgotten how handsome he was. She hoped he would come over when he realized they were there.

Odette's teenage granddaughter appeared with a basket of sliced baguette, two glasses and a carafe of red wine.

'*Merci*,' Briony said.

While they waited for their meal, a constant stream of people approached the table, offering their sympathy over Giselle and welcoming them back to the village. Once their *daube* arrived, people politely left them to eat in peace.

'Mum, there's a man over on the far end of the terrace who I feel I know, but I can't place him.'

Jeannie knew who Briony meant instantly but gave a quick glance, smiled and waved her hand in acknowledgement. 'Yes, that's Yannick.'

'Uncle Yannick? Dad's old friend and my godfather? Gosh, he used to be such a bear of a man.'

'Evette, his wife, died some months ago; she was a great cook. I suspect he's missing all the patisseries she used to bake. I'll go over and see him once I've finished lunch,' Jeannie said.

But Yannick came over to them as they finished dessert – a delicious tarte tatin – and Jeannie stood up to greet him, smiling and holding out her hands, which he took and held before kissing her on both cheeks.

'Yannick, fancy seeing you here.'

'Where else can I eat my lunch?' he said, returning her smile. 'It's lovely to see you here again, even though Giselle is no longer with us. Losing someone you love leaves a huge gap.'

Jeannie squeezed his hands. 'It does.'

Yannick turned to Briony. 'You look a lot like your

grandmère, who was a lovely woman. She's missed. It's lovely to see you too back in the village. *Bon*. We'll talk another day,' he said, looking at Jeannie.

'Come for lunch at Owls Nest tomorrow,' Jeannie said.

'*Merci*, but *non désolé*. I go tomorrow to Paris to visit Pauline, my daughter, for a day or two. You remember Pauline?' he asked Briony. 'The two of you had fun when you were small.'

Briony nodded. 'It would be lovely to see her again.'

'*Peut-être* if you both visit one day at the same time, it will happen,' Yannick said, turning to smile at Jeannie hopefully. 'We have lunch another day?'

'Definitely. We're here for another five or six days. I'll come and knock on your door before we leave,' Jeannie said.

'Please do that. Then we can have a proper catch-up.'

Watching Yannick walk away, Jeannie lamented the years he had been out of her life. He and Jeromé had grown up together in the village and they'd stayed friends even though their life paths had gone in different directions. But Jeromé moving to England permanently when he and she had married, followed by Yann marrying Evette, had meant that the close friendship between the men had changed and they had drifted apart. Holidays visiting Giselle once or twice a year were the only occasions they'd met whilst their children were growing up. In recent years, they'd barely seen each other at all. And now both Jeromé and Evette were gone.

Jeannie gave herself a mental shake. At least in the past year she and Yann had rekindled their friendship, talking and comforting each other via WhatsApp and emails about the loss of Evette and Giselle. An old friendship springing back to life that Jeannie was beginning to value more and more.

* * *

Briony was glad when they got back to the cottage after lunch, although she knew that Jeannie was expecting her to discuss what she wanted to do about her inheritance. Something she wasn't ready to do yet. She needed some time to herself. Besides, whilst on the surface everything appeared to be normal between herself and Jeannie, the last few hours had undeniably held an undercurrent of tension. Which had strangely increased after Yannick had come across to speak to them.

'It's too nice an afternoon to spend indoors,' Jeannie said. 'I'm going to pull some weeds.'

'I'm going to check on my emails,' Briony said.

Normally, she would have offered to join her mother in the garden, but this was the perfect opportunity she desperately needed for some thinking time on her own. And despite the weather being too nice to stay indoors, that was exactly what she planned to do. She was going to have a wander around the cottage in the hope that what she should do about her unexpected inheritance would miraculously manifest itself into her brain.

It had been Giselle's parents, who, in the years after the Second World War, had converted the two-hundred-year-old mas into the home it was today. Briony wandered out of the kitchen into the sitting room that came into its own in autumn and winter when it was too cold and dark to be outside. A low-ceilinged room with oak beams, a cream wood burner in the inglenook fireplace and two sets of double French doors set into the curved spaces of what had originally been high wooden doors for herding animals like goats and sheep in for shelter. Two Chesterfield settees and three matching wing-back chairs, lamps on several small tables and a writing bureau against the far wall by several shelves filled with books, framed photos and ornaments, gave the room an inviting feel. Briony had always loved curling up in a chair in this room and losing herself in a book.

Looking around, she remembered several magical childhood Christmases spent here, the smell of the greenery – holly, mistletoe and pine Giselle had placed everywhere – filling the cottage with its outdoor scent. They didn't come every year for Christmas, but summer holidays here were the highlight of Briony's school years until she finished college when the long summer holidays became a distant memory.

The dining room was smaller and had only one set of double French doors. The polished round table was big enough to sit ten around – more when the extension was slotted into the middle. The heavy wooden buffet contained all the crockery, including the fragile Limoges dinner service with its fine gold decoration that Giselle used at Christmas and on special days. Sets of delicate wine and champagne glasses were neatly stacked on the shelves.

The floor in both rooms was tiled with traditional red hexagonal terracotta tommetes and covered with several scatter rugs. One of Briony's happiest memories was seeing the table extended and loaded with food and wine the last time she'd been here in the cottage. She and Jeannie had come over for several days to help celebrate Giselle's eighty-second birthday. The cottage had been buzzing that weekend. So many people dropping in with presents, cards, champagne and flowers. Jeannie had decided that a full-on party would be too much for Giselle and had invited people for lunch aperitifs on the Saturday. For two hours, there was never less than twenty people out on the terrace as friends came and went.

It was that weekend the decision had been made for Giselle to move to England to live with Jeannie. A sudden thought struck Briony. Why hadn't Jeannie simply moved to France to look after her? Surely if Jeannie had always longed to live here, that would have suited them both better.

Returning to the hallway, Briony stopped to look at the painting hanging by the hall stand. Reputedly painted by Great-granny Marie-Louise, it was a scene of one of the cobbled streets in the perched village of Saint-Paul de Vence and perfectly captured the beauty of the ancient buildings. It was a painting Briony had always loved and one she'd thought about asking Jeannie if she could have as a memento of Granny Giselle. The thought that it was now hers made her smile.

Climbing the stairs to the first floor, Briony

trailed her hand along the smooth wood of the banister, smiling as she remembered secretly sliding down it numerous times as a child when Giselle was occupied in the kitchen or out in the garden with the chickens.

When she'd mentioned her childish pleasure to Marcus on the one and only time he'd come with her to France, he'd looked at her in disdain. 'That was the highlight of your holidays? Sliding unseen down a wooden banister in an old cottage.' Useless to protest she'd been six or seven years old at the time and it had been innocent fun.

That whole visit with Marcus had been a disaster as he hadn't bothered to hide his irritation with the place being inland. He wanted to be down where the action was happening, morning, noon and night. Especially night. A fifteen-minute drive to the coast was apparently unacceptable. She'd been so hurt by his attitude on that visit, but stupidly she'd pushed aside the doubts that were starting to niggle and married him two months later.

At the top of the stairs, she stood for a moment looking along the corridor. Four good-sized bedrooms and a bathroom were on this floor. Giselle's old room was the largest, with its en suite bathroom, and Briony decided to leave it for another day. Today she couldn't cope with the sadness that going in there she knew would overwhelm her. Jeannie was in the adjoining bedroom and her own bedroom was at the other end of the house with the main bathroom and the remaining bedroom.

Briony smothered a sigh and made for her own room. Maybe wandering around the cottage hadn't been such a good idea. Throwing up bad memories of Marcus was not helping her to sort out her thoughts.

Dropping down onto the bed, she lay there staring at the ceiling. The guilty feelings she'd been trying to suppress since breakfast immediately flew into her mind. She knew she didn't deserve to inherit the cottage. She'd been so immersed in her marriage problems during the last year of Giselle's life, she hadn't visited as often as she wanted to. Once she and Marcus had separated, it had become easier, but even then she'd often phoned, or made a Zoom call, rather than drive the twenty minutes to Jeannie's, citing being busy at work. She knew both Giselle and Jeannie were upset and sad for her that the marriage hadn't worked out, even though she now realised neither of them had liked Marcus. They tolerated him because he was her choice and they wanted to be supportive. But she was realising in hindsight how

Marcus had tried to separate her from the people she truly loved and the good things she had in her life long before she met him.

How many times during her life had she fantasied about living in France? Living in this very cottage? And now it was possible to do just that, she was fighting against it, saying it wasn't feasible. That her life was in England. But that wasn't strictly true currently, was it? No job. No permanent home.

As for Jeannie wanting to move to France and begin a new life, how could she deny her mother the chance to do something she clearly longed to do? Why was she, Briony, fighting it? Why didn't she suggest they came together? It would be a new beginning for the two of them.

But she needed a job. It was just over a week now since the redundancy and four or five days since she'd sent out an 'I'm unexpectedly available' letter to her contacts. And heard zilch back from any of them.

Briony sat up and reached for her laptop on the bedside table. Checking the job sites and the websites of some auction houses couldn't do any harm and might actually turn up an opportunity.

Half an hour later, Briony closed down the laptop and leant back against the bed headrest. Nothing.

Maybe it was time for a career change? As much as she'd loved her job, there had to be something else she could do. So many people worked remotely these days. Could she live in France and work for a UK company? Could she set up her own business? Become an entrepreneur? Again the question was, doing what? Living in France, her French would need improving. Granny Giselle had always been scolding her for not using the language she had tried to teach her all through her childhood. Briony gave a rueful sigh. If only she'd listened and tried harder with the language during those long summer holidays that she'd loved spending in the cottage with Granny Giselle.

She loved Owls Nest. Always had, and the idea of actually living here full-time was more appealing to her than Jeannie would ever realise.

As a dream it was irresistible. As a life plan, though, it would take a lot of thought and time to work through all the obstacles in the way of trying to put it into action, if she decided she wanted to follow her grandmother's wishes.

* * *

Jeannie was still working in the garden when Briony went downstairs an hour later. 'I'll give you a hand, shall I?' Briony said, seizing the pair of shears that Jeannie had temporarily abandoned and started to prune the overgrown oleander bush near the path.

'Thanks, I can't find the hedge trimmer, so I'm going to see if the strimmer works on the bottom hedge.'

To Briony's inward relief, with both of them concentrating on what they were doing, plus the noise of the strimmer, there was no chance of conversation between the two of them.

Once the oleander bush was cut back, Briony wandered happily down through the garden towards the oak tree with its hollowed-out hole in the trunk, cutting back various plants as she walked. Giselle had always maintained working in the garden was not only great exercise but also a great stress reliever, better than any medicine. This afternoon, Briony could agree with that.

Cutting through the ivy that was covering the trunk of the oak and pulling it away, Briony unexpectedly recalled Giselle's voice telling a teenage Briony, 'And hugging a tree for five moments is unbelievably therapeutic. You should try it when exams or life itself is stressing you out.'

Being a typical teenager, Briony had just smiled at her grandmother and teased her about being an old hippy. It wasn't until after her marriage to Marcus that she'd actually heeded Giselle's words and hugged a tree in desperation. Giselle had been right. It was therapeutic. Since then, whenever she felt stressed, she looked for a tree to hug. Marcus had seen her once hugging an ancient oak and had been remorselessly sarcastic about it. The thought of the words he'd flung at her still made her flinch whenever she remembered them, but it hadn't stopped her hugging a tree whenever the opportunity arose. Like now. Impetuously Briony flung her arms around the trunk of the oak tree she's just torn the ivy away from and hugged it tightly. Closing her eyes, she swore to herself that now Marcus was out of her life, his influence over her was also a thing of the past.

* * *

Sitting together on the terrace, Briony and Jeannie ate a light supper of ham with a green salad and some sliced baguette, washed down with a glass of red wine. Briony was conscious they were still both choosing their words and subject matter carefully as they spoke to each other. She wasn't yet ready to discuss her inheritance and she was grateful that Jeannie was clearly trying to give her time to think.

Jeannie started to stand up just as her mobile on the table pinged with a text message. She picked it up, read the message, smiled and put the phone in her pocket before starting to clear the table. 'I'm going to walk to the lake. Do you want to come?'

'No thanks, I'm going to have an early night,' Briony said, wondering who the text message was from while inwardly acknowledging it wasn't any of her business. 'Enjoy your walk. I'll finish clearing this and tidy the kitchen and I'll see you in the morning.' She knew her mother would realise that she was avoiding talking to her, but until she knew in her own mind exactly what she was going to do she didn't want Jeannie, whether intentionally or not, putting any pressure on her to decide one way or the other.

As she set off for the lake, Jeannie pulled her mobile out of her pocket and re-read the text message.

Le Ville Lumière and I miss you. Lunch at the weekend when I return?

Look forward to seeing you then.

Jeannie typed quickly and pressed send.

9

Elliot parked his 4x4 in front of his cottage and sat for a few moments thinking about his day. Shadowing Julian had been a useful exercise, giving him an opportunity to learn a little about how the practice was run and who was who. Not that he could remember many names. For the past few years, Julian had managed a team of three other vets plus himself, so now there would be five of them to share the busy rota, which hopefully would give everyone a lower workload, with all five of them rarely on duty at the same time. Two veterinary nurses and a receptionist made up the rest of the team and there was always a vet on call for emergencies.

Julian explained they were mainly a small animal clinic, as farms with actual livestock were few and far between in the area. 'There are a few goat and sheep farmers making cheese and, in winter, additional flocks of sheep are brought down from the mountains, but no dairy farms with cows in the immediate vicinity. The summers are too hot. There's an ostrich farm not too far from here that seems to be thriving though.' Weekday mornings were given over to routine operations, like castration of cats and dogs that had been booked in, whilst the afternoons were on a rendez-vous system for people to bring their pets in.

'And don't just expect cats and dogs,' Julian warned Elliot. 'We've had everything in here, from rabbits, snakes, donkeys, parrots, chameleons – even had a small pet tiger for a few visits until we managed to persuade the owner it would be better for everyone if it was in a zoo.'

Elliot had been impressed with the behind-the-scenes set-up, including an X-ray machine, a good-sized operating theatre, a recovery room with various-sized crates and beds, and the office with a professional coffee machine. 'Spend the majority of my evenings in here catching up with the paperwork,' Julian grumbled. 'I mainline coffee at times.' When

Elliot raised the question of Luna, Julian assured Elliot that he was happy for Luna to accompany him. 'Have to keep her out of the operating theatre obviously, but anywhere else, no problem. It'll probably be good for our image too.'

Elliot grabbed the bottle of champagne he'd stopped off in the village to buy from the passenger seat, opened the car door and jumped out. Tomorrow, he was assisting with a couple of female cat castrations in the morning and then he was the vet on duty in the afternoon. Tonight, he was going to celebrate his first day in his new job with Adam and Lucy.

Whistling happily, he walked across the yard to the farm. Luna was at his side as soon as he opened the kitchen door and he quickly made for the fridge and placed the bottle in the door shelf. 'A small thank you from me to you two, and also to toast the future,' he said, grinning at Lucy and Adam before starting to stroke Luna.

'The day went well then?' Lucy said, smiling.

'Yep and I've cleared it with Julian for Luna, so she can come with me starting tomorrow.'

Adam was already tucking into the toast and pâté Lucy had placed on the table and Elliot sat down and joined him.

'The fish pie will be ready in about five minutes, so don't fill up on the starter,' Lucy warned them.

Over supper, Elliot told them how his day had been, and they toasted his future before talk turned to Jeannie and Briony.

'Did Jeannie mention what was happening with the cottage – are they going to keep it or sell it on?' Adam asked.

'Didn't come up in conversation and I didn't like to ask. Briony seems nice, but both of them seemed a bit preoccupied.'

It was almost eight o'clock when Elliot pushed his chair back.

'Thanks for supper, Lucy. Now I'm gainfully employed again, I think it's time I started to cater for myself a bit more. Get out of your hair at mealtimes.'

'Don't be silly, at least get settled in at work first,' Lucy said. 'I know you, it'll be pizzas all the way and that's not good for you.'

Elliot grinned at her. 'You know me too well. Okay, Thank you. But I will have to start being more self-sufficient soon. I'm going to give Luna her evening walk down to the lake, shall I take Django as well?'

Adam shook his head. 'Lucy and I are going to

discuss her interior plans for the stables and we'll take him for a walk as we talk.'

The walk to the lake had become something of a nightly ritual for Elliot since the day he'd arrived on the farm. As the spring evenings stayed lighter longer, Elliot knew the evening walk would get later and later, but tonight mid-evening was a perfect time. Up through the farmyard, into the Top Field and then a gentle saunter down towards the lake. Ten minutes sitting on the bench, letting his thoughts drift as he watched the evening activity of the birds as the sun set had become a soothing end to his days. It was a special place that over the months had seemed to help him heal the hurt of the past year and begin to nourish hopes for the future. He always felt so much better when he turned for the cottage that he thought of as home these days.

As he opened the last gate, he glanced down towards the lake and saw a hunched figure on the bench. Damn. Briony. He'd retreat and go through the vines instead. But Luna had a different idea and was through the gate and streaking down the field before he could stop her. Elliot sighed. Luna was unlikely to come back when he whistled and it would be rude not to at least say good evening now that his presence would be known.

Perhaps Briony was getting ready to return to the cottage and he would still get some time down here alone after she left. Fingers crossed. But as he got closer, he realised it was an older woman. A woman who was stroking Luna with one hand and with the other desperately trying to wipe the evidence of tears from her face.

Elliot stopped and stood still until the woman had pushed her tissue back into a pocket and then he carried on walking slowly towards her.

'Hello, you must be Jeannie. I'm Elliot. I met your daughter, Briony, here yesterday. She received a warm welcome from Luna as well,' he said, giving her a smile.

Jeannie nodded. 'Yes, I'm Jeannie. Luna and I already renewed our acquaintance this morning up at the farm. Nice to meet you, Elliot.' She stood up. 'I'll leave you in peace to enjoy this beautiful oasis your brother has created.'

'Please don't leave on my account,' Elliot found himself saying. 'Luna seems to want you to stay.' He smiled at the dog, who was rubbing her face against Jeannie's leg. 'I promise not to annoy you with chatter. We can both sit with our own thoughts and watch the birds and listen to the noise of the cicadas.'

Elliot sat down on the bench. After a second's

hesitation, Jeannie joined him and Luna lay down in front of both of them.

A few moments later, Jeannie quietly broke the silence. 'Thank you for giving me time to try to hide my tears.'

Elliot gave a half shrug. 'I didn't see any tears.'

A minute passed before he spoke again.

'Lucy is a good listener if you need someone to talk to. She's patiently listened to me a few times over the past year when I needed to get something off my chest and out of my mind. No judgement or advice. Just a listening ear. And what goes in that ear stays there. Lucy doesn't tattle to anyone. Not even to Adam. I'm a good listener too.'

Jeannie didn't say anything immediately. The two of them sat there in companionable silence for a moment or two watching the birds fly to and fro, listening to the noise of the cicadas and the occasional frog's croak from somewhere near the lake. 'Sitting here alone, I realised just how much I miss Giselle and suddenly I couldn't stop the tears flowing.'

'It must be difficult for you returning to the cottage without Giselle being there,' Elliot said quietly.

Jeannie nodded and gave a muted mmm in acknowledgement. 'It does feel strange. Losing her was hard even if it was inevitable. We'd been friends from the moment we met nearly forty years ago. I never really thought of her as old or as my mother-in-law. She was simply Giselle, my friend. I miss her so much.' Jeannie bit her lip and tried to stop the tears from falling again. 'And right now I feel that I've let her down, handling something badly and upsetting Briony, which was the last thing I intended to happen.'

Unexpectedly, Elliot placed his hand on her arm. 'Shh. Turn your head slowly to the right and look at the bunch of yellow irises on the edge of the lake.'

'Oh,' Jeannie breathed. 'How beautiful, a kingfisher.'

Silently, they watched the bird for a moment before it suddenly took off, a streak of blue disappearing into the bushes at the far end of the lake.

Jeannie turned to Elliot, her eyes glistening, this time with happy tears. 'I expect you know the superstitions – I'd rather call them beliefs – surrounding kingfishers?'

When Elliot shook his head, she continued.

'They were Giselle's favourite bird. She always maintained that they are a symbol of peace and serenity. Not only do they signify a free spirit, they are seen as messengers of good news. To see one is very lucky.' She took a deep breath. 'Maybe everything is going to turn out the way Giselle would want it to.'

Elliot smiled at her, pleased that she had shaken off her tears, and recovered her equilibrium. Whether the sight of the beautiful kingfisher truly signalled good things on the way for both of them, only time would tell.

10

Briony woke the next morning determined to talk to her mum, to try to make sense of the situation. Jeannie was humming happily to herself as Briony walked into the kitchen. 'Morning. Coffee is ready. Toast okay today?'

'Thanks, toast is good. You sound happy.'

'I saw a kingfisher down by the lake last evening and Giselle always said they were lucky birds. It made me feel happy for the future.' Jeannie smiled at her. 'Did you sleep well?'

Briony nodded. 'Took time to drop off, but otherwise okay. And I love being woken by the dawn chorus.'

Sitting at the kitchen table sipping her coffee, she

waited for Jeannie to place the toast on the table and sit down with her. Time to address that elephant in the room.

'Mum, I know you said you'd be happy to sell up and come here to live on your own. But do you truly want to do that? It's not simply a ploy to keep the cottage available for me in case I sell it now, but sometime in the future I change my mind and regret not coming here to live?'

'It's not a ploy. I'd love to live here. I love the place,' Jeannie said. 'I tried for years to persuade your father to let us move back, but unfortunately, despite being born in this very cottage, he never wanted to return to live here. He preferred living in England. I could never understand that. It was one of the few things that we disagreed on.'

'After he died, you could have moved over, lived with Granny.' Briony looked at Jeannie. 'Why did Granny move to England so you could care for her for the last years of her life? Why didn't you come here? Save her the upheaval.'

Her words fell into a silence as Jeannie returned her look before answering. 'Isn't it obvious? I didn't want to leave you. I could see your marriage wasn't as happy as you deserved and I wanted to be around for you in case the worst happened. Granny felt the same way. She decided that she'd rather be with me and close to you rather than on her own in France.'

'Gee, thanks,' Briony said. 'Now I feel guiltier than ever. Granny could have stayed in her own home and you could have lived in France.'

'Don't. You have nothing to feel guilty over,' Jeannie said. 'Granny was happy living with me. As far as she was concerned, we'd made the right decision.'

'I did appreciate all the support when I left Marcus,' Briony admitted. 'But I wish I'd known the truth.' She picked up a piece of buttered toast and nibbled it before glancing at her mother. 'The thing is, I don't feel that I deserve to inherit the cottage.'

'Oh, for heaven's sake,' Jeannie said, trying to keep the exasperation out of her voice. 'Deserve has nothing to do with it. French law dictates you're the nearest relative, therefore you inherit the cottage. Giselle was so happy that it was going to a family member she loved.'

'I wish I knew what to do. I keep going round and round in circles. My heart says I'm so lucky to have inherited the cottage and to have the opportunity to live here in France. But my head says no. It's not practical. I need an income. It's going to take time for my French to be up to scratch again, I've used it so little for years.

So I need to work in England. I suppose I could work remotely online for a company there, if that's allowed.'

'I think you need to stop analysing things and listen to what you, in your heart of hearts, want. Things have a habit of working out when you give them time,' Jeannie said. 'Try to put it out of your mind for a day or two. We have an appointment with the notaire soon, maybe he will be able to explain if French laws allow you to work remotely for a foreign country whilst living here.'

'Not sure putting it out of my mind will work, but I'll try.' Briony hunched her shoulders and let them drop as she exhaled a deep breath. 'I just want to make the right decision for both of us.'

There was a short silence before Jeannie said, 'Shall we make a start today going through the cottage and Granny's things? It's not a job I'm looking forward to, but we have to do it, so sooner rather than later, I think. Then we can have a trip out to Giselle's favourite charity in Mouans-Sartoux with the clothes and books we need to get rid of.'

'Yes, let's do that,' Briony said, jumping up. 'We'll start with the sitting room, followed by dining room, shall we? Not quite so personal,' she added quietly.

The downstairs rooms might not be as personal a

room as a bedroom, but Briony soon discovered there was a definite problem in deciding what to get rid of and what to keep.

In the sitting room, she pointed out the things she'd like to keep to her mother. 'The writing bureau, the Chesterfield settees, maybe just one, maybe two of the winged armchairs, and a couple of the side tables.'

Walking through to the dining room, she continued.

'Definitely need to keep the dinner service and the lovely glasses, but not sure about the buffet, although it is a really nice nineteenth-century one,' Briony said, opening and closing the doors. 'And I love the round table. That's definitely a keeper. What about you? Anything in here you would like?'

Jeannie looked at her, surprised. 'First, I have a question – if you're not going to live here, what are you going to do with it all? Transporting it back to the UK is going to be expensive and right now you're not even living in your own home with somewhere to put things.'

Briony was silent for a moment. 'Basically, what you're actually saying is, before we can start to do anything, I have to decide: do I keep the place and move in, sell up, or agree to you moving over to live in Owls Nest?'

'That about sums it up,' Jeannie nodded.

Briony bit her lip thoughtfully. 'So, hypothetically speaking, would you want the cottage with the current furniture or would you bring your own if you were to move over?'

'Hypothetically speaking,' Jeannie said slowly. 'I'd bring a few pieces of my own, nothing major, as I would like the majority of the furniture here to stay in situ. It suits the cottage.'

'Okay. Maybe we should have started with Granny's personal effects rather than her furniture. But they're going to be difficult too.'

Briony gave a deep sigh. Trying to let things work themselves out didn't appear to be an option. She was definitely under pressure now to make life-changing decisions for both herself and her mother. If only there was a clear answer as to what she should do.

* * *

Lucy made sure Adam put on a clean gilet and combed his hair before they walked out to the field to make the short video to share with their YouTube followers on their so-far secret project.

'I'm a working farmer,' Adam protested. 'I'm not going to dress up around the farm.'

'You still need to look presentable,' Lucy said. 'Did you look at the questions I'm going to ask you so you've got your answers in your head?'

Adam nodded.

'Good. I've done an intro already, so when you're ready I'll start the video and ask the first question.'

Adam nodded as he opened the gate into the field and they both walked through.

'Gosh, they're really growing, aren't they?' Lucy said, looking at the rows of plants and their glossy green leaves. 'Okay, let's start walking and talking – I'm switching on. So, explain why we're growing avocados here in the South of France?'

'Traditionally, avocados are grown in hot countries like Mexico and Peru. Global warming is now a scientific fact and the South of France – already hot in summer – is going to get hotter. Consumer demand for avocados has risen rapidly here during the last few years and we buy tonnes of the fruit, which sadly means creating a large carbon footprint. If we can grow and sell them here, lowering that footprint is an immediate benefit. But they are not easy plants to grow, the ground has to be thoroughly weed-free and clean and checked for essential minerals like copper. Another environmental concern is water. Avocados need a steady input of water. The average rainfall down here on the Riviera is about thirty-two inches, which is roughly 812 mm. And that rain generally falls between October to May.'

'Is watering likely to be a problem for us?'

Adam shook his head. 'Thankfully, here on the farm, we have a lake fed by an underground spring, so I'm confident that water is not going to be a problem. Locals have assured me that the spring here has never dried up. And, certainly, over the last eighteen months since we planted the avocados, there hasn't been a problem with water.'

'How much of the farm have we given over to growing avocados?' Lucy asked.

'As it's an experimental crop, we've started with one hundred and fifty plants on one acre, which is roughly half a hectare. So quite small. But we do have plans to increase it to a full hectare. As you can see, they are planted in rows and each plant is twenty feet by twenty feet – or six metres – away from its nearest neighbour. So they do need quite a bit of land.'

'Why have we kept quiet about this project until now?'

'There was a lot of work involved in getting the ground ready, buying and planting the plants. Incidentally, the plants are grown in the Var, so they're local plants – no long air journey to get them here. We were warned that there was bound to be what they call gapping when plants die and would have to be replaced. So we wanted to make sure we had something to show for all the effort that has gone into establishing the future crop.'

'And have we lost many?'

Adam nodded. 'Yes. We've lost about thirty. The replacement plants seem to be doing okay.'

'So now we have told everyone, what happens next?'

'Well, nobody should expect to buy our home-grown avocados in the near future, We have at least two years before we can expect to see signs of fruit and then they have to reach a certain size. Could possibly be as long as another five years, but hopefully sooner. In the meantime, we have to maintain clean ground, provide adequate water, do some pruning, maybe grafting, and generally make sure they're happy plants.' Adam smiled at Lucy. 'It is not a quick crop and it is a lot of work. Fingers crossed, we can pull it off and help diminish that carbon footprint at least a little.'

'Fingers crossed indeed,' Lucy said before panning a general view of the crop for about twenty seconds before stopping the video. 'That's great. I'll edit it later and add a final voiceover.'

Adam gave a sigh of relief. 'Do I get a cup of tea now and the last piece of that coffee and walnut cake?'

11

After a busy but rewarding afternoon in the practice, Elliot arrived home in time to have a reviving shower and feed Luna before heading across to the farmhouse for supper. After supper, he'd take Luna for her evening walk before settling in for an early night. Standing under the power shower as he felt the stress of the day fall away, he wondered why he felt so tired. He'd worked on the farm with Adam on a daily basis since he'd arrived and considered himself fitter than ever.

In a moment of clarity as the hot water pounded his body, he realised he wasn't physically tired but drained with the mental effort of being around people, speaking French all day and hopefully building trust with his colleagues. He'd cut himself off from so many people when everything fell apart, it was harder than he'd anticipated getting back into a work routine and being around people who were still strangers all day.

As for building up a new network of friends here in France, that would either happen or it wouldn't. He gave a mental shrug. He wasn't quite ready yet to socialise away from the farm. Not that Adam and Lucy – particularly Lucy – would allow him to become a total recluse. He knew she wanted him to meet someone new and be happy. But he was determined to be careful whom he allowed into his new life and a close relationship with a woman was not going to happen any time soon.

Turning off the water, Elliot stepped out of the shower, quickly dried and dressed and, within minutes, he and Luna were on their way to the farmhouse. Tomorrow, he had the morning off and he planned to offer Adam a helping hand with anything that needed doing around the farm.

* * *

Lucy smiled as Luna bounded into the kitchen, closely followed by Elliot. 'How was your day?'

'Good. Yours?'

'Mine was good too. Actually persuaded Adam to record something for this week's video.'

'Not making a habit of it,' Adam muttered.

Lucy ignored him and pointed to the family whiteboard where important dates, notices and reminders for everyone were put and held in place with magnets. 'I met the postman this morning. You have mail.'

Elliot's heart sank as he moved across to the board. Slowly, he took the envelope with its English stamp and the loopy handwriting that he knew so well off the board. Thoughtfully, he tapped the envelope against his hand. His first thought was to mark it 'Undeliverable. Gone Away'. But the French postal service was unlikely to return it to the UK.

Lucy gave him a questioning look. She, like him, had clearly recognised Robyn's handwriting. Robyn, though, could write as many times as she liked, but he was no longer married to her and he was not remotely interested in anything she had to say.

Both Lucy and Adam watched as he tore the envelope into tiny pieces and threw them in the rubbish bin.

'You don't think you should have read it first?' Adam ventured quietly.

'No.' Elliot gave his brother a look and shook his head. 'And do me a favour please? If she sends any more, tear them up and throw them away without telling me, okay? I'm not interested in anything she has to say.'

Opening and reading the letter, whatever its contents, would mean Robyn was surreptitiously slipping back into his life, ready to take up space, mess with his head. There was no way he was going to allow her to do that. She had no place in his present life and no place in his future either. Robyn belonged in the past and that was where he intended her to stay.

* * *

After a pleasant but quiet supper with her mum, Briony set off on a longer walk past the lake and to the woods at the very edge of Adam's land. She hoped the fresh air and exercise would clear her head and help her to think straight. Her thoughts were a veritable jumble of memories of the past, mixed in with worries about finding a job and knowing she had to make a decision about the cottage soon. If nothing else, it wasn't fair to keep her mum waiting for a decision that would change both their lives. Especially when in her heart she knew the decision she had to take regarding Owls Nest.

Jeannie had made a valid point when she said that she didn't have anywhere to take the furniture she wanted to keep if she decided to sell the cottage. But the thought of not adding to all those memories that the settees, the table, the cottage itself, had all invoked of past family celebrations was upsetting. It was such a perfect family cottage.

She quickly pushed that particular thought out of her head. The fact that she had been married and should have had a couple of babies by now didn't bear thinking about. But, in truth, it was probably for the best that there had been no children, seeing the way things had turned out. Not that she could ever forgive Marcus for his despicable behaviour. Or the fact that her biological clock was now ticking down like a time bomb in reverse, silently extinguishing all hopes of her ever having a family. Bloody Marcus.

Reaching the beginning of the woods, Briony stopped and looked at the nearest trees. In the pale blue evening sky above, a buzzard was circling. The woods were a mix of oaks, beech, horse chestnut and the occasional silver ash, with the ground beneath them covered in a mush of dead leaves and twigs. Somewhere in the distance, she could hear the drilling sound of a woodpecker searching for insects. She stretched out and placed her hand against the trunk of a large oak tree, its bark thick and textured with age and rough with lots of creases and grooves.

Right now, when Jeannie's unexpected news about the cottage had tossed all her plans and thoughts for the future up into the air, she could really do with the happy, grounded feeling that hugging a tree always gave her. Hugging the tree in the garden the other day had been all too brief but here, on the edge of the woods, where there was no one around to see her and think she was mad, which was most people's reaction, was the ideal time.

Taking a deep breath, she slowly placed her arms around the trunk. It was too large a circumference for her hands to meet, but she gently squeezed the trunk. She closed her eyes and stood there breathing and trying to empty her mind. Time disappeared as she stayed hugging the trunk as her mind cleared and her thoughts drifted away. All she knew when she finally took her arms away from the tree was that she felt lighter, calmer and happier, the stress in her shoulders of the last few days magically banished. Giselle had been so right. It was therapeutic.

Walking slowly back to the cottage past the lake, Briony gave a sigh of pure contentment. It was so lovely here. How could she bear to sell the cottage and never again have the opportunity of enjoying the special place it held in her heart?

* * *

Leaving the farmhouse after supper, Elliot decided not to take his usual route down to the lake. The chances were that either Briony or her mother would be sitting there on the bench and tonight having to make small talk was not on his agenda. He wanted total solitude, a chance to banish all thoughts of Robyn, so he planned to take the track from the back of the farm and drop down to the woods from the other side, avoiding the lake all together. Luna loved the woods, chasing imaginary squirrels or racing after a thrown stick. For Elliot, it had the added bonus that nobody ever went there at this time. Luna stayed at his side as he walked and waited patiently whilst he opened the gate at the top of the second field and closed it behind them.

As he turned, he caught a glimpse out of the corner of his eye of Briony in the woods below, moving towards a tree, placing her arms around and hugging the trunk. Interesting. He wouldn't have thought Briony to be the tree-hugging sort, but you never could tell.

Quickly, he grabbed Luna's collar and slipped her lead on, not wanting her to run down and disturb Briony in her moments of absolute tranquility – or to alert her to his presence.

'Come on, Luna, let's get out of here,' he whispered. He knew how precious those fleeting moments of being at one with nature had helped him. Not that he'd ever hugged a tree, just taking long walks alone in the countryside was enough for him. Turning, he started to walk across the field that would take him back to the farm, leaving Briony in peace.

12

A beautiful Riviera morning greeted Briony the next day as once again she was woken by the dawn chorus. As the bird song quietened and the sun rose, she threw the duvet back and stood looking out of her bedroom window and gave a happy sigh. The sky was already developing that deep daytime azure without a cloud in sight. After a shower, Briony dressed and crept downstairs. Five minutes later, she was on her way to the village for breakfast croissants.

Barely seven thirty but the village's daily routine was already underway. The café's coffee machine was filling the air with the aroma of freshly roasted coffee beans being ground ready for the day's customers.

Odette, wiping down outside tables, waved at her as she went past. '*Bonjour*, Briony. *Ça va?*'

'*Oui merci. Et vous?*' Briony called back.

The boulangerie shop door was open and villagers were already leaving with their fresh baguettes and croissants and hurrying home for breakfast. She didn't recognise the woman behind the counter who smiled and greeted her with the welcoming 'Bonjour', that every customer received.

A few moments later and Briony was walking home, trying not to squash the warm croissants and wondering what it would be like to live permanently in the cottage and be a part of the local scene.

Jeannie was in the kitchen making coffee when Briony returned. 'Mm, still warm,' she said appreciatively, taking the bag of croissants from Briony and putting them on a plate.

Briony waited until they were both sat down at the table, and had coffee and croissants in front of them. 'Mum, we need to talk.' Briony took a sip of coffee before saying quietly, 'I've been thinking and...' She paused. 'I've made a decision about the cottage.'

Jeannie looked at her wide-eyed, anxiety written all over her face. 'Tell me.'

'I love the place and can't bear the thought of

selling it or being the one who lets it leave the family. So, if you are serious about wanting to sell up in England and move here, you can.'

'You're going to keep the cottage? Oh, thank goodness.' Jeannie brushed a tear away as she let out a deep breath. 'I was so worried you were going to put it up for sale.'

'It might come to that in the end,' Briony said. 'Depending on how much it costs to run and how quickly I get a new job.'

'Please don't worry about money,' Jeannie said. 'The house in England will sell and the proceeds will be enough...'

'No.' Briony shook her head. 'That is your money. The cottage is my responsibility from now on. If things get really tight, I might have to ask for a small loan, but if I do, I will pay you back, okay?'

Jeannie gave a resigned nod.

'There is one other thing about you moving in though, which I hope you'll be happy with.'

'Which is?' Jeannie looked at her and waited.

'I'm going to try to come to live here too. No idea how I'm going to manage it and earn money but...' Briony shrugged. 'There has to be a way.'

'My morning has just got better and better,'

Jeannie said. 'The thought of the two of us living here makes me so happy.'

Briony fetched her laptop and began to make lists for both locations, starting with France as they were currently in situ. The next hour flew by as the two of them planned the best way to deal with everything; there was so much to organise here in France and in the cottage.

'Don't forget we've got the notaire tomorrow,' Jeannie said. 'And our flight is booked for next Tuesday. I don't think we need to stay longer this time, do we? Be better to move over quickly and then sort the cottage out, yes?'

'Yes, I agree. I will email my landlord today and give him notice on the flat. Get that underway. I don't have many things, probably all go in half a dozen big boxes, so I can vacate it early and either come to you or return down here,' Briony said.

'I'll need a removal company to bring the small amount of furniture I want to keep – all your stuff can come over with that,' Jeannie said. 'I'm probably going to have to stay there for a couple of weeks – get the house on the market, pack up my personal stuff, decide what to bring here and sell the rest. I'll also need to tell the hospice they will need to find another volunteer to organise their library.'

'If I stay with you for a few days before flying back down, I can give you a hand packing up,' Briony said.

'Oh, I'm so excited,' Jeannie said. 'I can scarcely believe that in a few months you and I are going to be living permanently in Owls Nest. I wish I could wave a wand and make it happen instantly.'

* * *

Lucy poured coffee into two insulated non-spill mugs, added a spoonful of sugar to one and placed them in a wicker basket alongside a plastic container with biscuits and a bottle of water. Adam was busy doing the weekly stint of weed-clearing in the avocado field. She knew he wouldn't bother to stop and come up to the farmhouse for a mid-morning break so she'd walk down to him. She needed to talk to him and, taking him a coffee in the middle of a job, she was guaranteed to have his attention.

Django was instantly at the door when she picked up the basket and the keys. 'Extra morning walk today,' she said, locking the door behind her.

Adam smiled at her and dropped the hoe he was using to remove the weeds and aerate the earth around each plant when she reached him. 'You're a lifesaver. I was just thinking I could murder a coffee.'

They stood companionably drinking coffee and Adam devoured several biscuits.

Lucy took a sip of her coffee. 'I think – no I know, I'm going to need help this summer. It's shaping up to be our best summer yet. The gîte is already fully booked for July and August and most of September, and the early summer months are filling up too. I want to start advertising the stable gîtes soon, once I've furnished them, and hopefully we'll start to get interest and bookings for the summer.'

'Debs and Hannah were a great help last year,' Adam said.

'I know, but their student days are behind them. They've both got proper jobs now with limited holidays and there's going to be three gîtes occupied for at least several weeks this summer. That's a lot of weekly washing and cleaning. And if we go ahead with offering breakfast and dinner in the farmhouse too...' Lucy shook her head. 'I can't be everywhere, or do everything. Editing the YouTube videos is time-consuming. And we really need to think about finding someone to help man the *pèpiniére*. It really needs someone on hand to serve people who want to buy plants and pots.'

Adam nodded thoughtfully. 'Okay. There's bound to be someone local looking for a part-time summer job. Ask in the village, see if anyone is interested before we start advertising. And maybe Holly or Calvin would keep an eye out for customers in the *pèpiniére*.'

'I don't think that would work – definitely not for Holly. If she's in the middle of making a pot or something, we can't realistically expect her to stop and man the *pèpiniére*.'

'No,' Adam agreed. 'The person who helps you would probably need to know something about plants, wouldn't they?'

Lucy nodded. 'It's lucky we don't have any animals other than Django. Honestly, when you think about the amount of work a farmer's wife in the old days was expected to do – help with livestock, feed the family and any workers, help on the land, keep chickens. All with no modern conveniences. I don't know how they managed to fit everything in. I'm glad I live in the twenty-first century, that's all I can say.'

'Right, back to work.' Adam finished his coffee and placed the cup in the basket before casually asking, 'What d'you think Robyn said in that letter?'

'No idea,' Lucy replied, not at all surprised by the unexpected question. The brothers were close and Adam did worry about his younger brother.

'I sort of wish Elliot had opened the envelope before tearing it up. It's always better to know what the enemy is up to than not,' Adam said.

'Enemy?' Lucy said. 'Robyn's not his enemy. She's his ex-wife.'

'A bitter ex-wife, which makes her an enemy in my view,' Adam said. 'A woman scorned and all that.'

Lucy sighed. 'I suppose you're right, but Elliot was the one scorned in the end, not her. I understand him not wanting anything to do with her. She hurt him so much with her actions and I think he's right not to want to let her back into his life in any shape or form.'

'I hope not receiving a reply from him doesn't mean she takes it into her head to turn up here to talk to him face to face, that's all,' Adam said.

'That's a risk, I admit, but I honestly can't see what she'd get out of doing that. She literally emptied his bank account, as well as scuppering his career in England. He's got nothing left to give her.'

13

Jeannie drove into Cannes the next morning with a thoughtful Briony beside her in the passenger seat. 'Shall we have a coffee before or after our meeting with Monsieur Caumont, the notaire?'

'A quick walk along the Croisette before would be good. Get some sea air,' Briony said. 'Afterwards, we can have a coffee and maybe a stroll around Forville Marché if it's still on.'

'I'll park in the Palais des Festivals underground car park then, nice and central,' Jeannie said.

Ten minutes later, the car was parked and they were making their way along the Croisette in the sunshine. 'Have you met the notaire before?' Briony asked curiously.

'No, but I dropped Granny off there once for an appointment, so I know where his office is,' Jeannie said. 'He was recommended to Giselle by her friend Agnes whose husband died and the will got complicated when an illegitimate son showed up. Giselle said Monsieur Caumont was very correct but also understanding. Mind you, I think the fact that he had a twinkle in his eye and a sense of humour endeared him to her!'

'Do we know why he wanted us to come over for the meeting?'

Jeannie shook her head. 'No, but I suspect that French bureaucracy will need you to sign lots of pieces of paper so that he can close Granny's estate and formalise the transfer of the cottage over to you.'

'Is it far from here?'

'Not far. Shall we cross over and indulge in some window shopping in the luxury shops before we turn into the labyrinth of streets behind the Croisette and find his office?'

'I love how there are no prices on anything,' Briony said, minutes later gazing at a window display with just a single headless mannequin dressed with a beautiful floaty chiffon summer dress, a straw tote hanging from one arm with a scarf tied to its handle hung down towards the floor pointing to where a wide-brimmed sun hat and a pair of wedge sandals were casually clustered together as the perfect accessories. Beautiful daywear for the Côte d'Azur. 'I like the tote and the hat, but I love the wedge sandals. Knowing that I have to ask the price means I can't afford them.' Briony sighed.

Further along, they stood gazing in an estate agent's window.

'Something else out of our price range,' Briony said, gazing at luxurious villas and apartments, all with POA instead of an actual price. 'Not that I would want anything like that. Owls Nest is perfect for me.'

Jeannie smiled as she glanced at her. 'Good to hear. Let's find the notaire's office.'

And the two of them made their way back along the Croisette before taking a left turn into the first of the back streets.

The notaire's office, with its shiny brass plate, was easy to find and it was only minutes later that Monsieur Caumont was greeting them.

'Today I have to explain Madame Giselle Aubert's will and we have to sign a few papers. Nothing too worrying. I will translate so you know what you are signing. *D'accord*?'

Briony nodded. She might say she was bilingual,

but legal and medical expressions were hard to translate correctly.

'You know because you are her only direct descendant that you have inherited the property known as Owls Nest Cottage. *Mais*, you also inherit the rest of her estate, except for a small monetary gift to you, her daughter-in-law Madame Aubert,' he glanced at Jeannie.

For the next ten minutes, he explained the intricacies of French inheritance as they applied to Giselle's will. When he mentioned the amount of money that Giselle had left her in addition to the cottage, Briony was stunned. The notaire explained most of the money was invested and he suggested she leave it there for the time being. Finally, he pushed three or four pieces of legal paperwork across his desk to Briony and asked her to initial them before asking.

'What do you plan to do with the cottage? Sell or perhaps keep it as a *maison secondaire*?'

'I – we are moving over and living in it,' Briony said. 'I assume we can do that despite Brexit?'

'Yes, of course. You will need to apply for the now necessary long-stay visas, but I can't see that being a problem, especially with such a close French relative.'

'I was thinking I might work remotely for a UK company until my French is good enough to get a job here,' Briony said. 'Does France allow remote work for another country?'

'You need to apply for a different long-stay visa to do that as there are certain employment and tax rules you will need to abide by.'

'Is it complicated?'

Monsieur Caumont shook his head. 'I will help you sort the correct visa. Now, before I forget, do you both have a French bank account? Because you definitely need one if you are moving over and it would make things less complicated when I close Giselle's estate and legally transfer everything. Another plus would be there would be no exchange rates to worry about. I can organise one for you if you would like me to do that too?'

'Thanks, we'd appreciate that,' Briony said. 'I assume Granny had the cottage insured – is that still in effect? If not, can you organise at least temporary insurance for me please? When I move over, I can sort out all that kind of thing, but I'd hate anything to happen in the meantime.'

'Certainly, I'll make sure the cottage is insured. I hope to be in touch soon then,' and Monsieur Caumont stood up, indicating the meeting was at an end.

'Please don't hesitate to contact me if you need help with those visas.'

Leaving the notaire's office, they began to walk back in the direction of Forville Marché and went into the first coffee shop they passed. Briony ordered their coffees and as they sat down at a table in the window she looked at her mum. 'Did you know about the money Granny left?'

Jeannie shook her head. 'I knew she never appeared to worry when bills came in, but we never talked about money in general. I certainly wasn't expecting her to leave me anything.'

'I wasn't expecting to inherit the cottage, let alone the rest of it,' Briony said, as the waiter placed their coffees on the table. 'I'm stunned.'

'It will certainly relieve the pressure on you trying to get another job for a little while, you can take your time,' Jeannie said. 'And you already have your divorce settlement and also your redundancy money. So you have quite the cushion. Also, you no longer have rent or a mortgage to pay.'

'That's true,' Briony nodded. 'I think I'll take summer off. Enjoy settling in down here, practise my French as much as I can, sign up for a conversation class or something, and generally try to work out

what I want to do. We can have some days out together too.'

'Sounds like a good plan,' Jeannie said.

'Right now, I fancy a stroll along rue d'Antibes
when we've finished here. Have some celebratory
retail therapy to mark the occasion! Like a new pair
of shoes. How about you?' Briony smiled at her mum.

'If I see a pair of sandals I like I might buy a pair,
but there's a large Sephora store up there and I do
need some new foundation.'

'Come on then, drink up.'

The two of them spent a pleasant hour strolling
along rue d'Antibes. Briony found a pair of wedge
sandals that were even nicer than the ones she'd
spotted earlier that morning and were infinitely more
affordable. Jeannie splashed out on a pair of loafers
and in Sephora, she treated herself to not only a new
foundation but also a lipstick and a bottle of her
favourite perfume Chanel No.5. Afterwards, for the
final treat of the day, they had lunch in the oyster
restaurant down near the market.

It was mid-afternoon when they arrived home
and Jeannie made straight for the kitchen to make
some tea. Briony put the cushions on the terrace
chairs before carrying a parasol out of the shed and
slotting it through the centre of the table. 'Definitely

need the shade this afternoon,' she said as her mum placed two mugs of tea on the table.

'I've had a text from Lucy,' Jeannie said. 'We're invited for Sunday lunch this weekend. Twelve thirty for one.'

'We can't refuse a Sunday lunch invitation,' Briony said, smiling.

'I'll text Lucy back and accept. It will be a good time to tell them that you've inherited the cottage and we will both be moving here permanently. They've been too polite to ask what's happening, but I expect they're curious,' Jeannie said.

A cold breeze sprang up later that day and the two of them retreated to the sitting room for the evening. Briony, curled up on one of the settees, had headphones on watching a film on her laptop and Jeannie was reading on her Kobo, her mobile on the side table next to her. When a WhatsApp text pinged in Jeannie glanced at the ID and smiled before surreptitiously glancing at her daughter. Had she heard the message arrive? Unlikely, she was too engrossed in the film.

Jeannie stretched out her arm to pick up the phone and clicked on the message. It was a reply to one she'd sent Yann earlier that day.

Wonderful news. Is there a
timescale? I'm home now, so let
me know if I can help in any way.
Can we have lunch tomorrow? xx

Jeannie closed the phone down. She'd reply later when she was on her own. Once they were living over here, she'd have to have a serious chat with Briony. Explain and hope that Briony would understand and be happy for her, that this – this what? Her old connection with Yann was definitely growing from a comfortable friendship into something more, but it wasn't yet a true relationship, more of a liaison. Yes, liaison was probably the word.

14

Once she'd accepted Yann's lunch invitation, Jeannie decided that there was no need to be secretive about lunch with an old friend of her husband's.

'Yannick has invited me to have lunch with him today,' she told Briony at breakfast. 'Just in the village – I expect there will be a lot of other people I can catch up with there too. You could always join us?'

'You go and have a reminisce about the good old days. I might do a spot of weeding or just mooch around here, try to decide what to keep. Maybe open the garage doors and see what's in there. Why not?' Briony said as Jeannie shook her head.

'I shouldn't. There is so much stuff in there dating back years and years. Once you're living here, there will be time enough to open those doors, trust me on that.'

'That bad? Okay. What about the attic? Is that likely to be full as well?'

'No, I don't think so. The access isn't brilliant, although there is a drop-down ladder. The family never found it that easy to put stuff up there – the garage was definitely the easiest dumping ground.'

'I'll do some weeding this morning and then maybe take a look in the attic,' Briony said.

By the time Jeannie came out to say goodbye, Briony had weeded a couple of the flower beds and was starting on the pots. 'The car keys are on the hook if you decide to go out.'

'Thanks, Mum. I'm finishing up here and going for a shower. Have a good lunch. See you later.'

On the landing outside her bedroom, Briony glanced up at the ring in the ceiling hatch. Maybe her shower could wait. There was a long pole with a hook in Giselle's bedroom which fitted perfectly, as she'd known it would. She gave it a gentle tug, the hatch opened and she pulled it and the ladder down carefully.

The ladder was steep and Briony held the handrails on either side as she climbed slowly and hesitantly. A small roof window gave a little light into the attic which spanned the whole of the top floor of the cottage and was boarded. Standing near the top of the ladder, Briony looked around. At first glance, the attic appeared to be empty, but as she turned her head to look to her left, she saw two cardboard boxes tucked away out of sight in the corner of the attic underneath the sloping roof that was behind her.

Carefully, Briony stepped onto the boards and, bent double as there was no headroom, pulled both boxes nearer the open hatch. One was open and seemed to be full of papers and cards, the other had been closed, with the cardboard flaps tucked in under each other. Neither box was particularly heavy and Briony decided she'd take them downstairs and go through them. The open one she simply dropped through the space between the ladder and the hatch onto the landing floor. A veritable dust storm lingered in the air for moments after it landed. She put the other, bigger box closer to the edge before stepping back onto the ladder. Pulling the box closer and holding it against her chest with her left arm and hand, she began to descend. Her right hand was tightly holding the stair rail as she slowly felt her way backwards down the ladder. As her feet finally stepped onto the landing, she let out a long breath. She placed the box beside the other one and pushed the ladder back up and the hatch closed into position with a definite click.

After a quick shower, she took the boxes downstairs to the dining room and put them both on the table. The open box was full of a mixture of letters, newspaper cuttings, old birthday cards and lots of black-and-white photographs – mainly formal family pictures of people who were long dead. And underneath everything was an old lockable leather-bound five-year diary complete with its key.

The second box, when she took a peek under the cardboard flaps, seemed to be full of sketches and a couple of finished watercolours. Briony knew instantly that they were the work of her great-grandmother Marie-Louise; they were so similar to the one hanging in the hall. Carefully, she closed the flaps down again.

Why had all these paintings and photographs been put in boxes and hidden away? Briony picked up the diary. Who had owned this diary? What secrets did it contain? And would any of those secrets reveal the truth about why the boxes had been left hidden in the attic for what appeared to be decades?

* * *

When Adam left to drive to the nearest builders merchants for some supplies, Lucy took advantage of the quiet to edit her latest video blog in preparation for loading onto the channel at her regular time on Sunday evening. Once she was happy with the video she carefully scheduled it to go live Sunday evening at eight o'clock French time.

'Hi, anyone home?' Elliot called out as he opened the back door. Django shot out of his basket as Luna appeared and the two dogs greeted each other with enthusiasm.

'Coffee?' Lucy said.

'Please.'

'What you are you doing home?'

'My day off today. Thought I'd take Luna and explore Lac de Saint-Cassien. Still early in the year, so it should be quiet. The water adventure centres won't all be open yet.'

'It's a lovely day, wish I could join you,' Lucy said. 'What about tomorrow – are you on call? Sunday roast tomorrow as usual.'

'No, I'm not on call, I'll be here. Couldn't miss one of your famous roast dinners.'

After Elliot left, Lucy wandered down to see Holly, who had messaged to say her daughter was better and she would be opening the pottery today. If

Holly was happy, Lucy planned to film a short sequence of her working at the wheel fashioning one of the beautiful jugs she made and decorated and also showcase some of the pottery on the shop shelves.

Passing the empty workshop on the way, she sighed. Hopefully someone would take it on soon. Having it standing empty was such a waste.

* * *

When a text from Yann saying he'd pick her up at eleven-thirty pinged into her phone, Jeannie had smiled to herself. She'd been wondering what the locals would make of her and Yann lunching alone together. It would definitely be more relaxing to be in a busy restaurant where they were unknown.

Now, sitting next to him as he drove them down towards Cannes and then along the *bord de mer* towards Mandelieu-La Napoule, Jeannie's thoughts drifted down memory lane to the time when the three of them – Jeromé, Yann and herself – had been firm friends. Life in those early days had been so carefree.

She and Yann had got on from the first moment Jeromé had introduced the two of them. Something had drawn them together. Yannick had never heard

the term 'best man' and when Jeromé asked him to
be his, he had burst out laughing. He'd turned to
Jeannie. 'If I'm the best man you should be marrying
me!' A throwaway joke that the three of them had
laughed at. But Jeannie had registered the sad look in
his eyes.

When they'd met and married, Jeromé had been
six months into a two-year exchange contract with
the English office of the French financial firm he
worked for. When Jeannie had said how much she
was looking forward to living in France when he returned to the French office, Jeromé had looked at her.
'*Mais non*. We stay in England; my life is here now
with you. I have already accepted a promotion in the
English office.'

Jeannie remembered Giselle being upset at that
decision. She'd tried to hide it from Jeromé, pleased
that he was doing so well in his career, but had privately admitted to Jeannie that she'd been looking
forward to the day when the two of them moved back
to France. Once Briony had been born, Jeannie had
told Jeromé that she would like to take Briony to
spend most of the long summer holiday in France
with Giselle every year. As Briony grew, Jeromé insisted that they left Briony with her grandmother for

a fortnight in the summer whilst the two of them enjoyed a holiday on their own.

'We have the time for a short stroll to look at the boats if you like,' Yann said, breaking into her thoughts as he drove into a space in the car park of the Port La Napoule.

'I haven't been here for years,' Jeannie said as they walked the quay alongside the water, looking at the moored boats. 'It's much bigger and busier than I remember it. Do you still keep your small day boat here?'

Yann shook his head. '*Non.* I sell it. The expense as the marina expanded was too much. Pauline and I had some good times on it together, but Evette was never a keen sailor. Now I come to look at the catamarans and the other wonderful yachts. And occasionally bring a beautiful woman for lunch to the new restaurant.' He smiled at Jeannie and caught hold of her hand. 'I can't tell you how happy I am that you are finally coming to live down here and we can be in each other's life from now on.'

'We've been in each other's life for a long time,' Jeannie said quietly.

'*Oui*, but not in the way I would like.' Yann looked at her, a serious look on his face. 'Now I like to think, it is our time.'

15

Sunday morning, Jeannie and Briony had a relaxed late breakfast of coffee and toast out on the terrace. 'This week has gone so quickly. To think we've only got today and tomorrow left,' Jeannie said.

'Do you think we'll be the only guests at lunch today?' Briony asked.

'Elliot will be there, I expect.' Jeannie gave a small shrug. 'Other than that, I have no idea. Does it matter?'

'No. Just wondering.'

'How long do you reckon you're going to have to stay back in England?' Briony asked. 'I've just got to clear out my personal stuff in the flat and leave.'

'I certainly don't want to stay there for too long,

so I'm just hoping the house will sell quickly, not drag on for months,' Jeannie said. 'I know it's un-likely to be less than three months though. And I def-initely don't want to have to stay there all that time. I want to be down here.'

'You could do the completion on Zoom and just have the solicitor to do the proxy signing on your be-half,' Briony suggested.

'Brilliant idea. I want to be back down here as soon as I can,' Jeannie said. 'So once it's on the mar-ket, and the removal men are lined up to bring things over here, I can jump on the plane.'

'Think we may have a problem with cupboard space, if not room space, for any extra furniture,' Briony said thoughtfully. 'The kitchen cupboards here are already full. In fact, there is far more stuff than we're ever going to need. And we do need to sort out Granny's bedroom. Talking of which.' She glanced at her mum. 'Would you like to use that room rather than the one you're currently in? I'm quite happy in the room I've always had.'

Jeannie hesitated. 'It's a lovely room and it does have the en suite, but I think I'd prefer to stay in the one I'm used to.'

'Okay, but perhaps we should think about emp-tying the wardrobe and the chest of drawers in there so that if we have anyone to stay they can use that room.'

'We've got a couple of hours this morning, we could make a start?' Jeannie said.

'Good idea. Let's do that,' Briony said, finishing her coffee and standing up.

'Let's start with the wardrobe,' Jeannie said as they opened the bedroom door. 'Granny brought most of her clothes with her when she moved in with me, but she did say she'd left some good pieces over here.'

The good pieces turned out to be classic designer wear that Giselle had collected down the years, that both Jeannie and Briony eyed appreciatively. A Jaeger coat, two Hermès scarves, a black evening dress and a red one in a similar style both from Ralph Lauren, a long-sleeved white shirt, and a Chanel suit in the pale-coloured tweed material Coco Chanel was famous for. Clothes that would never go out of fashion and were of such good quality they were unlikely to wear out either.

'Granny loved dressing up for special occasions,' Jeannie said. 'Lunch or dinner at the Cannes Carlton was always an excuse.'

'How about we keep these rather than take them to the charity shop,' Briony said, looking at her mother. 'We could share these – use them on special occasions ourselves. They're such classic designs. We could each have a scarf to wear any time.'

'Let's do that.' Jeannie hung the designer garments back in the wardrobe. 'I think Granny would approve.' She reached up and took a box off the top shelf of the wardrobe and placed it on the bed before taking off the lid. 'Not sure what's in here. Oh, it's a handbag.'

Briony stared at the bag Jeannie was carefully taking out of a protective cover – a scarlet Longchamp leather tote. 'Ooh, I love this,' she said. 'It's beautiful.'

'I guess that's not going to the charity shop either,' Jeannie said with a smile.

'Definitely not,' Briony said. 'This has my name written on it – unless you would like it?'

Jeannie shook her head. 'It's more your style than mine and I have a feeling that Granny bought it with your birthday in mind.'

Briony sniffed in an effort not to cry. 'Best birthday present ever. I'll look after it, but I definitely intend to use it on a regular basis.'

The chest of drawers had a few jumpers and blouses folded up neatly that Jeannie decided could go to the charity shop. 'Right, at least we've made a start. Which scarf would you like? I'm going to wear mine today.' She held both the scarves out to Briony.

'You choose your favourite,' Briony said. 'I'm happy with either.'

An hour later, they locked the cottage door and made for the gate to walk up the track at the edge of the field to the farm.

'What a lovely setting for lunch,' Jeannie said as Lucy and Adam greeted them. She held out the bottle of red wine that she and Briony had chosen to bring as a small thank you. The table on the terrace under the wisteria-covered loggia at the back of the farmhouse had been covered with a pretty tablecloth with a jug of daffodils placed in the middle. 'You two have done amazing things to this place in such a short amount of time.'

'I had strict instructions from Lucy that the house had to be habitable within as short a time as possible, otherwise she'd leave me,' Adam said, smiling as he handed them both a glass of champagne. 'She's always maintained that one can put up with living on a building site so long as there is a functioning kitchen, a bathroom with lots of hot running water and a bed to collapse into at the end of long working days.'

'I was right too,' Lucy said, raising her glass. '*Santé*. It's lovely to have you both here.'

Elliot looked at Jeannie and Briony and smiled. 'Hi. Nice to see you.'

A couple of moments later, Lucy disappeared into the kitchen, brushing away any offers of help, and Jeannie was talking to Adam about how different the farm had been the first time she'd seen it nearly forty years ago. 'I always felt a little sad when we visited because it just got sadder and sadder down the years. You've really done something to be proud of pulling it back from the brink.'

Briony, standing slightly apart from them, wondered whether she should try to start a conversation with a silent Elliot standing at her side or join in with Adam and Jeannie about her own memories of the farm.

'How do you like the Renault 5 EV you've hired?' Elliot said unexpectedly.

'You're talking to someone who knows nothing about cars,' Briony said. 'But it's great to drive. Very nippy too,' she smiled. 'I've only driven it along the *bord de mer*, I suspect on the A8 it would be very hard to keep to the limit.'

'I keep thinking I should at the very least trade my diesel-guzzling Toyota in for something more environmentally friendly,' Elliot said. 'But the kind of car I need doesn't have a large enough range yet.'

'Maybe a hybrid to start with?'

'Possibly,' Elliot nodded.

Lucy reappeared at that moment. 'I hope nobody minds, but I haven't done a starter,' she said as dishes of roast beef, roast potatoes, Yorkshire puddings, vegetables and two large jugs of gravy were placed on the table for everyone to help themselves from. 'But there will be a cheese course, followed by dessert.'

'This looks absolutely delicious,' Jeannie said, helping herself to some pink beef and a Yorkshire pudding.

'Lucy's a brilliant cook,' Adam said. 'A couple of years ago, the girls and I tried to enter her for *Master-Chef*, but she wouldn't let us.'

'Too much pressure,' Lucy shuddered. 'It's going to be enough pressure cooking breakfasts and the occasional evening meal if any of the gîte visitors request one. I have to confess, I'm not really pushing the evening meal side of things – the next few months are going to be busy enough without adding dinner for strangers into the equation. I've started to ask in the village if anyone wants a part-time job for the holiday season. A Girl Friday sort. But nobody has applied yet.'

'I'd quite like a part-time job, if you would con-sider me,' Briony said, looking at Lucy. 'I'd be happy to be your Girl Friday.'

'Really?' Lucy looked at Briony, surprised. 'Does that mean you're going to be here all summer?'

'Yes. We haven't had a chance to tell you before, but because of French inheritance laws Granny Giselle has left Owls Nest Cottage to me.' Briony took a deep breath. Actually voicing their plans to other people made her believe it was definitely going to happen. 'Mum and I are going to move over perma-nently. A new beginning in France for both of us.'

'This is great news,' Adam said. 'When are you planning to move over?'

'We're going to go back as planned Tuesday morning. Then, once back in the UK, we'll start to close down things over there. I'm hoping to be back in about a week, to make a determined start on going through Granny's things, which is sad but a neces-sary thing we will have to do,' Briony said.

'I shall have to stay longer as I have to sell my house, which means sorting it out first and getting it on the market,' Jeannie added. 'But as soon as it's or-ganised I'm coming back. Easter is so late this year that, with luck, I'll be back around then, but possibly it will be early in May.'

'I'd be very happy to be your Girl Friday, general dogsbody, whatever you want to call it, for the next few months,' Briony said, looking at Lucy. 'It doesn't have to be regular hours – just when you need help.'

Lucy smiled happily. 'Consider yourself my Girl Friday when you get back. And thank you both. I can already feel the pressure coming off.'

'And, as well as Briony, I'll always be willing to help you out,' Jeannie said. 'Actually, Adam, I was going to ask you about the *pépinière*. There never seems to be anyone there to help. Maybe we could have a talk when I get back?'

'Look forward to it,' Adam said, smiling.

* * *

It was late afternoon before Briony and Jeannie said their goodbyes and made their way back home.

'What a feast of a Sunday lunch,' Jeannie said. 'I don't think I want anything else to eat today. Just a nice cup of tea out in the garden and maybe a walk to the lake this evening.'

'Sounds a perfect end to the day,' Briony said. 'Especially if I get to see your kingfisher.'

JEANNIE BOULBY

16

Briony and Jeannie spent Monday morning pottering around both the cottage and the garden. Knowing that Jeannie had a house full of furniture in the UK, they also tried to work out a plan of what would go where, which pieces Jeannie would sell in the UK and which she would bring with her. With very little success.

Sitting out on the terrace mid-morning with a coffee, Jeannie gave a sigh and looked at Briony. 'Tell me something – do you like Granny Giselle's furniture?'

'Yes,' Briony looked at her puzzled. 'Why?'

'It is your new home and you should be the one choosing how it is furnished.'

'But it's going to be your home too,' Briony protested.

'The thing is...' Jeannie paused. 'I don't think my furniture is going to suit the cottage – the things that are here now are so right for the place.'

'Shall we leave it until we get back to England and then decide?' Briony suggested.

'I think that is the best idea,' Jeannie smiled, re-lieved. 'A couple of things I do want to bring over are the cane garden chairs for this terrace and the wrought-iron table.'

'What about gardening tools?' Briony asked. 'Yours are in much better condition than the ones here.'

'Definitely bringing the tools. I'm looking forward to pulling this garden back into shape.'

'Have you had a look at the boxes I took out of the attic?' Briony asked, finishing her coffee. 'I left them on the dining-room table.'

Jeannie shook her head. 'No. What's in them?'

'One, which I'm really looking forward to going through when we get back, has lots of photos, letters, old birthday cards, some old-fashioned sheet music, a few tatty newspaper cuttings, and a locked five-year diary with a key. The other one is full of paintings, sketches, a couple of small, framed pictures, like the picture in the hall. I think they're all the work of Great-granny.'

'Intriguing,' Jeannie said. 'Have you opened the diary?'

'No. Diaries are such personal things, it doesn't feel right reading someone else's private thoughts, even after all this time. But I will once I'm living here.'

'I know a little about Dad's grandparents but not much. His grandfather was quite a stern, hard man, not a lot of time for other people. Jeromé adored his grandmother though. Said she was one of the gentlest, sweetest people he'd ever met, as well as being a talented artist when she was young.'

'Once I'm down here full-time, I'll try to do some family history research,' Briony said. 'Neither Granny nor Dad seem to have inherited her artistic talent, though, do they? I know Dad could draw a caricature with just a few strokes of the pen, but he never painted actual pictures, did he?'

'No. He wasn't interested in art at all.'

Jeannie's phone rang at that moment and she picked it up.

'Hi,' she said, and listened before speaking again. 'That would be lovely. Thank you. We'll see you then.' Turning to Briony, she said. 'That was Yann.

He's invited us to lunch in the village today. I accepted for both of us.'

* * *

Three-quarters of an hour later as they arrived at the village café, Yann was waiting to greet them and Odette showed the three of them to a reserved pavement table under the cover of a large parasol.

With a glass of rosé to sip, a bread basket and a large plate of charcuterie on the table to share between them as a starter, Briony sat back as Yann and her mum talked nostalgically about the meals they'd shared there with their respective partners, in the past. At one point, they both laughed and glanced at each other as if the two of them shared a personal special memory of that particular occasion. Thoughtfully, Briony sipped her wine and began wondering. Jeannie's voice brought her back to the present.

'I was telling Yann about the boxes you found in the attic. He's suggested that when we're back and settled here, we show them to him. His own grandparents were friends with Dad's grandparents, particularly his grand-mère and great-granny.'

'Brilliant idea,' Briony said, smiling at Yann.

Lunch developed into the typically French two-hour affair and it was late afternoon when they said goodbye to Yann and made their way back to the cottage.

'Shall we pack this evening, ready for an early start tomorrow?' Briony said. 'It still feels a little unreal that we are actually going to come and live here permanently.'

17

ENGLAND

Briony stayed with Jeannie when they arrived back in the UK. There was little point in sleeping in her own place, she just needed to clean it and pack up her few personal things and move out.

Briony finished cleaning and emptying her apartment and handed the keys back to the agency two days later. Mentally, she ticked it off her list. Now to concentrate on helping Jeannie.

First, the two of them went through the house from top to bottom, Briony making notes while Jeannie decided what furniture she'd like to take to France. In the end, there was only her favourite armchair, a couple of bedside tables, some lamps and two or three rugs. 'Are you sure about this?' Briony asked.

'I know you decided your furniture wouldn't suit the cottage, but what about your bed, for instance?'

'No, the bed in the cottage is more comfortable than this one,' Jeannie said, laughing. 'I'm hoping the house will appeal to a first-time buyer and they will appreciate the fact that it comes furnished. If it's a problem, I can always get a house clearance company in.'

'Okay. We'll put all the things you want to take in the dining room, I think; we're not using it. Now we need to start sorting through the smaller stuff – books, bedding, kitchen equipment, ornaments, cushions, clothes.'

By the end of the week, the local charity shops had received box after box of books, ornaments, miscellaneous things that defied naming but were deemed to be useful and clothes that Jeannie said she didn't want to keep. Despite all this decluttering, the dining room was overflowing with the furniture and the boxes earmarked for France. Briony tried not to think about where on earth everything was going to go in the cottage.

While Jeannie had a hair appointment one morning, Briony met up with Maeve for a coffee.

'Any news on the job front for you?' Briony asked.

'Sort of but...' Maeve pulled a face. 'The American company who took over have asked me back, said they made a mistake, but I really don't want to work for them after the way they treated us. What's to stop them doing the same again in six months?' Maeve gave the waitress a smile as she placed coffee and cakes on the table. 'But I don't have any real choice. There's just nothing around. Anyway, enough about me, what's happening with you? You're looking good, the French air obviously agrees with you,' Maeve said. 'Your mum still going to sell the place or did this visit change her mind?'

'Not exactly,' Briony laughed. 'I've inherited the cottage, not Mum, and guess what?' She gave a dramatic pause. 'We're both moving to France.'

'Wow, I wasn't expecting that.'

'Neither was I,' Briony said. 'But I'm excited now it's been decided. We've been busy getting Mum's house ready for sale and I'm heading back to France the day after tomorrow. Mum will fly out once the estate agent is sorted and the house is on the market.'

'I'm so pleased for you,' Maeve said. 'You've had a tough time recently.'

'You will come and visit, won't you? You and Brian – the girls too if they want to come. Just get yourselves on a cheap easyJet flight to Nice and come and have a holiday. Plenty of room in the cottage.'

'Sounds like a wonderful plan,' Maeve said wistfully. 'But it probably won't be this year, even if I do go back to Raise Your Hand Auctions.'

Briony looked at her friend. 'Have they offered you a rise, longer holidays?'

Maeve shook her head. 'I've said I'll go in tomorrow and talk about it. I suspect there will be a little pay rise but not enough to make much difference.'

'They've approached you to return so quickly, they obviously need your expertise on the system quite desperately. Don't just say thank you and return to your desk. Name the wage you want, the holiday period you want and tell them the hours you're prepared to work before asking for overtime. You might not get all three things, but...' Briony shrugged. 'Worth a try. You held that accounts department together and you were never given enough respect for that.'

Maeve was staring at her wide-eyed. 'When did you get to be so demanding?'

Briony shrugged. 'I'm not really, but it was very unjust the way they sidelined you with one of their American staff before making you redundant. Going back on your own terms would be different.'

'Are you going to work in France?'

Briony laughed. 'I'm going to be a Girl Friday for the summer,' and she quickly told Maeve about the farm and Lucy wanting help. 'Other than that, I'm going to enjoy my first summer in the cottage, improve my French and then in September I'll start looking around for a job. That's the plan anyway.'

'I did hear somebody once saying that their French improved no end when they took a lover,' Maeve said. 'Maybe that could be a bonus over the summer? A handsome Frenchman will sweep you off your feet and...' She wiggled her eyebrows suggestively.

'I already speak French, Granny and Dad insisted I learnt, although I admit I'm out of practice,' Briony laughed. 'So I don't need to take a French lover.' *Or any lover*, she thought silently. She glanced at her watch. 'I'd better get back. I've got the removal company coming to give us a quote in about an hour. Ring me tomorrow, let me know how it went. And remember that cliché – You're worth it!'

Walking home, Briony found herself wondering about the way a certain vet had sprung into her mind when Maeve had made the suggestion about a sexy French lover sweeping her off her feet. Which was silly, Elliot was English not French. Although she had to admit she'd thought him handsome on the two occasions they'd met.

This summer, though, was going to be all about laying the foundation for a new life in France. A life she intended to live on her own terms. After Marcus, there was no way she planned on letting a man back into her life any time soon.

18

SOUTH OF FRANCE

'Furniture for the main rooms, rugs, beds and lamps for the Stables are arriving today. Are you going to be around in case the men need a hand? They shouldn't, as it's mostly flatpack, but there is a lot of it. I'm hoping I can persuade them to put things in the rooms, so we don't have to move it ourselves. I'm definitely going to need help assembling it all.' Lucy smiled at Adam as she watched him eat his breakfast of scrambled eggs on toast.

Adam groaned. 'My favourite job – not.'

'I thought we could make a start late afternoon tomorrow, work until supper and then finish the next day. So if you can keep tomorrow afternoon fairly free?'

Adam gave Lucy a look. 'You weren't exactly asking me, were you? You already had it planned.' He shook his head. 'You are so bossy.'

Lucy grinned at him. 'With a bit of luck, Elliot will be able to help as well, so with two Alpha males on the case it shouldn't be too hard or too long a job. Briony is returning tomorrow, so her first Girl Friday job can be giving me a hand making up the beds and dressing the rooms.'

'I hope this Girl Friday business with Briony works out,' Adam said thoughtfully. 'I like Briony, but I'm not sure she realises what she's taking on working here. She's going to need to be pretty adaptable and hands-on with stuff. You going to give her a trial for a week?'

Lucy gave him a shocked look. 'No, definitely not. That would be so awkward. I've already told her the job is hers for the summer.' She gave a sigh. 'Trust me. It's going to be just fine, okay? She's going to fit in here well.' Lucy picked up the dirty breakfast plates and took them over to the dishwasher. 'Anyway, aren't you supposed to be helping Bruno in the vineyard this morning?'

'Yes, he needs a hand with the early pruning and shoot thinning that he tells me is essential in spring for a good crop in September. Also, the rows need a gentle hoe to keep the weeds down. All back-breaking work.' Adam stood up. 'I'll see you later.'

After Adam had left, Lucy made for her study and opened her computer. Time to do some editing of the next video and also to check on bookings for the gîte and prepare an advert for the Stables to go with the photos she intended to take once everything was in place over there. There was always so much behind the scenes and office work to do. Personally whatever Adam thought, she couldn't wait for Briony to arrive and share some of the workload.

* * *

Briony settled back in her seat, did up her seatbelt as instructed and waited for the plane to become air-borne. In just over three hours, she'd be back at Owls Nest Cottage – her very own home. If anybody had told her four weeks ago that her life was about to change dramatically, she would have said they were out of their mind. Even now, knowing that at the end of this flight she would be stepping onto French soil to begin a new and different life in the South of France, one that she'd never expected to happen, still felt strangely surreal. There was no doubt, though, that she was ready to embrace and enjoy her new life.

The plane gained height and soon they were flying above the clouds, something Briony loved. She found it exhilarating, if a little scary, seeing the clouds so close, rather than being on the ground looking at them from a distance.

The days in England had gone by in a whirl where she'd barely had time to draw breath. Between them, she and Jeannie had organised everything. The removal firm were collecting the things they'd decided to take to the cottage in a couple of days. Gerry, the owner of the removal company and an old friend she'd used on a regular basis to transport things for the auction house, had estimated it would take them several days to drive down through France. 'Not often we get these kind of trips. No point in rushing, we can take the scenic route,' he'd said with grin when he'd realised they weren't desperate for a quick delivery.

The estate agent had been and taken photographs and the house would be on the market within the week. He was hopeful of a quick sell, he'd told Jeannie, saying the house was a sought-after property in a good area that didn't come on the market very often.

Briony smiled to herself as she remembered Maeve's excited phone call after her meeting with the auction house. 'I did what you said – I asked for a substantial rise, definite working hours and four weeks holiday a year, plus of course Christmas, Easter and bank holidays. They didn't bat an eyelid. Oh, and I've got an office upgrade – one with a bigger desk and an actual window. I start next week.'

The captain's voice over the Tannoy broke into Briony's thoughts. Apparently, the weather in Nice was sunny and twenty-one degrees and they would be landing in approximately ten minutes. Turning her head away from the window, Briony took a deep breath, determined not to think about the narrow runway landing strip.

* * *

With only a carry-on bag, she'd hoped to be through passport control and customs quickly, but it still took over forty minutes before she was through customs and exiting the arrivals hall and making for the taxi rank. She'd decided not to hire a car because at some stage soon she would have to buy one. Until then she would walk to the village and get the bus into town. Thankfully, the taxi driver, although perfectly polite and smiley, was not chatty, as he concentrated on navigating the traffic and finding the slip road for the A8.

Half an hour later, Briony was standing outside the cottage and watching him drive away. Putting the key in the lock and opening the front door, she smiled happily. She was home and it felt so good.

19

Briony was sitting out on the terrace sipping a mug of tea and feeling happy to be back, but it also felt a little weird being there on her own. She guessed that was something she was going to have to get used to until her mum arrived. Life was going to be pretty full on anyway when Gerry arrived with the van full of their belongings. Briony couldn't help worrying where everything was going to go; she definitely needed to make space for her and Jeannie's things. Before the van arrived, she wanted to try to give the cottage a bit of a makeover, nothing drastic but start to put her own mark on it.

Lucy had invited her for supper that evening and suggested if she wandered up to the farmhouse early evening they could talk about the Girl Friday job before they ate. Briefly, Briony wondered whether she'd been a tad impulsive volunteering her services without knowing what the job would actually involve. Running the farmhouse and several gîtes, as well as filming for the YouTube channel and putting food on the table regularly, was a lot for one person, although Lucy seemed to thrive on it. Thoughtfully, Briony sipped her tea. She was looking forward to working with Lucy and didn't really mind what she did to help. Being busy for the next few months would be good and allow her to settle into her new life before she had to start making decisions about a future proper job.

She glanced at her watch. Just time for a reviving shower before she walked up to the farm.

The dining-room door was open and as she walked past, Briony saw the boxes from the attic still on the table. Maybe tonight when she got back she'd have another quick look.

* * *

Briony walked up the field track to the farm, carefully closing gates behind her. Lucy was setting the table under the loggia ready for supper and gave her a welcoming hug. 'You're back. All go well in the UK?'

'Yes, thanks. Mum's house is listed with an estate agent and a van will soon be trundling its way down through France with our belongings. Adam still working?'

Lucy pulled a face. 'I'm in his bad books. He and Elliot are down in the Stables currently cursing me. We had a big delivery of beds and sofas recently for the new gîtes there and they are, umm, putting the final pieces together.'

Briony smiled. 'Rather them than me. I either lose screws and fittings or have some left over. Never sure which is worse. Either way not ideal.'

'They should be up soon. I've made a big batch of spaghetti Bolognese to help placate them. But, meanwhile, it gives us a chance to talk. Are you still happy to come and help me?'

'Yes.'

'I need another pair of hands to help me run the farmhouse and the gîtes. So basically it's housework on changeover day, which is usually Saturday, and helping me in the kitchen occasionally, but I was also wondering about your computer skills? I never seem to catch up with marketing the gîtes so I could do with a hand there too.'

'I'm not a total computer expert, but I know enough to more than get by. I'm familiar with websites like Canva for making adverts, et cetera. I'm good at editing videos. And I quite like spreadsheets.'

Lucy's mouth fell open. 'You like spreadsheets? Are you mad? They are the work of the devil!'

Briony shrugged. 'I like things to be organised.'

'We'll have to have a session together on the computer, but first are you okay to work this Saturday for a couple of hours? I want to make the beds up in both No.1 and No.2 The Stables and dress the rooms. Put a few pictures up. Place cushions. You know the kind of thing. Also need to get some photos up on the website and start advertising them.'

'Sure. How many hours are you likely to want me every week? Regular or ad hoc when you're snowed under?'

'I was thinking about Saturday being a fixed day because it's normally changeover day and then one day in the week, Thursday perhaps, for some admin, but there may be more once the season gets under way, if guests want dinner or breakfast, so maybe a couple of hours some mornings – but if that's too much, just say.'

'Saturdays and Thursdays are fine right now. There is one thing. I haven't registered as a resident yet, so technically I don't think I'm supposed to work. So can I just be a friend helping you out occasionally until I've got my visa sorted out? The notaire is helping with that and setting up a bank account, so I'm hoping it won't be too long a drawn-out process.'

'Of course. Ah, here come the men. Time for supper.'

'Can I help carry food out?'

'That would be great.'

'Welcome back,' Adam said as he walked into the kitchen.

Elliot simply said. 'Hi,' before smiling at her.

Supper was delicious and Briony smiled as she listened to the banter between the brothers.

'Do you have a brother?' Lucy asked. 'I don't and when I first met these two, I couldn't believe how they sparred with each other, but I quickly realised most of the time it wasn't serious.'

'No brothers or sisters for me,' Briony said. 'I would have loved a sister.'

'Our daughters are as thick as thieves, always have been. Personally I'm waiting for when one of them meets the love of their life,' Adam said, smiling. 'They're so close, I wouldn't want to be the mister – as the old song says – who comes between them.'

'They'll be fine,' Lucy said, standing up. 'Apple

pie anyone?' she asked, picking up the empty spaghetti Bolognese bowl. Briony stacked the used plates and cutlery and followed Lucy into the kitchen. Lucy handed her small plates and a jug of cream. 'Thanks.'

Back out under the loggia, Adam had lit a couple of lanterns with citron candles inside to help keep the midges and mosquitoes at bay and placed them on the table and he and Elliot were talking cars. Briony took the opportunity to ask their advice as she placed the plates and cream on the table. 'Where is the best place locally to look for a reasonably priced car? Finding one is high on my to-do list.'

'Both Cannes and Antibes have garages with a big selection of second-hand cars that come with a good warranty,' Adam said. 'You shouldn't have any trouble getting one. Have a look on the internet too. When you find one, if you want either of us to check it out, just ask.'

'Thanks. I'd appreciate that.'

Twilight had fallen when Briony stood up to leave. 'Thanks for supper. I'd better get back to the cottage before it gets too dark. Stupidly I didn't think about bringing a torch.'

Elliot stood up. 'I'll walk you back down the track.'

'No, honestly I'll be fine. It's not really dark yet.'

'It's not a problem. I haven't walked Luna yet this evening,' Elliot said.

'Okay, if you're sure, thanks.'

The track was wide enough for the two of them to walk side by side as Luna bounded ahead. 'How do you feel about being back at the cottage on your own?'

Briony turned to look at Elliot, grateful that he had broken the silence. 'It feels strange without Granny Giselle and also knowing that it's mine. I suspect it's going to take me some time to settle. Trying to decide what to do with Granny's things is going to be hard and probably upsetting.'

'That must be difficult. It takes courage to begin a new life in a foreign country without adding in the poignancy of missing a loved one. My new life was thrust upon me unexpectedly too, but I didn't have to cope with grieving at the same time.' He glanced at her. 'All I can say is that I have discovered there is nowhere quite like France for nourishing a certain *joie de vivre* – you just have to give it time.' He gave her a reassuring smile.

'Thank you, that's good to hear,' Briony said.

They were almost at the cottage gate when Briony spoke. 'Can I ask you something?'

'Of course.' Elliot glanced at her and waited.

'I've wanted a pet for years, but it hasn't been possible until now, so I was wondering if...'

Elliot stopped and glared at her. 'I hope you're not going to ask to have Luna as she was your grandmother's dog. But if you were about to ask that, the answer is a resounding NO.'

Briony gave a startled gasp. 'No, of course I wasn't going to ask to have Luna. That would be cruel to you both. She's definitely your dog. I thought as a vet you might sometimes hear of dogs and cats needing to be rehomed, or you could point me in the direction of a local refuge. I'm not in any rush, it's something for the future when I'm more settled.'

She sensed Elliot's relief as he exhaled.

'Yes, we do occasionally need to find new homes for animals,' he said as he opened the gate into the cottage's garden. 'I'll let you know if that happens. Right, safely home,' and Elliot waited for Briony to walk into the garden before closing the gate. 'Goodnight.' And he strode off in the direction of the lake.

'Goodnight, and thank you,' Briony called out to his retreating back, wondering where the friendly, approachable man she'd sat at the supper table with had gone. The kind, chivalrous man who had offered to walk her home had vanished. She seemed to have this unique, unintentional ability to upset him when-ever they were alone together. It was a good job they were unlikely to be thrown together often and she determined whenever that happened in the future, she'd try to avoid saying anything contentious.

* * *

Elliot trudged his way along the path to the lake, berating himself for being so sharp and cold with Briony and jumping to the wrong conclusion before she'd finished speaking. The unexpected thought that dropped into his brain that she was going to ask to have Luna had made him speak impulsively out of turn. He couldn't bear the idea of not having Luna in his life. He knew it sounded fanciful to other people, but he and Luna understood each other.

The day he'd arrived to live on the farm, scarred by all the pain and trauma of the past months, Luna had bounded across to his side to greet him. Instantly becoming his dog. A warm feeling had spread through his body as he stroked her and she leant into him, her gaze never leaving his face. Seeming to tell him: 'It's going to be all right. You've got me now.' There was no way anybody was going to take her away from him.

As for Briony, he couldn't help but wonder what it was about her that got under his skin and made him act like he did. He sensed that she was a very likeable woman – a woman who, in the past, he would have been attracted to. Even now, when becoming involved with any woman was definitely not on his current agenda, he felt a certain desire to get to know Briony better. But it wasn't something he intended to act upon. Staying away from her as much as possible would be his best bet.

20

Briony was up early the next morning and made herself a coffee, which she drank sitting in the kitchen whilst trying to figure out how to organise herself for the next few days. Some food shopping was high on the list to get her through the weekend, so a visit to the village shop for essentials like cheese, eggs, yoghurts and some salad ingredients. Stocking up at the boulangerie with bread was also on her list. Tomorrow, Saturday, she was working with Briony in the Stables. Monday she'd catch the bus into Cannes, find a cash machine and get some more cash in euros, before doing a bigger *supermarché* shop and catching a taxi home.

So that left this afternoon and evening, and all

day Sunday, to potter around the cottage working out how to put her own mark on the place. Make it feel more like her home rather than still being Giselle's. Nothing drastic: move the furniture around in the sitting room, change the pictures, buy some new cushions and maybe new curtains for winter. She'd already decided that a pot of yellow paint to brighten up the kitchen was on the shopping list.

* * *

An hour later, Briony was back from the village, the shopping had been put away, the kettle was on and there were two slices of bread in the toaster for a late breakfast. Taking her breakfast out on to the terrace, Briony inhaled the fresh air as she looked around. The garden was going to need some attention too, but she knew Jeannie, a keen gardener, would welcome taking charge out there.

Once she'd finished her breakfast, Briony wandered into the sitting room. There was too much furniture in here for her taste, although she did love it all. Perhaps if she rearranged it, had the two Chesterfield settees facing each other, with one of the coffee tables in between, that would work. The writing bureau could stay where it was, an armchair could go either side of the French doors. Another one in the corner. And ornaments could disappear from the bookshelves, there were far too many.

The first problem arose when she tried to move the settees. They were too heavy, she needed a man's strength. Maybe Gerry when he arrived would help move them. So she left them where they were and moved the armchairs nearer the French doors, placing a small table on one side of each of them. The lamps that had stood on the tables she placed on the floor temporarily by the bureau. One was a beautiful art deco brass lady. That was definitely staying. She'd decide what to do with the others later.

Briony remembered seeing some empty boxes in the shed where the garden furniture had been stored. After fetching a couple, she started to take the ornaments down from the bookshelves. More space for books and photographs. As she worked, she realised a lot of the items, a mix of French and English, were collectable, if not quite to her own taste. Some old Limoges plates, a couple of French chalk-ware beautiful decorative figurines. Small things that would be snapped up in an auction, but for now they were going in a box until she could decide what to do with them.

Lucy sent a text that evening.

See you at 9 o'clock tomorrow
morning outside the Stables.

Briony popped one of the pizzas she'd bought in
the village into the oven and when it was ready settled down with a glass of wine at the kitchen table to
eat while she scrolled through cars for sale on the
internet.

21

'Good morning. Welcome to No.1 The Stables,' Lucy
said, unlocking the door as Briony arrived. 'We've got
a lot of work ahead of us this morning. I thought
we'd start with the bedrooms and work our way
down.'

The two bedrooms were light and airy. One had a
double bed, the other two singles that could be
joined together. Both contained a built-in wardrobe,
a dressing table and comfy chair placed by the
window with several cushions piled high on it. Curtains made of toile de Jouy had been hung at the windows. Matching bedlinen, feather duvets and pillows
had been placed on the bed, with bales of white
towels placed alongside.

Together, Lucy and Briony made the beds in both rooms before they arranged four cushions against the pillows, leaving two cushions on the chair. A soft rug was placed on the floor either side of the bed as a finishing touch.

'What d'you think, bedrooms okay?' Lucy said, glancing at Briony. 'I'd like to have bought better-quality furniture rather than flatpack, but with seven gîtes to furnish...' she shrugged. 'The plan is to slowly upgrade everything as the gîtes start to earn their keep.'

'I'd be very happy to book a holiday here,' Briony said. 'The bedrooms look great. The bedlinen and towels are of high quality, which is always a bonus.'

'Right. Downstairs.'

The next hour flew by as the two of them made the sitting room look inviting, with cushions on the chairs, a throw on the settee, a few scatter rugs and a couple of framed retro posters of Cannes and the film festival hung on the walls. Lucy had already put crockery, cutlery, cooking utensils, tea towels, hand towels, kitchen paper and dishwashing tablets in the kitchen.

'I always put a welcome basket on the counter for new guests.' She glanced at Briony. 'I was wondering too about making up a folder of local attractions.

The Tourist Information centre have lots of brochures. I think holidaymakers would find it useful.'

'Definitely.' Briony nodded. She looked through the kitchen window. 'Is there an outdoor eating space?'

'Yes,' Lucy said, opening the kitchen door. 'There's a small barbeque out here, a table with a parasol and half a dozen chairs. Adam is going to pop some potted plants over from the *pépinière* before the first guests arrive to make it look a bit prettier. Oh, and a potted plumbago or two outside the front doors. Ready for No.2? The layout is a carbon copy of this one,' Lucy said. 'I think we've got time before lunch.'

As they repeated the process, albeit with a different colour scheme and retro posters of Antibes in No.2, Briony asked, 'Do you have many bookings for the season yet?'

'The Cider House – the first gîte we opened last year and the only one I've done any advertising for – is booked for the whole of July and August and most of September, with a smattering of bookings throughout the early summer months and Easter. Some is repeat business, which hopefully means I'm doing it right,' Lucy said, smiling. 'If I could get the

Stables advertised and maybe get a booking for Easter, that would be good.'

'It's only three weeks away,' Briony said. 'But I suspect a lot of people wait until the last minute at this time of the year to see what the weather is likely to do.' She took her phone out of her jean pocket. 'Shall I take a couple of shots? You can try them with your normal advertiser.'

'Please snap away. After lunch I'll show you what I've been doing up until now.' Lucy glanced at her watch. 'I'll leave you here and get back up to the farm and start organising some lunch. Can you lock up when you've got enough pics?' And Lucy held the gîte keys out. 'Lunch will be ready in about ten minutes. See you then.'

'I didn't expect you to feed me,' Briony said, surprised.

'Perk of the job,' Lucy said and left her to finish taking photos.

* * *

Briony took a couple of pictures of all the rooms from different angles before locking the door and making her way across to the farm. Adam was sat at the kitchen table scrolling on his phone and glanced up as she entered after knocking. 'Hi. Don't worry about knocking in future.' Seeing the gîte keys in her hand, he pointed to the keyboard near the pantry door. 'They live up there.'

Lucy placed three bowls of soup on the table, a plate of charcuterie, a cheese board and a pile of crusty bread. 'Lunch is served,' she said cheerfully, placing a jug of water and glasses on the table. 'Bon appétit.'

Briony hadn't realised how hungry she was and tucked in eagerly.

'I'm going to the *supermarché* on Monday, would you like a lift?' Lucy asked as she broke off a chunk of bread. 'Monday there is always an antique market in Forville, which I like to have a look at when I get the chance.'

'I remember wandering around that market several times with Granny. It's probably the reason I ended up in the job I did,' Briony laughed. 'I have to warn you, I do need to stock up on lots of things at the *supermarché*. I also need to find a cash machine.'

'There's one quite close to the market,' Lucy said. 'If not, there is one at the *supermarché*.'

'Brilliant,' Briony said.

After lunch Lucy took Briony up to her office and switched on her iMac computer. The two of them spent the next half-hour going through the marketing Lucy had been doing.

Briony downloaded the photos from her phone glanced at Lucy. 'If you are serious about trying to get Easter bookings for the Stables, how about something like this?' She pulled a picture up and started to type.

> The early bird may traditionally get the worm, but the latecomer will get the holiday bargain! Visit our website to see the newly finished gîtes that are ready for their first visitors this Easter. New introductory price!

'It's a bit corny, but with the right pictures and the right price on the website, it should work. Schedule it to post several times on Facebook, Instagram and Blue Sky over the next week and there should be some interest.'

'I'll see what I can do this evening,' Lucy said. 'Unless you have time to stay this afternoon and work on it?'

'Have you got Photoshop on the computer? Good. I'll sort an advert out for you. If you're happy with it, try and upload it this evening. You'll need to add the

Stables to the booking form on the website with the prices and everything.'

Briony made several small Canva adverts with the photos she'd taken. After Lucy had given her the password for the website, she'd made a few adjustments to it, as well as adding the booking form for the Stables. Now it was up to Lucy to approve what she'd done, decide where she wanted the adverts shown and then schedule the days and times.

It was late afternoon when Lucy poked her head around the office door. 'Time you were off. Want a cuppa before you go?'

'No thanks,' Briony said. 'You wouldn't have an umbrella I could borrow, would you?' During the afternoon, the weather had changed and looking out of the window Briony could see a gentle drizzle was now wetting the ground.

'Of course, lots in the utility room.'

Downstairs, Lucy handed her a brightly coloured umbrella.

'Mind how you go on the track, it can get slippery in places. See you Monday.'

Once back at the cottage, Briony dried herself off and started to think about a meal. For some reason, she really fancied a cheese and tomato toasty, something Giselle had made for her many times in the past when she'd been staying with her. She opened a couple of the units under the work surface. Bowls, plates, Kenwood mixer, and right at the back a modern version of the sandwich maker she remembered. Result, and she set to work to make a toasty cheese sandwich.

Briony had barely finished the delicious sandwich when her mother rang, anxious for an update and to tell her how things were progressing at her end.

'Gerry is coming Monday to start packing up my personal stuff, before loading the furniture and everything I'm bringing into the van. He's booked the overnight ferry for Thursday. He's still planning on taking his time and he thinks he'll probably arrive with you either the following Tuesday afternoon or Wednesday morning.'

'Okay, so that gives me just over a week to make some room for things,' Briony said. 'Has the house gone on the market yet?'

'I've got the first viewings next week. The agent says the advert in the paper has generated a lot of interest, so fingers crossed,' Jeannie said. 'How's your first few days gone?'

'Good. Started to clear the sitting room a little. Had my first day as Girl Friday today, and Lucy and I seem to work well together. She's giving me a lift to the supermarket on Monday so I can stock up on food and stuff. When do you reckon you'll be able to get back here?'

Jeannie sighed. 'Not sure. I can't wait to get back down and help you sort out the cottage. It's cold here too. Not seen the sun since I returned.'

'It's raining here at the moment, if that makes you feel any better,' Briony said laughing. 'Right, I'm going to have a quick walk to the lake before it gets dark. Talk soon. Love you, Mum. Bye.'

22

The rain had slowed down when Briony pulled on her wellington boots and an ancient waterproof coat of Giselle's still hanging on a peg by the back door and set off for the lake.

Nearing the lake, she saw Elliot standing on the edge. She hesitated. Maybe she should turn back. Elliot deserved time on his own as much as she did. Besides, she wasn't ready for another skirmish with him. But Luna had already spotted her and raced over. Mindful of Elliot's reaction the last time they'd spoken, Briony tried to curb her own enthusiasm for seeing the dog, as well as keep the conversation on safe neutral ground – like the weather.

'Everything always smells so fresh after a rain

shower,' she said, sniffing the air and smiling brightly at him as she looked around. 'Too late for sun, so no possibility of a rainbow this evening.'

'We'll have to make do with the rainbows on your boots,' Elliot said.

Briony giggled and glanced down. 'Luckily I've got small feet as they were in the children's department. One of the few advantages of only being five feet nothing,' she said.

'How's sorting out the cottage coming along?' Elliot asked.

'Slowly. I'd made up my mind to rearrange the sitting-room furniture but didn't get past the first hurdle of moving the Chesterfield settees; they are so heavy. I'm going to have to wait until Gerry and the removal van from England arrive in about ten days. So, in the meantime, I'm boxing up miscellaneous stuff instead. I'm going to start on the kitchen cupboards next.'

'I can give you a hand with the settees if you'd like me to,' Elliot offered.

'Oh, I couldn't ask you to do that.' Briony shook her head instantly, hoping she'd managed to hide her start of surprise at the suggestion. 'The rain is getting heavier again. I think I'm going to make for home.'

'You didn't ask, I'm offering. No time like the

present. Come on, you can show me the inside of Owls Nest, I've always wanted to see inside the cottage and at least we'll be out of the rain,' and Elliot started to walk in the direction of the cottage, Luna trotting at his side.

Briony stared after him for several seconds, unable to fathom why he'd made such an unexpected offer. There had to be more to it than just wanting to view the cottage. She saw him glance back to see where she was, so she started hurrying to catch him up.

Unlocking the kitchen door, shortly after, Briony said, 'Welcome to Owls Nest. Hang on, I'll find us both a towel. And one for Luna as well.'

Once they'd dried off the worst of the rain, Briony led the way to the sitting room.

'It's not looking its best with all the boxes, I'm afraid.'

Luna, following them into the room, gave a short bark and made straight for the armchair Briony had pushed into a corner, jumped up on it and curled herself into a ball.

Elliot went to call her off, but Briony stopped him. 'I'd forgotten that was her chair when Granny sat in this room. It must be strange for her to be back in the cottage.'

Elliot gave a brief nod. 'Yes. Now, what is it you want to do with the settees?'

Briony explained she'd like them to face each other, in front of but not too close to the log burner with the coffee table in between them.

Five minutes later, the two of them had pushed the Chesterfields into the exact position Briony had wanted and they stood considering the arrangement. 'I think that works, don't you?' she said, turning to Elliot. 'Thank you so much.'

'It looks good.' He glanced into the dining room and saw the boxes on the table. 'Do you want those boxes moved somewhere?'

Briony shook her head. 'Not right now, thank you. I'm planning on going through them soon and it will be easier to spread the contents out on the table. Would you like a coffee or a glass of wine as a small thank you for your help?'

'No thanks, I'd better get Luna get back to my place – make sure she knows where home is these days.'

'Oh I'm sure she knows,' Briony said smiling, thinking he was joking, but Elliot had already whistled Luna to his side and was striding towards the kitchen. Briony sighed. 'Thanks again,' she said as Elliot opened the back door. 'I'm really grateful.'

'Glad to help, goodnight,' and Elliot and Luna were gone.

Briony wandered back into the sitting room and sank down on one of the settees. It had been kind of Elliot to help her move the furniture, but Luna making herself at home so completely had obviously upset him. How on earth was she ever going to persuade him that neither she nor Jeannie would ever separate him from the dog who obviously adored him?

23

Standing in the house that was feeling emptier by the day, Jeannie was suddenly swamped with unexpected doubts about leaving. Was she really doing the right thing moving to France, even though it was what she'd often dreamed of doing of down the years? She'd lived in this house for nearly thirty years and it had been a lovely family home for all those years. It was hard to envisage walking out of it to begin a new life, albeit in a country and cottage she'd grown to love.

But nothing in life stayed the same forever. Briony had moved out, Jeromé had died, Giselle had moved in a few years later and now she was gone too. After

Briony had grown up and flown the nest, she and Jeromé had enjoyed being just a couple again until his unexpected early death in his fifties when the house had seemed so, so empty. Those early years after he'd passed had been lonely as she'd struggled to come to terms with being a single middle-aged woman. Having Giselle move in with her for what turned out to be her final year and a half had been a turning point – she'd felt needed again and there was a purpose to her life.

And now there was this new life in France planned for her and Briony. Jeannie couldn't kid herself that her purpose there would be to look after her daughter. To help maybe, but it was only fair that from the beginning they led independent lives whilst sharing a home. Had their own interests, their own friends. Hopefully, Briony would meet a new man too, someone who would treat her properly, love her and they would have a family together before it was too late.

As for the new unexpected complication in her own life, maybe the best thing would be to walk away from getting involved. But Jeannie wasn't sure that she could do that. The chance for her to be part of a couple again was too tempting not to at least see if there was a possibility of reigniting certain feelings that had by necessity been smothered and un-acted on in the past.

Jeannie sighed. So many people seemed to reinvent themselves, find new partners and become happier when they shook off their old lives and started anew. But what if it didn't work out for her? What would she do then? She'd pick herself up and dust herself down like she had done countless times in the past when life had thrown a curveball. Briony and she were as close as any other mother and daughter she knew. Living in France was going to be good for them both.

The mobile in her pocket rang at that moment. She glanced at Caller ID. Yann.

Smiling, she pressed the button and accepted the call. After all, if you don't take a chance, nothing changes.

With all the unwanted ornaments and knick-knacks boxed up, after a late breakfast eaten on the terrace, Briony decided to start on the kitchen cupboards. She took the last box from the garden shed and emptied the cupboards under the work surface. Lots of terracotta dairy bowls of various sizes, wonderful for salads and fruit, glass bowls, cooking trays, cake tins and crockery. Briony pulled the Kenwood mixer out, that was definitely staying, and she placed it on the counter.

The box filled, she grabbed the garage key off the hook in the corner of the kitchen where it lived. Maybe she'd find some empty boxes in there.

Pushing the key into the lock and pulling the wooden door open, Briony braced herself for what she'd find.

Her mum hadn't exaggerated. Old-fashioned bicycles were hanging on the wall, including one that Briony remembered riding into the village years ago. There was even an old wooden handcart hooked over two large brackets in the far corner, as well as galvanised water buckets, a tin bath, several dog baskets, garden implements and a large parrot cage. How old was that? Briony couldn't remember ever seeing or hearing about a parrot being in the cottage.

What on earth was she going to do with all this stuff? Not to mention everything from the house that she was packing up. Clearing the cottage was turning into a nightmare project.

Turning to leave, she saw some empty boxes thrown into the corner nearest the door. She might as well take them and carry on clearing the kitchen of unwanted dishes.

By midday she'd run out of boxes and also energy. She planned to have a hot reviving shower followed by lunch and a few relaxing hours in the garden reading, with maybe a walk down to the lake later. She needed to get into a routine of walking so that when she eventually had a dog it would be second nature to go for two walks a day.

It was a gorgeous evening when she opened the field gate and set off. The sky was still blue, although the sun was beginning its descent; the air was balmy and a perfect temperature for a walk.

Reaching the lake, Briony stopped and listened. The cicadas in the trees were extra noisy this evening and there was the usual crowd of robins, chaffinches, tits and sparrows flying back and forth between the nearby trees and shrubs. Briony walked out along the wooden jetty and stood looking over the lake and at the rowing boat moored alongside. Giving in to a sudden urge, she stepped slowly and carefully into the boat and sat on the central wooden plank. Tonight there were several ducks on the water in the middle of the lake and she watched them bobbing around for a while.

She closed her eyes and took a deep breath. It

was starting to feel more and more that the decision to move here had been the right one. Her mum would be back soon and together they could sort the cottage and garden out. Working with Lucy for the summer was going to be fun and...

Suddenly there was the noise of a huge splash and the boat rocked. Startled, Briony instinctively put a hand out and grabbed the side of the boat as she opened her eyes. Luna was in the water swimming, whilst Elliot stood to one side looking embarrassed.

'Sorry if Luna startled you.'

'No worries. At least she didn't try to join me in the boat,' Briony said, laughing. 'I love seeing her, but we must stop meeting like this. Two days in a row people will start talking.' Oh dear, the look on his face told her he was not amused by her comment. Quickly, she changed the subject. 'No sign of a dog for me yet?'

Elliot shook his head. 'No, sorry.'

Carefully, Briony stood up, accepted the hand Elliot held out to help her and stepped back onto the jetty. 'I'd better get back. I'll leave you to enjoy the peace and quiet.'

'Please don't let me chase you away,' Elliot said.

'You're not. I've had a busy day, so an early night is on the cards.'

'Goodnight then.'

'Night.'

With an inward sigh, Briony turned away to walk home. What was it about Elliot that got under her skin? Or, to put it another way, why had there been an unexpected frisson through her body when she'd taken his hand?

24

Lucy had suggested that she picked Briony up Monday morning from the cottage. 'No point in dragging you up here when I'm going to be driving past your door. Nine o'clock okay?'

Briony was waiting outside the front door of the cottage as Lucy drove down. 'Good morning,' Lucy said brightly. 'Hope you had a good weekend?'

'Yes, thanks. I made a start on sorting out the cottage. Moving furniture around, putting some of Giselle's things into boxes. I will have to decide what to do with them later, but for now I've squeezed some of them into the garage. The rest are in the sitting room.' She sighed. 'I hadn't realised Granny was such a hoarder.'

'House clearing can be hard,' Lucy said sympathetically. 'I'll make my way to Forville Market whilst you go to the cash machine. We can meet up there and you might find somebody who can come and do a mini house clearance for you. Take away the furniture you decide not to keep.'

'Thanks, good idea. How was your Sunday?'

'Busy. Those tweaks you did to the website and the social media promo posts you did seem to have garnered us some attention. Lots of likes and visits to the website. I'm hoping there will be a couple of bookings as a result later today.'

Once in Cannes, Lucy parked as close to the market as she could, and pointed out the street where Briony would find the cash machine. 'See you in the market.'

Briony made for the cash machine and joined the queue of three people.

Putting the cash safely in her bag, she made for the market hoping that she'd have time to have a quick look around before Lucy was ready to leave. Despite the noisy foreign chatter around her, Briony felt herself relax. Alongside the auctions for Raise Your Hand, she'd also organised mini festivals and markets like this one had been in her life for years. Lots of stalls with a mixture of antiques and bric-abrac, a rare book stand, lovely French linens and artisans offering furniture restoration services. She wandered around for a few moments, soaking up the atmosphere before stopping by a stall with smaller objet d'art nicely arranged on a velvet cloth. Briony smiled at the woman standing behind the stand as she looked at a small brass antique French carriage clock, priced at two hundred and fifty euros.

'*Bonjour.* Can I help you?' the woman said.

Before Briony could answer, Lucy was at her side. 'Hi, are we ready to hit the *supermarché*?'

Briony nodded and picked up one of the business cards that were on the table. '*Merci.* Do you have a shop in town?'

The woman shook her head. 'No shop – business rents are too expensive. I'm here every week and also in Antibes in summer.'

'Thanks again,' and Briony turned away, not wanting to delay Lucy, who was clearly ready to leave. 'Sorry I didn't mean to keep you waiting,' she apologised. 'I tend to forget the time in places like this. I was in my element.'

'Did you find anyone to help clear the cottage?'

'No, I was so busy looking at actual items for sale that I forgot to look.'

Briony was quiet for the short journey to the big out-of-town *supermarché* situated above Antibes.

'Penny for them?' Lucy said, glancing at her as she drove into a parking place.

'They're worth more than a penny,' Briony smiled. 'I've had an idea that I need to think through properly before I discuss it with anyone. Quite possibly it could be the stupidest idea I've ever had, in which case I shall never tell a soul.'

'Okay. Let's shop before it gets too busy,' Lucy said.

Pushing a large trolley each they made for the store and did just that. An hour later both trolleys were filled, although Briony's took the prize for containing the most diverse shopping. DIY stuff, like pots of paint, sandpaper, brushes nails, hammer, a battery-driven screwdriver, all were nestled in with the food shopping.

'Can I treat you to coffee and cake, or even an early lunch as a thank you?' Briony said, once it was all loaded in Lucy's car.

'I'd better get back,' Lucy said regretfully. 'I've a mountain of emails to sort through. We'll have lunch out another time.'

Once she was home, and the shopping was put away, Briony made herself a coffee, opened a packet of choc chip cookies and sat out on the terrace in the sunshine, turning her idea over and over in her head.

Wandering around the market this morning, she'd had what she could only think of as a light-bulb moment. Could she become a brocante trader in France? Buy things and sell them in markets.

She'd have to start slowly. Get to know her customer base, their likes and dislikes. Different things would appeal to the Riviera tourists in the summer – things they could carry easily on the flight home. Although not an expert on anything she knew a little about lots of items. She had an eye for good quality and she'd surprised herself this morning wandering around how little bits of knowledge about certain pieces had drifted into her mind.

That little brass carriage clock, early nineteenth century by a French horologist, was a case in point. She knew the woman had seriously underpriced it. It was worth double what she was selling it for. Briony knew because a similar one had gone through the auction rooms a couple of months ago, not in as good a condition and without its original leather carrying case which the one in the market came with.

The thought of being her own boss and doing something she loved was quite intoxicating. Getting an entrepreneur business of selling second-hand items off the ground would take a lot of planning and hard work, which she knew she was more than capable of doing. One of the biggest questions that would need answering early on was did she need a shopfront? Or could she just have a stall in various markets throughout the year? Another question was – where would she find stock?

Briony laughed out loud. So many of Giselle's things she'd been boxing up would be regarded as collectable by other people. She already had more than enough stock to start her off in fact.

Finishing her coffee, Briony stood up. She'd keep mulling it over for a few days, get everything straight in her mind before mentioning it to anyone. What she really needed to do this week was to find herself some transport. Time to do some serious searching of the internet.

25

Briony made her way up to the farm later that afternoon, hoping she'd catch Adam or even Elliot. Elliot's Toyota wasn't by his cottage so he clearly wasn't around. Fingers crossed that Adam was in the house and not out working in the vineyard or down in the avocado field.

Opening the farm door, she called out, 'It's only me. Can I come in? I need your advice please.'

'Yes of course,' Lucy answered. 'Everything all right? I've just made a pot of tea, would you like a cup?'

'Please,' Briony said, happy to see Adam sitting at the kitchen table, tea and biscuits in front of him. 'I hate to be a nuisance, but I think I've found a vehicle on LeBonCoin.'

'LeBonCoin, the great French treasure trove of online advertising of all things for sale everywhere in France,' Adam said, laughing.

Lucy handed her a mug. 'Exciting. What kind? What colour? I know that's a very girly thing to ask, but colour is important.'

'It's a 2012 Renault Kangoo. One owner since new; 104,000 kilometres on the clock. Colour red. Three thousand two fifty euros. Is it too old to buy? It sounds a good deal to me, but I know nothing about cars.'

'Those Kangoos go on forever. There's one in the village that is at least thirty years old,' Adam said thoughtfully. 'If it's been well maintained and has a current *control technique*, the age doesn't really matter. Where is it? And is it a private sale or a trader?'

'It's actually quite local – Cannes la Bocca. And it's a private sale. Which was why I was wondering whether you could telephone and ask the questions you know I should ask, and then would you possibly have time to take me to see it if you think it's okay?'

'If you give me the number, I'll ring now,' Adam said.

Briony gave him the piece of paper she'd scribbled the number on.

She sipped her tea listening to the technical questions Adam was asking and wondering whether the answers were good or bad. Adam gave a smile as he finished the call with a cheerful '*D'accord. Merci beaucoup.*'

'It's certainly worth a look,' Adam said. 'The owner has told me where it is and we can go and see it any time. I'd take you this evening, but Bruno is arriving soon for one of our regular vineyard progress meetings. Elliot should be home any time soon, I'm sure he'd be happy to take you. Otherwise I can take you in the morning.'

'Tomorrow morning will be fine,' Briony said, swallowing her disappointment at the delay. 'If you're happy to take me.'

'I'll come and pick you up after breakfast,' Adam said.

'Thank you, I really do appreciate it,' Briony said. 'See you then. Have a good evening.'

She'd been home less than ten minutes when there was a double toot of a car horn outside. Curiously, she opened the front door to find Elliot in his 4x4 with Luna looking out of the back window.

'Adam tells me you'd like to look at a Kangoo.

Jump in and I'll take you. He's rung the owner and told him to expect us.'

'Oh but I...' Briony stopped. She didn't want to be on tenterhooks, wondering if she was going to say something that would upset him. But she really did want to see the car. 'I'll just get my bag.'

As they drove down towards the coast, Briony said, 'I hope Adam didn't put pressure on you to take me. But I'm really grateful.'

Elliot gave a small shrug. 'He knew I was the best person to look at this car – I had one years ago in the UK. It was a great car.'

'Did Adam tell you how to find where we're going?'

'I've put the directions in the satnav. Basically we've to head for the *bord de mer*, and then take Boulevard Leader up towards the Croix des Gardes and the house we want is about two kilometres up on the left-hand side.'

Fifteen minutes later, they were pulling up behind the red Kangoo itself, with the owner, Francois, sat inside waiting for them.

After some introductions, Elliot took the car for a test run and came back smiling. 'It's a good one,' he said. 'The *control technique* was done only last week, which is good. Just drive up the road and back to make sure you can see over the steering wheel, you being five feet nothing.'

'Cheek!' Briony said, hiding her surprise at how relaxed Elliot was with her this evening.

'The seat is quite low,' Elliot said, grinning at her.

Briony drove the car up the road, did a three-point turn in a layby and drove back down to Elliot and Francois, smiling happily.

'Francois says you can have the car for three thousand euros,' Elliot said. 'He thinks you'll give it a good home.'

'Yes please,' Briony said, holding out her hand to shake on the deal. 'I'll give you a deposit and come back tomorrow with the rest of the money if that's all right. I don't have any insurance yet.'

Francois promised to have all the legal papers for the transfer ready to sign and the *carte gris*, the French version of the logbook.

Sitting in the passenger seat as Elliot drove them back to the cottage, Briony gave a contented sigh. 'Thank you so much, Elliot. I know you're probably tired after a day at work and the last thing you needed to do was drive me around.' She hesitated and glanced across at him. 'Can I cook you supper as a way of saying thank you? Nothing fancy – you have a choice of pasta or pizza – but I do have wine.' Elliot had been good company tonight and he clearly knew about cars, Kangoos in particular.

There was a short silence and Briony waited for him to refuse her offer, but to her surprise he accepted.

'Thanks, a bowl of pasta would be good. I'll drop you off, take the car back and walk down with Luna, give her a little bit of exercise.'

* * *

After Elliot had dropped her at the cottage, Briony rushed inside and started to organise supper. First, she set her favourite soft jazz playlist playing, and hummed happily along with it. It was nice enough to sit outside, she decided and set the table on the terrace with cutlery and wine glasses. She lit a couple of anti-mosquito candles and opened a bottle of red wine before going back into the kitchen and quickly making some garlic bread as a small aperitif, tossing a green salad together to accompany the pasta, grating some parmesan cheese and topping up the olive oil and the balsamic vinegar in their respective containers.

Luna arrived before Elliot and barked impatiently at the garden gate to be let in. Briony laughed and lifted the latch and the dog was immediately at her side wanting a stroke.

Elliot arrived half a minute later and handed her a piece of paper. 'I forgot to give you this. I made a note of the registration number and *carte gris* details, you'll need those to arrange insurance before you bring Pascal home.'

'Pascal?'

'Your Kangoo's name. Typically French, don't you think?'

'Yes, it is. Thank you. Come and sit down. Have a glass of wine while I go and put the pasta on. There's some garlic bread to stave off your hunger pangs whilst the pasta cooks.'

As they sipped a glass of wine and nibbled the garlic bread, Elliot looked at her. 'I hope you're happy with Pascal, but are you sure it's what you wanted? It's a useful vehicle, but it's more of a van than a car.'

'True.' Briony was silent for a few seconds. 'Originally I planned to get a new or newish car on contract, but I saw the Kangoo and I knew it would fit in perfectly with some new plans I might be making. Although I haven't actually decided on whether or not these plans are workable or even whether it's a good idea.' She realised she was verging on talking nonsense when she caught Elliot's amused glance.

'Sorry that wasn't very clear, was it?' She picked up the wine bottle and topped up both their glasses. 'I'll fetch the pasta. Then I'll explain why I bought Pascal.'

As she placed the bowls of pasta on the table, she said, 'I haven't mentioned my idea to anyone else yet, so it will be good to get your reaction, good or bad. Being Lucy's Girl Friday for the summer is great, but eventually I'm going to have to have some sort of other income. The only thing I know anything about is the second-hand trade, antique, vintage, however you want to describe it, having worked in it for nearly ten years. Owls Nest is full of collectables and everyday French items that people like to buy. Granny had a really good eye, but it's not necessarily things that I would want, so I already have enough stock to start in a small way.'

Elliot listened intently as she told him about her light-bulb moment in the market. 'I'd obviously start slowly, but Pascal will be a great asset in picking up larger items when I find them. And if in the end I decide running a brocante is not viable, he will make a fine run-around second car for Mum and me whether I buy a newer car or not.'

'You obviously know there are a lot of amateur dealers down on the coast, working the vide greniers and the smaller markets,' Elliot said thoughtfully. 'You'd be one step ahead of them with your knowledge. Premises?'

'I was thinking I could use the garage as a store and do the weekly market in Cannes for starters. And maybe the one in Antibes. I'd really like a base, but I know rents down here are extortionate.'

'Why don't you have a word with Adam about the empty renovated artisan outbuilding? I know both Lucy and Adam are keen to have it occupied.'

'That would be brilliant. I'll definitely ask.'

As the light started to fade, and they stayed chatting and sipping their wine, Briony felt a ripple of happiness spread through her. These kind of evenings had never materialised with Marcus. Too quiet. Too boring for him. Tonight had been anything but boring. This was the kind of evening she'd always longed to spend with someone special. Elliot had been good company and the evening had flown by. It was a long time since Briony had enjoyed an evening so much. Which was surprising really, considering how awkward their earlier meetings had been.

As a pair of owls started to call out to each other, Elliot stood up. 'I need to walk Luna to the lake and home again before it gets too dark.' To Briony's surprise, he unexpectedly leant in and kissed her cheek. 'Goodnight and thanks for supper and a lovely evening.' Before Briony could even utter a response, the garden gate had closed behind him and Luna.

Briony stared after them. French people were always greeting and saying goodbye to each other with cheek kisses. It was just something that Elliot had adopted living in France. He had not meant anything by it, but it did feel as if a tentative friendship had started to be cemented over a simple supper. Briony sensed, hoped, that given time they could become good friends. Because that was definitely all she wanted, wasn't it? Friendship not a relationship. After Marcus, she was not going to rush to let another man into her life.

Briony sighed. She would have loved to accompany Elliot to the lake if he'd suggested it. A walk would have rounded the evening off nicely. But Elliot had probably had enough of her company for one day.

She cleared the table, loaded the dishwasher and went upstairs. It had been a lovely evening, she wasn't going to spoil the memory of it by being disappointed at not being asked to go for a walk.

* * *

Elliot walked slowly to the lake with Luna trotting ahead of him, his thoughts chasing each other round and round. Why hadn't he suggested Briony accompanied him on this walk? It would have prolonged the evening nicely. What was he afraid of? She was good company. Tonight had been fun, he'd learnt a little more about her and realised she was nothing like Robyn – different values, different morals. If only he'd realised in the beginning that Robyn's hopes and dreams for the future were so different to his own, it would have saved a lot of heartbreak, especially where children were concerned. Throwing a stick into the lake and watching Luna retrieve it, Elliot sighed. Why was he so wary of becoming friends with Briony? She was definitely someone he'd already inwardly admitted to himself that he'd like to have in his life but the timing was all wrong. Too soon after Robyn. Too soon after moving to France. He simply didn't need, or want, the complication of a woman in his life whilst he concentrated on getting his career back on track. Not even one as attractive as Briony, with her understated natural beauty and her quirky footwear.

26

The next morning, Briony walked across the farmyard towards the artisan buildings. Elliot's suggestion last night that she should ask Adam about the empty one had stayed in her mind. It would be perfect. The three individual buildings were all slightly different and the empty one looked to be the biggest of the three. Holly was in her workshop with the door open, but Calvin had a notice pinned to his door apologising for 'Closure Exceptional'. As Briony approached, she could see Holly was hand-painting flowers on some plates. She glanced up as she saw Briony. '*Bonjour.* Lovely to see you again.'

'Hi. You too. That's beautiful. You're very talented.'

'I'm hoping the tourists will like them,' Holly smiled.

'Is this your only outlet?'

Holly nodded. 'Yes, for now. In the summer, Adam puts a sign out on the road which attracts passers-by, and last year when The Cider House gîte was open for the first time, the holidaymakers staying there bought several pieces. To be honest, I don't want too many customers as I couldn't cope. The idea has always been to use this place as more of a workshop, build up stock and then find outlets in town. The downside is I could do with earning more money all year round. But it's really a hobby at the moment, not a proper business, so...' Holly shrugged.

'Hopefully having more holidaymakers in the Stables this year will help then,' Briony said.

'Yes. And when the third workshop is occupied that should bring more people up here.' Holly dipped her brush in the paint and Briony realised she was holding her up.

'I'll let you get on, I have to go up to the farmhouse and see Lucy. See you again soon.'

She'd rung Lucy earlier asking if she was free to come for coffee and Lucy had immediately invited her up to the farm, saying there was a cake in the oven she couldn't leave. Briony sniffed appreciatively as she opened the kitchen door. 'That smells good,' she said.

'Apple cake. There's a slice with your name on it,' Lucy said.

'Have you ever thought about opening a little café up here?' Briony asked. 'Afternoon tea and cakes. I bet once word got around you'd be busy.'

'A café is on the list, but I keep pushing it further and further down because it's just another thing that would fall on me to organise and run and there aren't enough hours in the day all ready. But now I've got a Girl Friday, you never know.' Lucy smiled. 'Did you want to talk about anything in particular or just wanted some company?'

'Both really. I need to arrange insurance for my car before I can collect it later today, so was hoping you could give me a number? And you remember that idea I said I was thinking about and I'd tell you when I'd really thought it through? Well, I was wondering whether your third empty artisan building was still up for rent? And if it is, can I see inside it please.'

'It is still available for rent,' Lucy said, cutting two slices of the apple cake. 'Why?'

Briony took a deep breath and told tell her about

her brocante idea. 'Being my own boss really appeals and the only thing I know anything about is the world of antiques and collecting. Packing up so much of Granny's things made me realise too that she'd been quite an astute collector. But right now the cottage is just full of boxes and there's more arriving from the UK in a few days. The garage is already stuffed, so I could use some extra storage space for a few weeks even if you don't want to rent it to me permanently.'

As she finished speaking, Lucy gave her a worried look. 'Does this mean you don't want the Girl Friday job?'

'No, of course not,' Briony said hastily. 'I wouldn't let you down like that. I've said I'll do the summer and I will. The brocante thing is going to take a little while to get up and running.'

'I'll have to run your idea past Adam, but I'm sure he'll agree to you renting the unit and running a brocante from there,' Lucy said. 'If he doesn't, we can always find you some storage space somewhere. I really like the sound of the brocante though. Right, let's get your car insured. Adam is going into town this afternoon, and said to ask you, would you like him to run you in to collect it? And check the paperwork is all in order? He can pick you up at about three thirty?'

'That would be great, thank you. I'll let Francois know. I was going to catch the bus into town and then get a taxi up to the Croix des Gardes, but a lift would be lovely and a lot quicker.'

After leaving Lucy, Briony walked home and spent some time tidying her room and the kitchen before taking the garage key off its hook and going to check on an idea she'd had.

Once in the garage, she stood as close as she could get to the bicycle hanging on the side wall. Rusty in places, with its paint flaking off and bald tyres, it wasn't worth repairing to use. But cleaned, rubbed down and painted in the French colours of red white and blue, its basket on the handlebars filled with geraniums, it would make an attractive talking point outside the shop. Frustrated because there was no way she could possibly get the bike off the wall, she closed the garage up and went back indoors. Until she could move the boxes out of both the sitting room and the garage, there was very little she could do. She'd have to be content with working on her plans, making to-do lists on her laptop and trying to make room somewhere in the cottage for the furniture and boxes that were due to arrive soon. And she'd open that pot of Sunflower Yellow paint she'd bought in the *supermarché* and give the kitchen a makeover.

* * *

The post that morning had brought envelopes of papers from the notaire, both for her and her mother. Briony took Jeannie's upstairs and placed it on the dressing table in her room, ready for when she returned. Opening her own, she found the notaire had included a list of the papers she would need to provide for various visas, as well as her new bank details. All she had to do now was go into the bank, make herself known and sign the papers and then she could download the app onto her phone. Her French debit card and chequebook would take about another ten days to arrive.

Before leaving England, she'd changed a substantial amount of money into euros, anticipating a need for them. It was good to know that access to cash for day-to-day living would be available soon. She'd drive in tomorrow to go to the bank. She had enough cash to pay Francois from the stash she'd brought over with her from England and with what she'd taken out of the cash machine. Once she'd signed the papers at the bank, she could transfer some of her rainy-day money into her new French euro account.

Waiting for Adam to pick her up later that after-noon, Briony resolved to try to play it cool and not immediately ask about the artisan unit. She'd barely got her seatbelt done up before Adam himself raised the subject and pointed to the large key on the dashboard.

'Happy for you to have the last artisan unit. It's a little bit more expensive than the other two because it's bigger, but Lucy can give you all the nitty-gritty when you sign the lease. We don't have many stipula-tions about what you can and can't do. So long as you are here in France legally with a visa and everything, don't employ anyone who isn't, run a legit business, pay your taxes and definitely don't sell drugs, you're more than welcome to the unit.'

Briony laughed. 'Thank you. I think I can safely say I can adhere to those rules. The visa stuff will probably take a few weeks to sort, but it is already in hand. Monsieur Caumont, the notaire, has offered to help and has sent me a list of things I need to do.'

'Lucy wants to discuss something else with you, but the unit is yours. You'd better put the key in your bag. Don't lose it. I do have a master key for all the units, though.'

* * *

Briony drove home carefully on the wrong side of the road and continued up the road to the farm. She was positively buzzing with ideas, but first she needed to find out what Lucy needed to discuss.

Lucy came out when she heard the car. 'How was your first drive?'

'Bit nerve-wracking, but I'm back in one piece. Adam said you wanted to talk to me about the unit. He's given me the key so I'm guessing I can have it, but that there's a but?'

'Don't look so worried,' Lucy said. 'The artisan unit is yours to run as a brocante; it's just that I have a request I hope you will agree to.'

Briony looked at her and waited, hoping the request wouldn't be too serious or too expensive for her to agree to.

'I would like to video you for my YouTube channel from the beginning like I did when both Calvin and Holly moved in. Tell my followers a little about yourself as you organise the space and get the business up and running and also in the future when you are open. Would you have a problem with that?'

Briony shook her head. 'No, not at all. It would be some promotion for me too. I want to start bringing up the boxes from the cottage tomorrow. I can't move in the sitting room. Is that the kind of activity you want to film?'

Lucy nodded. 'Yes. I'll film the unit empty and you carrying in the first of the stock. Only need a moment or two.'

'Okay. It'll be early tomorrow morning because I want to go into town by about ten o'clock.'

'Give me a toot when you arrive and I'll come straight over,' Lucy said.

As Lucy went back into the farmhouse, Briony took the key out of her bag and made her way across to the artisan unit. Holly had shut up shop and left and the closed notice on Calvin's unit was still in place. Unlocking the sturdy wooden door, Briony pushed it open. Standing in the entrance, she surveyed the inside of the building for the first time. Empty and bigger than either of the other two, Briony could see it was an ideal size. The stone walls had all been re-pointed, the floor had beautiful Provençal terracotta tommetes and there were two light fittings hanging from the ceiling crying out for vintage chandeliers to be fitted. It would make the perfect base and showcase for the brocante she was already visualising in her mind.

* * *

Briony was up early the next morning and pulled on some old jeans and a sweatshirt. It took her half an hour to load up the Kangoo with the boxes from the sitting room. She carefully drove up to the farm, turned onto the drive and made for the unit, giving a joyful toot-toot as she parked.

Jumping out of the car, she took the key out of her pocket and unlocked the door, pushing it open as Lucy arrived.

'Morning. Are you excited?' Lucy asked.

'Yes.'

While Lucy took some shots of the empty building, Briony began to lift the boxes out of the car and carried them into building. Once Lucy had filmed her carrying in half a dozen boxes, she switched the phone off and helped her carry in the rest. Finally, the Kangoo was empty and Briony closed and locked up the building.

'Thanks for your help,' she said to Lucy.

'Pleasure. Want to come up to the farm for a bite of breakfast?'

'I don't really have the time,' Briony said, 'but thanks for the offer.'

'See you tomorrow then, if not before.'

Briony drove home feeling happy. That was an hour well spent. Time for a shower followed by breakfast and then she'd brave driving Pascal into Cannes in for the first time and go to the bank and sign the papers.

27

The last thing Elliot needed when he got home after a hard day was for Lucy to hand him another letter from the TV company when, with Luna at his side as usual, he popped into the kitchen to say 'Hi' to them both. He took the letter with a resigned, 'Thanks.'

'You look exhausted,' Lucy exclaimed. 'You staying for supper?'

Elliot shook his head. 'No, thanks. Had an early supper with Julian. It's been a manic day today. The veterinary practice has been so busy. How the hell Julian managed with only the four of them beats me. Anyway, you two okay?'

Adam nodded. 'It's been one of those days here too. Non-stop phone calls and people turning up on the door. Didn't get half of what I wanted to get done today.'

'Day off tomorrow, I can give you a hand,' Elliot offered.

'Sure? Would be grateful but don't want you knocking yourself out.'

'A walk down to the lake with Luna for half an hour now, a good night's sleep and I'll be as right as rain,' Elliot said, hoping that would turn out to be true.

'Come up for breakfast in the morning,' Lucy said. 'Full English is on the menu.'

Elliot looked at her. 'God, Lucy. Any time you get tired of my big brother you can move in with me.'

'Ow, watch it, kiddo,' Adam said.

'See you both in the morning.' Elliot shoved the letter in his pocket and turned to leave, Luna instantly at his side.

Elliot took the back farm track down to the woods and the lake, hoping that he wouldn't bump into Briony. He still hadn't sorted out his feelings in regard to their friendship. He knew that he wasn't ready for anything too serious yet, but surely he could cope with bumping into her occasionally? He'd enjoyed the evening she'd cooked supper more than he'd enjoyed an evening in a long time.

As for the letter currently in his pocket, he'd hoped his silence would have told the TV company that he wasn't interested. When he got back to the cottage, he'd write an email telling them he didn't want to be involved and not to contact him again. He stood still for a moment, closed his eyes and took some deep breaths. He could feel the stress building up again even simply thinking about everything that had happened.

When he opened his eyes, Luna had gone ahead and was down on the edge of the woods being petted by Briony. Despite how he'd hoped he wouldn't see her, he felt a small smile breaking across his face and he hurried down towards her. The memory of seeing her hugging the tree flashed into his mind.

'Which tree are you hugging tonight?' he said, smiling, the words out of his mouth before he stopped to think. Briony didn't know that he'd seen her that day. The look on her face told him he was in deep trouble.

Briony gave him a hard stare. 'I didn't think there was anyone around. You saw me? Watched me? Sounds a bit stalkerish to me.'

'I'm sorry,' Elliot said. 'I definitely was not stalking you. I promise as soon as I saw you, I turned back. I didn't watch you for a single second. I didn't want to disturb you in your moment of...' he shrugged, not knowing what to call it. 'Your moment of quiet contemplation.'

'Thank you for that,' Briony said, staring at him. 'You look stressed. I think you need to hug a tree.'

'What? I definitely do not need to hug a tree,' Elliot said, turning away.

'You do. It's surprisingly therapeutic. And it's scientifically proven to make you feel happy. You can't knock something or ridicule it, if you have never tried it,' Briony said, a challenging edge to her voice.

There was a silence for several seconds before Elliot slowly turned back to face her. 'Scientifically proven, eh? Okay. Which tree?'

Briony turned and pointed to the trunk of a large oak. 'That one. You need to banish sceptical thoughts and empty your mind. Close your eyes and hug the tree.'

'How long do I hug it for?'

Briony shrugged. 'You'll know when you're ready to stop hugging. I'll keep Luna with me. Go on.' Her hand waved him in the direction of the tree.

Shaking his head in disbelief at what he was about to do, Elliot moved towards the oak tree. A quick hug and he was out of here. Standing under the tree looking upwards at the developing canopy of green leaves, Elliot closed his eyes, stilled his thoughts and reached out to place his arms around the trunk of the tree. His fingers began to trace the grooves of the rough bark under his hands before he stilled them and leant into the tree. His breathing deepened and he could feel himself becoming calmer.

He had no idea how long he stayed like that before he opened his eyes, let his arms drop to his sides and turned to face Briony.

'Well, there you go, Mr Sceptical. Feel happier? Less stressed?'

Elliot gave a surprised nod. 'I do actually.'

'That will be the calming phytoncides chemicals that the tree emits. No need to thank me,' Briony said. 'I need to get back. Night.'

'Night,' Elliot said. 'And thank you,' he called out to her retreating back. Briony raised an arm in acknowledgement but didn't turn around.

* * *

The next morning, Briony smiled to herself as she ate her breakfast, remembering Elliot's obvious embarrassment over the tree hugging. Expecting him to walk away, she'd been surprised when he'd accepted the challenge she'd thrown at him. The fact that he'd stayed hugging the tree for several minutes had to mean that he had connected with not just the tree but with mindfulness deep in himself. Now the question was – would he do it again? She doubted that she'd ever know the answer to that question.

After breakfast, Briony set off for the farm for her second Thursday as Lucy's Girl Friday.

Lucy was on her own in the kitchen when Briony walked in.

'Let's go straight to the office,' she said. 'I'm hoping you can do a couple of hours' admin this morning?'

'Whatever you want me to do,' Briony said. 'Did we get any firm bookings for the Stables?'

'Yes, thanks to you. Both are booked for Easter. The Cider House has a repeat booking, so for the first time all three gîtes are booked. There's also been several bookings for next month too, as well as enquiries for later in the year.'

'That's great.'

'I've got your lease here ready for you to sign.' Lucy opened a folder and took out a piece of A4 paper. 'It's just a formal agreement between the three of us, protects you and us. It's a one-year lease, with an option to renew, three months' notice on either side, rent is due quarterly and a quarter's rent is paid as a refundable deposit when you leave, provided the unit is left in a good state. You sign there and date it and I'll do the same here. Happy?'

'It's really happening, isn't it?' Briony said as she signed the paper. 'I can't chicken out now, can I?'

Lucy looked anxious. 'Are you having second thoughts? I can tear up the lease right now if you want me to and we'll forget it was ever mooted.'

Briony shook her head. 'Oh no, I really want to do this. It's just a little scary thinking about having my own business.'

'I know that feeling,' Lucy said sympathetically. 'Adam has always been his own boss, but when I married him, I found the uncertainties of being self-employed overwhelming, but it soon became a way of life for me. It'll be fine, you'll see.' Lucy put the lease back in the folder. 'Have you got a name for the business?'

Briony shook her head. 'No. I'm going to have a brainstorming session with the laptop soon!'

Lucy handed over the lease.

'Thank you,' Briony said before glancing at Lucy. 'Can I talk to you about Elliot?'

Lucy gave her a surprised look. 'Of course.'

'He was extremely kind and helpful over Pascal, I

made supper as a thank you and we had a good evening. I thought we were becoming friends, and then I met him down by the lake yesterday and he was stressed and horribly moody at first if I'm honest, although he was better before I left him. Is he like that with everyone, blowing hot and cold, or is it me that rubs him up the wrong way without meaning to?' Briony shook her head. 'I can't make him out.'

Lucy sighed. 'He's not really been himself since all the trouble last year. He used to be as even-tempered as Adam. Nothing ever fazed him. I've noticed, though, that the slightest thing can set him off these days. Since he's been working again, he's been a lot better, but I do know he had a letter yesterday which wound him up. And also Robyn – his ex-wife – has been trying to get in touch.'

'Well, it's a relief it's not just me,' Briony said.

'I probably shouldn't say this,' Lucy said quietly. 'I think the problem is that since Robyn, he has had trust issues and he's frightened of getting too close to anybody at the moment and keeps backing off.'

'Okay.' Briony nodded. She could identify with that, although she wasn't about to say that to Lucy.

'You'll need to give him time if you want to be friends.' Lucy gave Briony a quizzical look. 'I don't know whether you know, but Robyn was – is – an investigative journalist, and TV presenter, she's all over the media sites on the internet,' Lucy said. 'Maybe do your own investigation of what she writes? Might give you some idea of what she put him through until he tells you himself. Cup of tea and a slice of cake before you leave?' she said as she strolled to the kitchen.

Briony stared after her. Lucy clearly wasn't going to gossip about her brother-in-law but had indicated that if she really wanted to know she could find out for herself with a couple of clicks on the computer.

28

Thursday afternoon and Elliot was in the recovery room at the practice checking on the three cats and one rabbit that had been neutered that morning and could hear Julian talking gently to a crying woman in his consulting room.

'Jill, you've got enough to deal with. Leave Meg here with me and I promise to find a good solution. Don't worry.'

'Thank you so much, Julian, I'm at the end of my tether, I don't know what to do for the best. I feel terrible about Dad and Meg...' Her voice faded as Julian walked to the door with the woman and waved her goodbye.

'Don't suppose you'd like company for Luna,

would you?' Julian said a minute later. Elliot turned to find Julian standing in the doorway holding a spaniel on a lead. 'Sad story. Meg here is eight, lovely dog. Known her all her life. Harry, her owner, has Alzheimer's and is about to go into care.' Julian sighed. 'Jill, his daughter, has four children, one with special needs, and a husband who works away. She's barely keeping things together. I've promised I'll find a new forever home for Meg. Any ideas? I was joking about Luna needing company, but...?'

'Can't you keep her?' Elliot said.

'In a heartbeat, but with three dogs at home already,' Julian said, 'I'd be pushing my luck, but if we can't find a home, then I will have her.'

Elliot bent down and stroked the dog who was sat quietly at Julian's feet. Luna padded in to see what was going on and the two dogs sniffed each other. Watching them interact, Briony suddenly popped into his mind. 'I'll take her home with me. I know somebody who might take her,' Elliot said. 'No promises though.'

'Vaccinations and everything are all up to date. Jill doesn't want anything for her – just a good home.'

'She'd have that where I'm thinking of asking.'

'Why don't you finish now and get off and find out,' Julian said. 'Be a weight off my mind.'

'Okay. I'll just pick up a bag of food and a couple of bowls and I'll be off.'

The two dogs settled happily together in the back of the 4x4 and Elliot drove home. He decided not to forewarn Briony but to simply turn up with Meg and see how they both reacted to each other.

* * *

Briony was sitting out on the terrace after work, a cup of tea and a biscuit in front of her, mulling over Lucy's words and thinking about Elliot, when he surprised her by calling out 'Hello,' walking round the side of the cottage.

'Good, you're home. I did think you might still be up at the farm. I've brought someone to meet you. Stay there, I'll be right back with Luna.'

Briony stayed where she was, mystified.

Luna raced around the side of the cottage and bounded up to her for a cuddle. Briony's heart skipped a beat when Elliot appeared with a spaniel on a lead.

'I'm hoping you're still thinking about getting a dog?' he asked. 'This is Meg. She's an eight-year-old springer spaniel and she needs a new forever home.'

Briony got up and went over to the white-and-liver-coloured dog, who regarded her with big brown eyes before tentatively sniffing her hand. 'What's her story?'

'She was brought in this afternoon by the daughter of her owner, a long-time client of the practice.' Elliot quickly told her the sad story while Briony started to stroke the dog gently. 'Julian has known Meg all her life and has promised the daughter he will find her a new home. She's good on the lead, her recall is good and she's friendly with other dogs. She's a little overweight at the moment as she hasn't had much exercise recently.'

'She's lovely. She and Luna seem to get on too. Do you want to let her off the lead? Let her explore a bit and play a little with Luna. The garden is secure.'

Elliot smiled as he let Meg off the lead.

'There is a problem though,' Briony said. 'I can't take her tonight. I don't have any dog food in the house. Although maybe you could spare some of Luna's? I can replace it tomorrow.'

'I bought some. It's in the car, together with her dog basket and cushion that Jill left with Julian, dog bowls and a new toy.'

Briony looked at him and laughed. 'What would you have done if I'd said I'd changed my mind about having a dog? In fact, I really should change my mind. I'm going to be so busy for the next few months, I really don't have time for a pet.'

Elliot looked at her and gave her a slow smile. 'But you won't change your mind, will you? Because you've already made her welcome. Shall we take her for her first walk to the lake?'

'Have you got time? That would be lovely.' Briony clipped Meg onto her lead and they set off. It was a lovely spring evening and Briony gave a happy sigh. Elliot too seemed happy as they strolled along. 'We always had a dog when I was growing up and I've wanted my own dog for so long, I can't believe it's finally happened, thank you.'

Elliot shrugged. 'It's difficult when you're working. Dogs like company.'

'Oh, I wouldn't leave a dog on their own – I would have taken it to work with me, like you do with Luna, and like I plan to do with Meg. No, Marcus, my ex-husband, was allergic. At least that's what he always said. I'm not totally sure it was true. I think it was one more lie among many. Anyway, now I've got Meg and I'm so happy. Will you tell your boss to tell the lady I'll give her a good home.' She paused and glanced at him. 'D'you think once Meg's settled that her old owner would like me to visit with her? Or is it likely to upset him?'

'Difficult one. I think he's quite ill,' Elliot said. 'I'll ask Julian and see what he thinks. That's kind of you to think of it, though.'

As Luna reached the lake, she went straight in as usual for a swim. Briony could feel Meg straining on the leash to join her. 'Not today,' she said quietly. 'Next time we come, maybe. You and Luna are going to have such fun.'

When they got back to the cottage, Elliot fetched the sack of dog food from the car and suggested the correct amount for Meg and after he'd left, Briony fed her. Early evening and she was curled up in her dog basket sleeping the excitement of the day off, whilst Briony ate her own supper.

Briony's mobile buzzed. 'Hi, Mum. How's things?'

'Gerry is catching the ferry tonight as planned,' Jeannie said. 'He should be with you sometime early next week. He's going to text you the night before.'

'Great,' Briony said. 'How did the house viewings go? Any interest?'

'I've accepted an offer from a young couple.'

'Gosh, that was quick,' Briony said. 'Brilliant. So you'll definitely be back down for Easter? I've bought a car, so let me know your flight details and I'll be there to meet you.'

Jeannie sighed. 'That's turned into a bit of a problem. Everyone seems to be jetting away to the South of France for Easter – most flights are full. But I've found a late-night one. So I'm going to book a taxi rather than drag you out at that time of night. Or I might ask Yannick. He has offered.'

'I really don't mind meeting you whatever time you land. Let me know what you decide,' Briony said. 'Just looking forward to having you back here.'

'I'm looking forward to being there too. How are things down there?' Jeannie asked. 'What sort of car did you buy?'

'It's a Renault Kangoo. Quite old and looks more like a van with windows than a car, but it's been well looked after. I've got lots to tell you when you get here. It's better to do it face to face,' Briony said. 'There is one other thing I have to tell you now – and I hope you're okay about it. I – we – as of tonight, now have a dog. A spaniel called Meg. Hang on, I'll send you a photo. She's gorgeous. You're going to love her too.' Briony quickly took a photo of Meg in her basket and sent it to her mum. 'Elliot turned up with her tonight needing a new home and I knew instantly I was going to have her.'

'Ah, she looks at home already,' Jeannie said. 'I can't wait to meet her.'

'Also, before I forget to tell you, one of the best

things is, I've heard the owls,' Briony said. 'I think they are still nesting in the tree.'

* * *

Jeannie finished the call wondering what Briony hadn't wanted to tell her over the phone. She'd sounded upbeat, though, especially when she mentioned having a dog, so she'd take her word for it that everything was good and not worry. Now she had one more phone call to make. She opened WhatsApp and pressed his name. Yann answered within two rings.

'I hope you were serious about meeting my flight whatever time it was because I've finally managed to get a seat on the last flight to Nice the Thursday before Good Friday. Due to land at eleven ten. Briony said she'd meet me at whatever time I land, but I really don't like the thought of her out driving alone at that time of night, so I said I was going to ask you, but I can always get a taxi rather than drag you out if you'd rather not. I don't want to be a nuisance.'

'Jeannie, you will never be a nuisance to me. Like you worry about Briony being out alone at night, I'd worry about you in the same situation. I'll be there at whatever time you land,' Yann promised.

'Thank you,' Jeannie smiled, knowing he would be.

'There is something I need to tell you when you're here. Something we will have to discuss.'

'Tell me now?'

'*Non*. I wait until you're here. It is something good, so do not worry.'

'Okay. See you soon,' she said, ending the call. It was a wonderful feeling having someone in her life again who truly cared about her and wanted to protect her. She had no idea how Briony was going to react to her news. News that she too thought would be better told face to face rather than over the phone. She couldn't deny, though, that she was looking forward to telling Briony about her feelings for Yann and explaining how happy she was to explore this unexpected development in her own life.

29

Friday morning when Briony woke she found Meg curled up on the bed beside her. 'What are you doing up here?' she said. Two big brown eyes regarded her sorrowfully, while a tail began to rhythmically thump the bed. 'You know the number one rule is no dogs on beds. You're supposed to be in your basket in the kitchen. But I like your company, so we'll ignore that rule.'

She stayed there for several moments fussing Meg before getting up and pulling on some clothes to let the dog out into the garden. After breakfast and a shower, she'd walk up to the farm and introduce Meg to Lucy, Adam and Django before settling down to do some more box-checking and organising as well as trying to finalise a business plan.

Briony clipped the long lead onto Meg's collar and went up through the fields, letting Meg stop and sniff and familiarise herself with her new surroundings. Up at the farmhouse, she knocked on the kitchen door and called out. 'Okay to bring my new dog in?'

'Of course, we're looking forward to meeting her,' Lucy said. 'Elliot told us last night you were giving this beautiful girl a new home,' and she immediately bent down, stroking Meg. Luna and Django wandered over and Meg stood patiently, her tail wagging.

Adam looked up briefly from his laptop. 'Morning and hello Meg,' he said before returning his attention to the screen with a groan. 'I sincerely hope they've got this long-term forecast of a late frost warning for Easter wrong,' he said. 'The leaves on the vines have unfurled beautifully and the buds are starting. The avocados too are showing new leaf growth. Frost is the last thing we need. Bruno tells me a late spring frost in April 2017 was the worst in France for over twenty-five years. Down here the damage was bad enough, but it caused absolute devastation further upcountry.'

'Is there anything we can do to protect the vines?' Lucy asked.

Adam shook his head. 'Not really. Bigger vine-yards have lots of short-term protection options, like oil heaters, large paraffin candles, setting fire to vine pruning or even straw. We're lucky that the vineyard is on a south-facing slope, so it should retain the heat of the day. Temperatures drop to their lowest close to the soil and create a so-called temperature inversion. Might start praying for warm sunny days but cloudy night skies that would offer some insulation to the buds.'

'Could you buy a load of straw?' Briony asked.

'Wrong time of year. There's never a lot of straw available down here and farmers that do use it have used last year's straw over winter and are short of it. I have rung around but haven't found any.'

'Fingers crossed the forecast is wrong – they often are, aren't they?' Briony said, trying to be optimistic.

'Météo France are usually on the ball,' Adam said. 'We can only hope they're being extra cautious warning everyone and they've made a mistake.'

After leaving the farm, Briony walked Meg down to the lake and for the first time let her off the lead by the water. A typical springer spaniel, Meg instantly jumped into the water enthusiastically even without Luna being there to egg her on. Briony smiled at Meg's antics. She looked so happy swimming around.

Briony held her breath when she called her to come out of the lake in case her recall wasn't quite as good as Elliot had said, but Meg came and quickly rewarded her with a wet shower.

'Come on then, Meg, let's get you home and get both of us dried off.'

With Meg in her life now, Briony was determined to spend time with her making sure she settled and was happy in her new home, so over the next few days they developed a routine. Their early-morning walk to the lake was usually on their own, but in the evenings, Elliot and Luna often turned up at the cottage and the two of them walked the dogs together. Luna and Meg were firm friends now and keeping them out of the lake was impossible – where Luna went, Meg was bound to follow and vice versa. Briony inwardly admitted to herself that she missed Elliot as much as Meg missed Luna on the days when Elliot didn't get home early enough for an evening walk. Not that she would ever tell him.

As well as working up at the farm on Saturday and walking Meg twice a day, the days began to fly by for Briony. She was determined to sort through the boxes in the garage before she moved any of them up to the unit. It would be better to see what they contained first. Slowly she was working her way to the back of the garage, where she could see some folded-up trestle tables that she hoped would be useable.

She soon had three separate piles of boxes: one for the brocante, one for rubbish and one full of things she wasn't sure whether to sell or keep. She was hoping her mum would take a look and help her decide. Meg curled up happily alongside her in the garage or wherever she chose to work.

A couple of times, Briony went up to the units. The first time was to tell Holly and Calvin that she was going to be their new neighbour and was looking forward to being there with them. Both Holly and Calvin were thrilled with the news that the third unit was going to be opened.

'That is good news,' Holly said. 'And a brocante is sure to bring more people up to the farm.' Both wished her good luck.

The second time she went up to the unit was to try to work out a plan of how to make the best use of the space and how to display items. The trestle tables from the garage, if they were useable, could be covered with some vintage material and there was a shelf unit on the landing in Owls Nest that would be useful. Slowly but surely her new life in France was taking shape and Briony was enjoying every minute of it.

30

There was still no sign of Elliot and Luna on Monday evening a week later as Briony and Meg walked to the lake. Briony began to wonder if something was wrong. Lucy hadn't said anything when she was up at the farm on Saturday and she hadn't liked to ask, figuring that Lucy would have mentioned if something was amiss. Elliot was probably simply busy, although surely he still had to walk Luna?

Back at the cottage, Briony spread the contents of the open box from the attic onto the dining-room table. Carefully, she sorted it into piles: letters, postcards, photos, birthday cards and random bits of paper and several Cannes Film Festival programmes from the late forties and fifties. The five-year diary she put to one side before trying to decide what to do with everything.

The Film Festival programmes would make an interesting display somewhere in the cottage once framed. She knew too that they were infinitely collectable and would sell instantly to film buffs. To her surprise, many of the postcards were photos of New York and most were blank. Some had simple phrases written on them 'This would make a wonderful painting' or 'This place would inspire you'. Sometimes in the corner of the card were the initials 'EM'. Lots of unused postcards were photos of Paris between the two world wars. Several newspaper cuttings about the social life on the Riviera in the early thirties were on the very bottom.

The black-and-white photographs were mainly formal family pictures of people who were long dead. There were a couple of a pretty young girl with incredibly sad eyes that caught Briony's attention. She picked up a formal marriage photograph mounted in an old-fashioned fold-over cardboard frame. Was it the same girl? Who was she?

Deep in thought, Briony picked up her phone when it pinged with an incoming text.

Been enjoying the scenery too much! ETA midday Wednesday. Have the kettle on. Dying for a good cup of tea. Gerry.

Briony smiled as she read the text. Gerry was well known for his tea addiction.

But as she put her phone down, she could feel herself starting to panic. Where was all the stuff from England going to go?

* * *

Wednesday morning and Briony was ready and waiting with a large plate of pain au chocolate and plenty of tea bags when Gerry and his mate drew up outside the cottage.

'Great place you've got here,' Gerry said, jumping out of the cab of the lorry. 'Quite fancy moving to France myself. Seen some beautiful places on our drive down. Loved Carcassone, which is why we're a day late. Right, cup of tea and then we'll unload.'

Watching Gerry unlock the van doors half an hour later, Briony's initial thought was 'Mum hasn't brought much furniture' but then she realised just how many boxes there were stacked in the van. And then there was her own stuff, some of which she hadn't seen since she'd left Marcus.

She showed Gerry the dining room and suggested he put all the boxes in there and she and Jeannie would sort them out at their leisure. It was almost summer and most meals would be eaten out on the terrace for the next few months so they wouldn't be using the dining room anyway.

After the van was unloaded, Briony asked Gerry if he would mind dragging several things she wanted to work on out of the garage and into the garden for her. The bicycle she remembered riding as a child, the wooden handcart and the parrot cage were soon outside the garden shed.

Gerry turned down her offer of food. 'Going to go and take a look at Cannes. Have something to eat down there. Find somewhere to stay before heading back tomorrow. I'm thinking the wife might like a holiday down here sometime.'

Briony paid Gerry, gave him a generous tip and waved him goodbye before turning back into the cottage. So much to do! But first she needed something to eat and then she'd spend the next few hours starting to sort out some of the boxes before taking Meg for her evening walk. Sitting out on the terrace with some slices of baguette and a cheese salad and a small glass of rosé, Briony gave a happy sigh as she looked down the garden towards the owls' tree. Things really were starting to come together now for this new life in France. Her mobile rang at that moment and she hurriedly picked it up when she saw the English number.

'Maeve. How lovely to hear from you. How are you? I'm so sorry I've not been in touch. How's the new old job going?'

'Surprisingly well,' Maeve said. 'Much better than I ever expected it. How's life in France?'

'Busy, busy,' and Briony gave her friend a potted version of her life since she'd arrived back, the plans she had for a brocante and the fact she now had a dog. 'Gerry delivered all of our things today. I'm just having a bite to eat before tackling a few boxes and taking Meg for a walk. Hopefully meeting up with Elliot and his dog Luna, the two dogs play together really well.'

'Stop. Who is Elliot?'

'The good friend who found me Meg. He's a vet and lives here on his brother's farm. He's helped me a lot since I moved into the cottage.'

'Single? Handsome?'

'Yes to both of those but he, like me, is recently divorced and neither of us are looking for a relationship at the moment, so like I said, a good friend. How are the girls?' Briony asked before Maeve could ask more probing questions. Thankfully Maeve took the hint and the conversation moved on to other things.

The call ended five minutes later with Briony promising to keep in touch more and reminding Maeve that she had an invitation to visit whenever she wanted to. Thoughtfully Briony finished her wine and took her dirty dishes back into the kitchen. Time to make a start on unpacking her old life and starting to merge it into her new life here in France.

31

That evening after unpacking a couple of her boxes with clothes in and filling the wardrobe in her bedroom, Briony set off with Meg to walk to the lake, hoping that this evening Elliot and Luna would be there. It was over a week now since the two dogs had had a good play together.

There was no sign of anyone as they reached the lake and for once Meg was happy to stay at her side on the lead as a disappointed Briony sat on the bench. Briony closed her eyes and let her thoughts drift. Thoughts of how much her life had changed for the better recently. Thoughts of how grateful she was to Granny Giselle. Thoughts of how happy she was now she was no longer married to Marcus. Thoughts of Elliot. Thoughts of how much she missed seeing him. Thoughts about looking Robyn up on the internet kept coming into her mind, but she pushed them away. It felt sneaky and somewhat underhand to Google Elliot's past. After all, she'd never talked to him about her own past or the major effect Marcus had had on her life. Briony cut that particular thought off. She would not go there.

Perhaps if she opened up more, Elliot would respond in kind. She'd hazard a guess though that if it was searchable on Google, then his problems had been played out in the public eye, whilst her own had been suffered in private. Not even her mum knew the whole truth about their divorce.

A voice gently broke into her thoughts. 'Give you a penny for your thoughts? Or are you asleep?'

Briony opened her eyes, startled. 'No, I wasn't asleep, just miles away. I didn't hear you coming and Meg didn't warn me either. How are you? Meg's missed Luna recently.' Easier to say Meg missed Luna than to admit she had missed him.

'Julian and one of the other vets have both been off ill, so it's been full on at the clinic,' Elliot said, sighing as he sat down on the bench beside her. With Luna off the lead, Meg was frantic to be free too, so Briony unclipped her and the two dogs dashed for the lake. 'Luna's missed her walks down here with Meg too. I've had to walk her in the park near the practice. I hope your thoughts before I disturbed you were happy ones,' Elliot said.

Briony nodded. 'They were mostly. These days my barbarous thoughts about my ex-husband are getting less and less thankfully. I haven't yet reached the stage of being able to forgive him, though, and probably never will. To do that I have to accept the fact that I'm probably never going to have the children I've always wanted because of his lies and actions.' She took a deep breath. 'Sorry, more information than you need about me and my darkest thoughts. Let's talk about something else.'

'Sometimes barbarous thoughts about one's ex partner are totally acceptable,' Elliot said quietly. 'I've often thought murderous thoughts about Robyn. Still do occasionally – more often than is healthy, if I'm honest.' There was a short pause before he continued. 'So, how are the plans for the brocante coming along?'

'Slowly. I've taken some stock up to the unit and once Mum is back I'm planning on working out a layout and starting to display stuff. Mum's good at that kind of thing, so between the two of us we'll soon have it ready.'

'When do you plan to open? Will you make a bit of a fanfare about it?'

'I was originally thinking about the first week in May, but I've changed my mind. I'd rather get Easter out of the way. Late May or early June in time for the summer season would be better. Gives me a little more time to organise the correct visa and also to find some stock that hasn't come out of the cottage. As for a fanfare, I'll have to think about that. Maybe an advertorial in the *Nice Matin*.'

'Don't forget if you need a helping hand you only have to ask,' Elliot said.

'Thank you, but you're busy enough with the practice by the sound of it.'

'Never too busy to help a friend when I'm around.' Elliot gave her a smile as he stood up. 'Come on, I'll walk you and Meg back.'

As they walked, Briony silently admonished herself for telling Elliot she had barbarous thoughts about Marcus. Still, he had responded with an understanding comment. Maybe another day he would confide in her about his problems with Robyn.

32

The Thursday morning before the Easter weekend Briony made her way up to the farmhouse to spend a couple of hours doing admin in Lucy's office. Not only did Lucy want everything to be as perfect as possible for the holidaymakers in the gîtes, she also lived in fear of double-booking one of them. Briony, now in charge of the bookings diary and the spread-sheets she'd created, double-checked and assured her everything was correct for the weekend.

Afterwards, they both went to look over all three gîtes. As they strolled across the farmyard afterwards, Lucy told Briony to take the afternoon off. 'But I'll see you Saturday morning for a final check and to put the welcome baskets out, as well as to help me greet the guests. In theory, guests will arrive at different times, but in practice I expect there to be some overlap.'

'It's going to be fine,' Briony said.

'Last season with only the one gîte was easy,' Lucy said. 'Now it's three it seems much harder to organise. Maybe I should suggest Adam doesn't renovate any more cottages. Three gîtes is more than enough to run.'

'I think when we've got two or three changeover days done, we'll have a routine and it will all be plain sailing,' Briony said.

'I hope you are right,' Lucy said. 'Before I forget, would you and your mum like to come up for dinner tomorrow evening and meet Debs and Hannah?'

'I'd love to, thank you, and I'm sure Mum will too – provided she actually turns up before Easter. Now stop worrying. I'll see you tomorrow evening and then Saturday morning for work.'

* * *

Whilst Adam went to pick up Hannah and Debs from Nice airport, Lucy walked along the hallway to do a final check on their room. Growing up, they'd always chosen to share a bedroom and they were still insistent on sharing when they came home together. Lucy and Adam had shrugged and gone alone with it, although privately Lucy did wonder what would happen if they both came home with a boyfriend at the same. So far that hadn't happened, but the spare guest rooms were always ready, just in case.

She was looking forward to having Debs and Hannah home for a few days and catching up with their lives, but it did mean pushing her weekend routine aside. Not that she minded, she loved having them home filling the farmhouse with laughter and noise. The house always felt so empty in the hours after they left. Now they were both working full-time, it was rare to have them both home together and she intended to make the most of their company this weekend. Besides, Easter was going to be a busy weekend, so her routine would be out of the window.

The room the girls shared was large and had originally been two rooms which Adam had knocked into one and created an en suite bathroom with both a bath and a shower unit. Light and airy, its windows overlooked the main farmyard and the driveway. There were two single beds with a bedside table in between, a large double wardrobe and a chest of drawers with a lovely vanity mirror Lucy had found in a local brocante, standing in the centre of the top.

Satisfied that the room was ready, Lucy went on downstairs to the kitchen.

After a *supermarché* shop yesterday, the fridge was stuffed with everything for Easter, plus the treats the girls liked – greek yoghurts, different cheeses, little pots of their favourite chocolate mousse – and the salad drawer was stuffed with enough lettuce, tomatoes, onions, avocados, asparagus, broccoli, carrots and courgettes to feed a mountain of hungry people. A large leg of lamb was in the fridge ready for the traditional Sunday Easter roast. A large piece of pork with an old-fashioned muslin cover over it was in the pantry ready for their Good Friday evening meal.

Lucy gave a happy sigh. She did love it when the family were all together and she could spend most of her time in the kitchen cooking food for them.

* * *

Once back home, Briony made herself a cheese sandwich and a cup of tea for lunch and sat out in the garden to enjoy it. Meg curled up happily at her feet, alert for every crumb that might be dropped. After lunch, Briony stayed out in the garden and sanded the ancient handcart down and afterwards gave it a coat of plain white paint, deciding that all the colour should come from an explosion of flowers that she'd get her mum to plant in the cart.

A quick shower to get the paint off her hands and she sat down on the terrace in the shade to start reading the five-year diary, something she'd been promising herself she'd do for days now. Her conscience was still troubled by the fact that diaries were such personal things, not meant to be read by anyone else but the owner. On the other hand, a lot of history was gleaned from such journals and she really longed to learn more about the history of both her family and this wonderful cottage that was now hers. There was always the chance too that the diary had never been used. That all she'd find would be blank pages.

She inserted the key and carefully turned the lock. A faint click and she lifted the leather cover. There was a handwritten inscription on the first page.

Always remember as my friend Henri Matisse would say, 'Creativity takes Courage'. Forever your friend. EM.

Briony puzzled for a few moments over the EM

initials before remembering so many of the postcards she'd found in the box bore the same initials.

Slowly and carefully, Briony started to turn the pages. She soon realised that the diary was more of a journal with infrequent entries and even a few pencil sketches – something which banished her guilty feelings over reading someone else's diary. It wasn't full of personal thoughts and dreams, although there were a few scattered on its pages. Cryptic entries, though, were frequent. Some pages simply recorded a trip. 'Went to Antibes today with EM.' Another, 'How I wish I could have gone to the Carlton with EM for lunch today.' On another page in the middle of the journal, the words, 'EM says the Windsors were thrilled with the party she organised for them last night' jumped out at her. Was that a reference to the Duke and Duchess of Windsor? Surely not.

Lots of entries referred to 'EM' meeting well-known figures, like Noël Coward, Aly Khan, Picasso. But there was no real clue as to whom the journal had belonged to – until the name Albert appeared, when Briony realised the owner could be Marie-Louise, her great-grandmother. 'Albert says EM is not a respectable woman and he has forbidden me from seeing her.'

Briony turned the pages and read an entry in the

middle of the journal which was so personal it made her catch her breath. 'Albert is pleased that I am "with child", as he calls it. He says it will put a stop to my antics. I will love this child when it arrives and hope that I am able to give it a happy life.' If Great-grandmother Marie-Louise was the writer of these last two sad entries, then the baby had to be Giselle.

Briony closed the diary with an aching heart, resolving not to read any more until later.

When she walked Meg down to the lake that evening, Briony's head was still full of the diary entries she'd seen. Elliot and Luna were there already and she sighed happily as she joined them.

'Have you had a good day?'

Elliot nodded. 'Quiet for some reason. Maybe everyone has taken their dogs and cats on holiday. How about you?'

'Amongst other things, I painted the handcart. And I've sorted through some more boxes.'

'Meg is looking good now she's getting more exercise. She's settled in with you so well,' Elliot said as they both sat watching the dogs enjoying another evening swim in the lake.

'She has. I love her to bits. I think Mum is going to adore her too.'

'When is Jeannie arriving?' Elliot asked.

Briony shrugged. 'I have no idea. I've been waiting for her to ring and tell me what time to pick her up. I missed a call from her last night, but when I rang back she didn't pick up and then this afternoon I got a brief text. "All well. See you soon. Love Mum." And that was it. No date, no arrival time. No information at all. It's so out of character for her.' She shook her head. 'It's Good Friday tomorrow. I thought she'd be here by now. She did say she was having difficulty finding a flight. But not a word since, so I just don't know what is going on.' She gave Elliot an anxious glance. 'Either something has happened or there's something going on that she hasn't told me about yet.'

33

Jeannie was trying not to feel guilty as she sat in the Departure lounge Thursday evening waiting to board her flight. Last night she'd pressed Briony's number intending to tell her about the plan she'd made, but then her nerve had failed her and she'd cut the call before Briony could pick up. Then she'd doubled the guilt by not answering when Briony had called several times today by letting it go to voice message. Briony had only left one message and Jeannie knew from the stress evident in her voice that she was worrying about the silence. Hopefully, the brief text she'd sent in response would stop her worrying too much. She also hoped Briony would understand when she explained.

Jeannie glanced at her watch. Surely her flight should be boarding by now? She glanced at the flight departure board and saw that boarding had been delayed by half an hour. Jeannie groaned to herself. It was the last flight of the day to Nice, due to land at eleven ten. It was going to be gone midnight before she walked into the Arrivals Hall at Nice.

She took her phone out and typed a message.

> Boarding is currently delayed by half an hour. It's going to be a truly late night. Shall I get a taxi instead?

She pressed send. Her phone rang almost immediately.

'No taxi. I promised to meet you and I will, however late the plane is. Does Briony know you're flying over tonight?'

'No. I plan to surprise her in the morning.'

'I know she will be pleased to see you, but I'm worried about her reaction to me meeting you tonight and the news you are planning to tell her. I think I should be at your side when you talk to her.'

'I'd rather explain things on my own,' Jeannie said. 'And then together we can adjust to the new order of things. I promise you it will be fine. I'll see you soon – hopefully today, not tomorrow!'

Jeannie bit her lip as the call ended. How hard could it be telling your grown-up daughter that her soon-to-be sixty-year-old mother was thinking about embarking on an affair with an old friend. In theory, not hard at all. In practice? Well, she'd find out soon.

The Nice flight finally boarded an hour later. Jeannie slept through most of the journey, waking only to hear the captain's voice telling them they were approaching Nice and apologising for the lengthy delay.

It was 1 a.m. when Jeannie finally walked into the Arrivals Hall. She smiled with relief when she saw him waiting patiently. 'I'm so sorry Yann. Thank you for waiting.'

He pulled her into a tight hug. 'I'm just glad you are here now. Come on, let's get you in the car and home – well, back to my house anyway.'

It was nearly nine o'clock when Jeannie woke the next morning, briefly disorientated as to where she was when she didn't recognise the curtains at the window. She'd been so tired last night when Yann had carried her case into his spare bedroom, wished her '*Bon nuit*' and left her to sleep. Seeing the time on her watch, Jeannie hurriedly got out of bed and made for the en suite.

A quarter of an hour later, she headed downstairs to the welcome smell of coffee and croissants. 'Morning. I seem to have overslept. That bed is very comfortable,' she said as Yann kissed her on the cheek. 'I'm so sorry, I know you said you have to be in Cannes this morning.'

'It's fine,' Yann said as he handed her a coffee and a croissant. 'We'll have this and then I'll drop you over to Owls Nest and carry on from there.'

* * *

Briony was busy in the garden rubbing the bicycle down ready for painting when Meg gave a sharp bark and stood up looking towards the side path. 'Stay,' Briony said, putting her paintbrush down and getting ready to greet whoever it was.

'Briony, I'm back,' Jeannie called out as she appeared around the corner.

'Mum, how did you get here? And why didn't you tell me you were coming? I've been worried sick, not hearing from you.'

'I'm sorry about that,' Jeannie said. 'I ended up on a late-night flight and I didn't want to drag you all the way into Nice. Yann offered to pick me up, so I accepted. I'm glad I did because the flight was delayed and didn't land until after midnight and it was nearly one o'clock before I was through to Arrivals. I wouldn't have liked you to be hanging around at that time of night.'

'You stayed the night at Yann's? Did he bring you here now? Why didn't he come in?'

'He has an appointment in Cannes, otherwise he would have stopped for a coffee.'

'It's Good Friday,' Briony said. 'Nowhere will be open. Oh, of course, for reasons I can never understand, it's not a holiday in France, is it?'

'So this is our new dog? She's rather beautiful.' Jeannie bent down to stroke Meg, who had come forward to her, tail wagging furiously.

'Yes, this is our Meg,' Briony said. 'She is lovely and has settled in so well. She and Luna love each other.'

Jeannie looked up at Briony. 'Do you and Elliot walk the two dogs together?'

'Yes. Recently he's been too busy at work, but usually it's three or four evenings a week. It's not a big deal,' Briony said, not wanting her mum to start thinking that she and Elliot were more than friends. 'The dogs get more exercise playing together.'

'I'll just pop my case up into my room and then you can tell me everything that has been going on,' Jeannie said, straightening up.

'You might find your room a little crowded. I got Gerry to put a couple of boxes with the things I thought you might want up there, but I haven't re-arranged the room. There's a letter from the notaire on the dressing table for you too. Should have your new bank details in it.'

'I slipped a packet of hot cross buns in my bag,' Jeannie said. 'Good Friday without hot cross buns is not on and I've never found them in France.'

'I'll put them in the kitchen. We'll have them with coffee and you can tell me all your news.'

Twenty minutes later, warm hot cross buns were on the terrace table and the coffee was made. 'Welcome back and here's to the future,' Briony said.

'Why are you painting an ancient bicycle?' Jeannie asked curiously, looking towards the garden shed. 'That old handcart looks freshly painted too. Is the parrot cage also going to be upcycled?'

Briony took a deep breath. 'I've got some exciting news. I've decided that I'm going to use my knowledge of antiques to open a brocante. I know I'm not an expert in any particular branch of antiques, but I know a little about a lot of different items. Importantly, I know a couple of experts who I can always ask for advice. I've rented the empty artisan building on the farm from Lucy and Adam,' Briony said, anxiously watching her mother for her reaction.

'What a brilliant idea,' Jeannie said. 'You know I'll help you as much as I can.'

'I was hoping you'd say that. We'll walk up later and I'll show you the inside. I've taken up some boxes from the garage and stuff from the house, but I was waiting for you to return to make sure I'm not planning on selling anything you want to keep. The handcart and the bicycle are going to be turned into flower containers and one or the other will be placed outside the unit. The parrot cage, still thinking about that. Do you remember ever seeing a parrot here in the cottage?'

Jeannie shook her head. 'I don't remember there ever being a parrot here, but I do remember your dad saying his grandparents had one when he was little. He hated it flying free around the cottage.'

'Sounds like I've got a vintage parrot cage then,' Briony said, laughing. 'Must be worth a fortune. Those hot cross buns were delicious. Are you ready to walk up to the farm now?'

'I need to talk to you first,' Jeannie said. 'About

Yann,' she added when Briony raised her eyebrows at her.

'He's more than a friend, isn't he?' Briony said, remembering the look that had passed between the two at the lunch in the village the first week they were here.

'He wants to be,' Jeannie said slowly. 'How do you feel about that? I don't want you to feel I'm forgetting your dad.'

'Mum, Dad's been gone for several years – of course I don't think that. You're only sixty this year, you've got lots of years ahead of you. If you have feelings for Yann, then go with the flow. See what happens. You deserve to be happy with someone new. You've both known each other a long time, it's not as if you're two strangers having to get to know each other. When did you start to grow close?'

'After your dad died, both Yann and Evette telephoned me every couple of months. When Evette passed, Yann continued to telephone me, especially after Giselle moved over when he regularly phoned to talk to her. As her health declined, he'd talk to me. He knew how I was feeling, what I was going through. He's a very kind man,' Jeannie said, hesitating, wondering just how much she dared to tell Briony. 'And I do like him a lot. I always have, but I never expected to be able to have a relationship with him.'

'I'm sure Dad would be pleased at the thought of his best mate taking care of his wife.'

Briony pushed her chair back, stood up and began to clear the lunch things. Jeannie started to help her, knowing that was one remark she didn't dare to acknowledge or answer. Because the truth was she knew that Jeromé would have been far from pleased about this particular new man in her life. He'd always done his best to keep them apart.

'Easter Sunday lunch – invite Yann,' Briony said. 'We can do roast lamb – and I can thank him for collecting you from the airport. And then I shall grill him about his intentions regarding you!' Briony laughed at the expression on her mum's face.

'Don't you dare,' Jeannie said, laughing as Briony's words cut through the tension she was feeling.

34

Briony and Jeannie walked up through the fields with Meg so that Jeannie could see inside Briony's unit. Both Holly and Calvin were open and they met Holly's daughter, three-year-old Carla, for the first time. Carla immediately wanted to pet Meg, who rolled over for her tummy to be scratched.

'I'm planning on opening the brocante in time for the summer and when I'm ready, I'm going to do an advert in the *Nice Matin*. Hopefully I'll be able to have an advertorial rather than a straightforward advertisement,' Briony said to Holly and Calvin. 'I was thinking of taking a picture showing all three units to use in the advert, are you both happy with that?'

Calvin agreed instantly. 'Great idea. Happy to chip in with the cost.'

Briony, who had seen the fleeting look of worry cross Holly's face and realised she couldn't afford to offer anything, said quickly, 'No. I'm not asking either of you to contribute to the advertisement. But rather than picture one unit, it's better to show everything that is available up here. You okay with that?' she added, looking at Holly.

'Thanks, that's great.'

Leaving the units Briony and Jeannie made their way back down through the farm fields to the lake, where Meg went for a swim and Briony and Jeannie sat on the bench.

'Before I forget, Lucy has invited us for supper this evening up at the farm. She wants us to meet Hannah and Debs, their daughters. I did accept on your behalf.' Briony looked at her mum. 'Are you free or have you arranged to meet Yann?'

Jeannie shook her head. 'No. I'm free.'

'Good.'

'It's lovely here. Giselle loved it by the lake. I wonder...' Jeannie stopped.

'What are you wondering?' Briony said.

'Granny's ashes came over with Gerry,' Jeannie

said quietly, looking around. 'They are in one of the boxes in my room. Maybe this would be a lovely place to scatter them? She loved the garden too, so perhaps there would be better. What do you think?'

Briony was silent for half a moment, trying to think which place would be better. 'For selfish reasons, I think the garden. I like the idea of her being close, staying in a place she loved that is now mine.'

'That's what we will do then. Scatter her ashes down near the old trees under the owls' nest in the garden.'

'Just the two of us saying a final goodbye? Or do you think we should have a little memorial gathering for people here? I know Granny wasn't a fan of either funerals or memorials.'

'I think the two of us. Although I think Yann would like to be with us – he knew Giselle all his life and was very fond of her.'

'Shall we do it Easter Sunday then, when hopefully Yann will be with us?' Briony suggested.

Jeannie nodded. 'Perfect timing.'

Back at the cottage later, Briony showed Jeannie the posters and the postcards from the attic box and Jeannie started to study the photographs. After about five minutes, she shook her head. 'Sorry. I give up. I did think I might be able to work out if there were any photos of your dad's grandparents, but I can't. I think these are from before the war and even earlier. I think the girl with the sad-looking eyes could possibly be Giselle's maman and Jeromé's grand-maman, but...' she shrugged. 'Who knows.'

'Let's open the second box,' Briony said. 'We might have more luck with that one. I'm pretty sure it has a lot of Great-granny Marie-Louise's paintings in there.'

Inside, they found paintings of all descriptions – landscapes, portraits, views of villages, cottages, the Mediterranean – even a couple painted in the Cubism style. But the ones they both fell in love with were the Impressionism. All the paintings had the same small signature in the bottom right-hand corner of the painting as the one hanging in the hall: Marie-Louise.

* * *

Early that evening, Briony and Jeannie walked up to the farm with Meg. 'Isn't the weather glorious today?' Jeannie said as they made their way onto the terrace to join everyone. 'So much warmer than the UK was yesterday.'

Adam nodded. 'Thankfully, the last few nights

have been warmer, but Météo France are still issuing a frost warning over Sunday night and Monday morning. Downgraded but still a worry.'

'It does mean, though, that the avocados are likely to escape any damage and hopefully the vines will too,' Lucy said. 'Fingers crossed that we get warm sun and blue skies for the weekend, but cloudy nights would be good. The girls will be joining us in a moment. Right now, they're trying to persuade Elliot to drive them into Cannes after supper.'

'I've given in,' Elliot said, appearing on the terrace, accompanied by the girls in question. 'It's easier than trying to argue with them. So no wine for me this evening.'

'Honestly, they can wind you round their little fingers,' Lucy said, handing the glass of rosé intended for him to Debs.

'As their godfather, I feel duty-bound to be nice to them.'

'Don't let them drag you out at midnight. They can get a taxi back. Or Adam will go down for them.'

'Jeannie, Briony, let me introduce you to Debs and Hannah,' Lucy said as the girls appeared. 'And then they can give me a hand with getting dinner on the table.'

Briony found herself on the opposite side of the

table to Elliot, who was sitting between the two girls. Taking a sip of her wine, Briony looked over the top of her glass at the three of them. Clearly good friends despite the age difference, she saw a different side to Elliot. A side that she really liked and hoped she would see more of in the future.

35

Briony was up early on Easter Saturday morning to walk Meg to the village for breakfast croissants. She knew that Jeannie planned on taking the dog to the lake later in the morning for her proper walk. Jeannie had coffee ready when she got back and they sat out on the terrace in the early-morning sunshine. Afterwards, Briony changed into a pair of white jeans and a red striped Breton top and headed for the farm.

Lucy had asked her to be there for nine o'clock and charged her with putting the welcome baskets in each gîte and doing a final check that everything was good and ready for guests. The guests for the Cider House were due to arrive around mid-morning. Lucy would welcome them and then Briony would take them across to the gîte. Neither of the guests for both the Stables gîtes had given an arrival time so it was a question of waiting and seeing who arrived first. All the guests were to be invited for an informal aperitif on the farm terrace at six o'clock.

Briony wandered back to the farmhouse kitchen after she'd done the final check and found Lucy busy making small pastry nibbles for the evening get-together.

'You will come up too, won't you?' Lucy said. 'You're part of the team now.'

'Yes, I'll be here. Can I do anything right now?'

'You could finish loading the dishwasher for me and start it off,' Lucy said. 'While I remember too – can you come up on Tuesday morning about ten o'clock, instead of Thursday? The Cider House guests are only here for a long weekend so we'll need to strip the beds and everything. The Stables are both empty next Saturday.'

'That's fine,' Briony said. 'What about...' She paused as they both heard a car drive onto the yard. 'Sounds like some guests have arrived.'

Lucy sighed. 'Can you go? I really need to finish these pastries. Tell them I'll pop over to see them in about half an hour. Too early for the guests in the

Cider House. If it's the Dunkling family, they are in No.2. Anyone else, No.1.'

Briony left Lucy to her baking and went out to greet the guests.

* * *

Jeannie tidied up the breakfast things once Briony had left and generally pottered about the cottage for an hour. She thought about ringing Yann and inviting him for Easter Sunday lunch before deciding she'd take Meg on a walk through the village and surprise him at home.

Odette called out a cheerful 'Bonjour' and several people waved to her as she walked through the village towards Yann's cottage, a short five-minute walk on the outskirts. Jeannie smiled happily. She was already loving living in France.

As she approached Yann's house, she smiled as she saw the garden which she knew had always been Yann's pride and joy. Her smile vanished as she saw a van parked on the small driveway and Yann watching a man hammering a For Sale sign into the flowerbed to the side of the front door.

Yann turned and saw her. 'Jeannie, what a lovely surprise.' He hurried to her side.

'You didn't say you were moving away?' Jeannie said, looking at the board.

'I'm not. Well, I am hoping to move, but not far. Come on in and let me explain. Let's sit out in the garden,' Yann said.

As Yann ushered her through the house and out into the secluded back garden, Jeannie felt a strange shiver of apprehension. She'd realised the night she'd spent in the house after Yann had picked her up from the airport that this was still Evette's house. Her handiwork, her taste, was still in evidence. The wallpaper, the paintings, even the lampshade hanging over the hallway, had all been chosen by Evette. The tiles in the bathroom she remembered Evette asking her advice on and she'd been so proud of her modern bathroom. Yann had changed nothing. The last time Jeannie had been here when Evette was still alive, she'd welcomed her with a huge smile and thrown her arms around her. Now it was Yann drawing her close and kissing her cheeks.

'To what do I owe this surprise visit?' he asked with a smile.

'You're invited for lunch tomorrow,' Jeannie said. 'If you're free of course?'

'Thank you, of course I'm free to have lunch with you.'

'There is one thing we'd like to do Sunday morning. We've decided to scatter Giselle's ashes in the garden near the trees at the bottom. I know you were very fond of Giselle and we wondered whether you'd like to join the two of us?'

Yann's arms around her tightened. 'I'd be honoured. Thank you.'

'I've also told Briony about us becoming closer and she is happy for both of us.'

A relieved smile passed over Yann's face.

'I have to warn you, though, that at lunch tomorrow she may tease you with questions about your intentions.' Jeannie paused. 'Having seen that sign outside, I must admit I have a few questions of my own.'

'That's what I want to talk to you about.' Yann looked at her. 'Evette has been gone for eighteen months now. Like you will never forget Jeromé, I will never forget Evette and the life we had together, mainly in this house.' He paused. 'I need to move on. Everywhere I turn, there are memories – mostly good, I admit – but I want to make some new memories with you. I hope one day that we will be living together, maybe even married,' he shrugged. 'I don't know if that will happen, but I do know that I can't ask you to stay in a house that is still full of Evette. I want somewhere that the two of us can be happy together, making our own memories. Do you understand?'

Jeannie nodded. 'Yes, of course I do. Are you going to buy in the village or somewhere else?'

'I thought we could take that decision together. Sometimes I quite fancy a complete change from village life – an apartment on the Croisette in Cannes, *peut-être*. But you've only just begun your village life, so it is something we need to discuss, yes?'

Jeannie nodded. 'Yes, it's definitely something we need to talk about.'

* * *

The French guests staying in the Cider House arrived at midday as expected and Briony welcomed them, gave them the guided tour and left them to settle in. She was walking back across the yard to the farmhouse, when an Audi sports car drove into the yard and stopped. An attractive woman slid gracefully out, her slim white jeans with pale blue-white designer polo shirt tucked in accentuating her figure. She closed the car door and stood looking around. Briony walked towards her.

'Can I help you?'

The woman moved her sunglasses down so that she was looking over the top of them at Briony. 'Perhaps. I'm visiting a friend.'

'Which gîte are they staying in?' Briony asked.

'I forget the name. Maybe something like the Hen House, the Corn Store or even maybe the Pig Sty.'

Briony stiffened. Calling one of the gîtes the Pig Sty was not nice – and the Corn Store was Elliot's cottage. She had a sudden feeling she might know who this woman was. Elliot's 4x4 had been parked outside his cottage earlier, but whether he was indoors or over at the farm with Adam, she had no way of knowing. What she did know, though, was that both Elliot and Adam needed to be told about this woman.

'You're looking for Elliot?'

'Yes. Don't worry. I am happy to wander around until I find him.'

'I'm not sure he's at home at the moment. I hope you don't have to wait too long,' Briony said as she turned away and casually made for the farmhouse. Opening the door, she was relieved to see both Elliot and Adam looking at some data on Adam's laptop.

Adam looked up with a frown. 'Hi. You look a bit flustered. Do you want Lucy's help with one of the guests?'

'No. All the bona fide guests are fine, but there is a woman wandering around looking for her "friend". She mentioned the Corn House, although she inferred that maybe it had changed its name to the Pig Sty. I think it's your ex-wife,' she said, looking at Elliot.

Elliot clenched his fists and turned to leave.

Adam put a hand on his arm. 'Calm down, bro. We don't want a scene in front of any of the guests. I can come with you and ask her to leave and threaten her with the police for trespassing if she doesn't go.'

Elliot shook his head. 'No need to come with me, there won't be a scene, I promise.' And he turned and left the kitchen with Luna.

Briony exchanged a glance with Adam, who shrugged resignedly, before they both watched Elliot as he crossed the yard towards the Corn Store, Luna walking as close as she could to him, clearly sensing the tension in his body.

* * *

Robyn had found Elliot's 4x4 outside the Corn Store and was leaning against it as Elliot approached her. 'Thought this would be your vehicle. Hello, Elliot.'

'What the hell are you doing here, Robyn?' Elliot said. 'If you are here to cause trouble, I have to warn you, Adam is prepared to call the local gendarmerie and have you escorted off the farm. And regardless of whether you intend to cause trouble or not, I have nothing to say to you. So perhaps you'd like to leave now.'

Robyn shook her head. 'I'm not here to cause trouble. I wanted to see you and to have a civilised conversation with you.' She glanced around as she saw both Adam and Briony, as well as two guests from the Cider House, all standing around and watching the two of them. 'A private conversation.'

Elliot sighed and gave in to the inevitable. 'You'd better come in then,' and he opened the door to his cottage. 'Five minutes. You say what you've come to say and then you leave.'

* * *

'So why are you here?' Elliot demanded as he and Robyn stood in the main room of the Corn House.

'Do I have to have a reason to come?'

'Damn right you do.'

Robyn shrugged. 'I simply thought we could have lunch, have a chat, mend some fences.'

Elliot stared at her. 'I do not want to have lunch with you, have a chat or mend fences. What do you want?'

There was a short silence before Robyn spoke.

'You've been offered a TV follow-up to the programme that—'

'The programme that ruined my life in England?' Elliot interrupted. 'That programme? The one I have no intention of being involved with? Which, incidentally, the producer already knows.'

Robyn gave a brief nod. 'Yes. That one.'

'So, again – why are you here?'

'To persuade you to accept the job. I asked if I could be considered for the presenter's job and the producer said yes – with one condition. You have to accept the job. He thinks that the two of us working together would give the programme, what he called, "an extra dynamic". So full disclosure here. If you don't accept the job, I don't get mine either.'

Elliot gave a short cynical laugh. 'Work with you? Are you for real?' He shook his head. 'No. Never. You are wasting your time even thinking that you can get me to change my mind.'

'You're being offered the chance to clear your name once and for all. Get rid of the "guilty by association" tag that you acquired.'

Elliot shook his head. 'The people that matter know the truth. And I've made a new start away from all the lies that were bandied about. I have no intention of dragging them into the light again.'

'But you—'

Elliot held up his hand. 'No. You've asked. I've refused. Your five minutes are up – you can leave. I'll walk you to your car.' Elliot turned away from her, but Robyn made no attempt to move.

'If you don't take the job, I...' She paused and Elliot turned to look at her.

'You what?'

'I lose my chance to present another TV documentary. I've been blacklisted by every other company.'

'You expect me to be sorry about that after what happened to me with your last documentary where you failed to tell me the truth about what you were actually doing?'

'No, I don't need you to be sorry, but we were happy together once and I was hoping that perhaps, for old times' sake, you'd help me.' Robyn sighed. 'I need the job. I've run out of money and I seem to be unemployable in the world of TV production.'

'Let's be honest here. Us being happy together

didn't last long enough for me to feel nostalgic about those few years. Especially after the decision you made regarding our baby,' Elliot said. 'If things are that bad work-wise, maybe you should think about a change of career?'

'I loved being a TV presenter, but I guess I could go back to being just a freelance journalist,' Robyn said.

'I'd advise you to find a pen name if you do that,' Elliot said, staring at her. 'Time to go.' This time when he moved to open the front door, a subdued Robyn followed him.

By the time they'd walked across the farmyard and Elliot had opened the car door for Robyn, he could tell that she'd pulled herself together and the successful, confident act she presented to the world was firmly back in place.

Robyn slid onto the driver's seat, switched the engine on and lowered the window after Elliot closed the door.

'Goodbye, Robyn, I hope you manage to sort out your life,' he said. 'Mine is good now and I wish you the same, although somehow I doubt you'll ever be truly happy.' He turned to walk away when Robyn called out.

'Elliot – you know that abortion I had that upset you so much? You shouldn't have been – it wasn't your baby anyway.'

* * *

When Elliot and Robyn had disappeared into the Corn House, Briony had joined Lucy and Adam keeping an eye out through the farmhouse window.

'I wish she'd hurry up and leave,' Adam muttered. 'The longer she's here, the more I worry.'

'I'm trying to work out why she's here,' Lucy said. 'The only thing I can think of is that somehow it's connected to that letter Elliot received, wanting him to get involved with some TV programme or other.'

'The door of the cottage is opening,' Briony said quietly.

The three of them watched as Elliot escorted Robyn to her car, opened the door for her, waited while she got in and closed the door.

'He just said something to her,' Adam said. 'I hope to hell it was along the lines of *never contact me again*. At last he's walking away.'

'Hang on,' Lucy said. 'She's determined to have the last word. Now she's off.' They all watched silently as Robyn drove out of the yard and disappeared.

'I don't like Elliot's body language,' Adam said, sighing. 'He looks absolutely shattered. What the hell has that bloody woman done to him now?'

Briony watched as Elliot began to slowly walk towards the farmhouse. As much as she wanted to help, to comfort him, she knew it wasn't her place. Elliot needed his brother and his family around him.

Briony gave Lucy a quick look. 'I'm sure Elliot would appreciate some private time with you two. I'll disappear for a bit. See you later.'

She was already on her way to the door when Elliot walked in visibly upset. Briony gave Elliot a gentle smile as he walked in and closed the door behind her.

* * *

Briony left Jeannie sitting in the garden with Meg when she walked up to the farm for the Saturday evening welcome aperitifs for the guests. 'I shouldn't be more than an hour,' she said. 'Pizza and a glass of wine on the terrace when I get back?'

'Sounds like a plan,' Jeannie said.

As Briony got close to the farm, she could hear

the quiet hum of conversation out on the terrace. Lucy and Adam were talking to the couple staying in the Cider House and the Dunkling family arrived at the same time as she did. Briony quickly went into work mode pouring drinks, as Lucy made her way over to introduce the Dunklings to the other couple. There was no sign of the family who were staying in No.1 The Stables. There was also no sign of Elliot or the girls.

Briony helped herself to a glass of lemonade from the jug on the drinks trolley Lucy had placed near the table and walked over to Adam. 'No Elliot?' she said quietly.

Adam shook his head. 'Debs and Hannah have taken him to Cannes to cheer him up. He was in a bit of a state.' He glanced at Briony. 'My money is on them not succeeding after what she told him. Bloody Robyn and her antics.'

Before Briony could comment, the family from No.1 appeared and whilst Lucy poured them drinks, she started to hand around the nibbles that were on the table, but her mind was far away, thinking about Elliot. She couldn't help but feel that he would need more than an evening out on the town with his god-daughters to regain his peace of mind after Robyn's visit. The numb, closed-off look on his face earlier

when he'd walked into the farmhouse had told
Briony just how much he was hurting. She knew
there was nothing she could do to help him but her
heart ached for him in a way that surprised her. She
longed to simply reach out, put her arms around him
and hold him tight. Impossible, of course, they were
just friends.

36

Briony was up early on Easter Sunday and walked Meg to the lake. She'd been there no more than five minutes thinking about Elliot and what had happened yesterday, when he and Luna appeared.

'I was hoping you'd be here,' Elliot said, bending to let Luna off the lead as Briony released Meg. Both dogs raced off to the water.

'Me too.' Briony smiled. 'Did the girls manage to take your mind off things last night?' Looking at the shadows under his eyes and the pallor of his skin, she could guess the answer.

'I don't remember; they plied me with drink,' Elliot said ruefully.

'I'm guessing then, alongside a headache, those

murderous thoughts about your ex are still filling your thoughts,' she said.

'How did you guess.' He sank down wearily onto the bench. 'I've realised that my ex-wife is what people call "a real piece of work".' He glanced across at Briony. 'I think it's more than time for me to tell you about my marriage. I doubt that Lucy has said anything to you about my problems of the last year or two.'

'You're right.' Briony hesitated before continuing but decided honesty was always best. 'Lucy did infer that the internet would have the details.' Briony felt Elliot stiffen beside her. 'But I didn't go looking. I figured that if you wanted me to know you'd tell me yourself. Besides, the past is the past.'

'Thank you for not googling me.' Elliot nodded ruefully. 'The past is the past – until it comes back and deals you another killer blow that knocks you sideways – which is what Robyn did yesterday.' He exhaled a deep breath. 'To begin at the beginning. Our marriage had already hit a rocky patch soon after our first anniversary. I realised that I should never have married her, but being old-fashioned and taking my marriage vows seriously, I thought we should try to work things out. I even hoped we'd get back the feelings we must have had for each other in the beginning and could think about having the family that I've always wanted. Thankfully, it didn't happen because it would have been simply compounded the problem.' Elliot shook the thought away.

'It would,' Briony said quietly.

'Robyn came home one evening and said she'd been asked to present a programme about vets and veterinary practices. And one of the practices she was going to be filming at was the one where I had recently started to work. I wasn't overly thrilled at the thought of TV cameras following my every move and asking questions, but I didn't have a choice. The boss had agreed to do the show and we were expected to co-operate.'

'It must have been difficult, especially when you were dealing with a sick animal, to have a cameraman hovering.'

Elliot nodded. 'It was. But it got worse. What they were actually after, film-wise, was an exposé of certain vets for malpractice.' He took a deep breath. 'I'd only been at the practice for three months and I had no idea of the things that were suspected to be going on behind the scenes there and in other practices in the county. And were finally proved to be true.'

Briony gazed at him, horrified. 'Were you accused

personally of malpractice when you were totally innocent?'

'No. But I got smeared with it because when the owner of the practice realised that I was married to Robyn he accused me of setting him up, and I unwittingly became the scapegoat of the whole thing. When he publicly fired me, people believed that I was the one guilty of the malpractice – not him.' Elliot closed his eyes and rubbed his face.

When Briony reached out and touched his hand, he took hold of it and gripped it tightly.

'Given time I could probably have understood to a degree why she didn't warn me about the type of documentary she was making – although I think she should have told me. I would never have gone to that practice. But what really broke up my marriage in the end was the fact that in the middle of all this going on, Robyn had an abortion, telling me it was her body, her choice. I knew I could never forgive her for that. We should at least have talked about it. But guess what?' Elliot took a deep breath. 'As she was driving away yesterday, she gave me that final knockout blow. She told me that the baby she had aborted wasn't mine.'

Briony gave a shocked gasp. 'She'd been having an affair? Became pregnant, let you believe you were the father, before having an abortion? That was un-believably cruel of her.'

They both sat silently for several moments, Briony realising that Elliot was close to tears, if not crying. She searched for ways to comfort him.

With Elliot still holding her hand tightly, Briony stood up. 'Come on, you need a therapeutic hug with a tree,' she said, catching hold of his other hand and pulling him up. 'Hugging a tree always helps in stressful times.'

'I'd rather hug you today,' Elliot said quietly. 'May I?'

Briony smiled at him but shook her head. 'An-other time. I think today you need a tree hug more,' and she took him over to the big oak.

To her surprise, he didn't protest but slowly raised his arms as if in a daze and placed them around the trunk of the tree, closing his eyes, Briony stifled a sigh of regret as she moved away to keep an eye on the dogs. Elliot would never know how much it had cost her to refuse him a hug. She'd longed to hug him, to comfort him, but an inner instinct told her that he was more in need of some of those calming phytoncides from the oak tree than a hug from her.

Another woman in his arms when the actions of

his ex-wife were continuing to hurt him so much was not necessarily a good idea. Especially when her own feelings towards him were all over the place. Deep within herself, Briony hoped that one day soon Elliot would want to hug her for no other reason other than he liked her. And when that happened, she'd happily hug him back.

37

When Briony and Meg got back to Owls Nest, Jeannie had finished her toast and coffee breakfast and was busy peeling potatoes ready for lunch. She glanced up as Briony walked into the kitchen. 'You all right? Long walk?'

'No longer than usual, but Elliot was at the lake and he wanted to talk.'

'Ah, how is he after yesterday's upset?'

'Thinking murderous thoughts about his ex-wife,' Briony said. 'But otherwise he's okay. I did invite him for lunch, but Lucy and the family are expecting him. Can I just grab a coffee before I start peeling vegetables?'

'Of course. Time for toast too if you want it. I'll join you with another coffee,' Jeannie said.

By the time Yann arrived carrying a bottle of champagne, bunches of flowers and Easter eggs for them both, everything was prepped and both the dauphinoise potatoes and the lamb were ready to go in the oven.

Jeannie thanked him and put the bottle of champagne in the fridge to chill, taking out the one she'd placed there overnight.

'I thought we could toast Giselle with a glass after we've scattered her ashes,' Jeannie said quietly. 'She was very fond of a glass of champagne. So shall we take this cold one out to the terrace and open it when we've said our final goodbyes?'

Out on the terrace, Jeannie placed the bottle in the wine cooler that Briony had put on the table with three glasses and turned to pick up the urn from the low wall at the end of the terrace. Silently, the three of them made their way to the trees at the bottom of the garden, stopping in front of the oak with the hollowed-out branch.

Carefully, Jeannie took the lid off the urn and slowly began to shake the ashes free. Whilst Yannick stood at her side, his eyes closed as he said his personal goodbye to Giselle, Briony softly recited the first verse of 'Remember', the Christina Rossetti poem.

'Remember me when I am gone away, Gone far away into the silent land; When you can no more hold me by the hand, Nor I half turn to go yet turning stay.'

Jeannie finished scattering the ashes and the three of them stood silently for a moment or two before Jeannie said, 'Time to open the champagne, I think,' and she led the way back up to the cottage.

After raising their glasses in a final toast to Giselle, they sat out on the terrace sipping their champagne and eating a few nibbles that Jeannie had placed on the table.

Briony looked at Yann. 'I have to confess that I – we did have a small, ulterior motive for inviting you to lunch today.'

'You did?' Yann said. 'I promise my intentions towards Jeannie are strictly honourable.' His eyes twinkled as he smiled at her.

Briony, a little embarrassed and realising that her mum had told him about her reaction, laughed. 'It's really nothing to do with me and mum is happier than I've seen her for years. We have some questions about Dad and Granny Giselle's family we hope you may be able to answer. We want to show you some old, mainly black-and-white photos, and see if you could name any of the people in them. I know you're a different generation and would have been quite young, or not even born, when some of the photos were taken, but maybe your grandparents or Dad's grandparents are in the photos and you'll recognise them,' Briony said. 'Basically I'm hoping you can help solve a mystery for us.' She got up. 'I'll fetch the box with everything in.'

'I'll do my best,' Yann said, glancing at Jeannie. 'Did Jeromé or Giselle never share any family history with you?'

'Jeromé rarely. Giselle occasionally mentioned her mother Marie-Louise, but I've never seen a family album of photos. And so far nothing has turned up as Briony has been decluttering the cottage.'

Briony returned and put the box on the table and took out the diary and the photos and placed them on the table alongside it.

Yann riffled through a few photos gently before smiling and picking up a formal photo of a wedding group. 'This is my grandparents on their wedding day. And that couple in the background are Marie-Louise and Albert – your great-grandparents,' he said, looking at Briony. 'It's not a very clear photo of them, let's see if there is a better one.' Discarding a few photos, he picked up the photo of the young girl with the sad eyes. 'This is Marie-Louise as a young girl. She kept that sad look all her life. Lovely lady.' He shuffled a few more of the photos. 'Ah, here she is on her wedding day with Albert, her new husband.' Yann glanced at Jeannie. 'Did Jeromé never talk to you about them? I think they were both dead by the time you came into his life.'

Jeannie shook her head. 'He said once he adored his grandmother but hadn't cared much for his grandfather. Said he was a bit taciturn and didn't have a lot of time for children.'

'That's how I remember him too,' Yann said. 'My grandparents were friends with them, largely, I suspect with hindsight, because my grand-maman tried to keep an eye on Marie-Louise. It wasn't a particularly happy marriage, I don't think.'

'I'm curious to know why Marie-Louise stopped painting when she was young,' Briony said. 'I do wish we'd found these photos before Giselle died. She might have been able to give us some answers, even tell us why everything was hidden away. Do you think she knew about the box in the attic?'

Yann rubbed his face thoughtfully. 'I'm pretty sure there was some sort of scandal in the village in the late nineteen-thirties. You have to remember that village life here was a very closed one, not like down on the coast, where it was already the playground of the rich and the famous. Did you say something about solving a mystery?'

'Yes. There are lots of postcards – Paris and New York mainly – with the initials EM on and in the diary journal the writer mentions EM all the way through.'

Yann reached out and picked up the diary. 'Was this in the box as well?'

'Yes. But it was never kept as a proper diary, it's just comments at irregular places in the book. And a particularly sad one near the end about being pregnant,' Briony said. 'I'm certain that it belonged to Marie-Louise.'

Thoughtfully, Yann slowly turned a few of the pages near the beginning of the diary. 'I would agree Marie-Louise was the owner of this journal,' he paused. 'And I also think the mystery EM was probably American. Judging by all the name-dropping in the journal and the parties, I think she was one of the very first celebrity figures in the twentieth century. I think she was part of the village scandal too somehow.' He shrugged. 'I can't be sure – it was all so long ago and happened before either Jeromé or I were born. So I only know stuff that was passed down through the generations, truly family legends. But I vaguely remember mutterings about an American woman who became friendly with Marie-Louise, much to Albert's annoyance.'

'Well, at least we're fairly sure now that Marie-Louise was the owner and writer of the journal, and the baby she mentions was Giselle,' Jeannie said. 'We'll have to be content with that for now, I think. I need to go and check on lunch.'

Briony started to pack the photos back into the box. Picking up the photo of Yann's grandparents' wedding, she held it out to him. 'Would you like this one?'

'Maybe a copy would be nice,' Yann said. 'Thank you.'

'I'll organise one for you.'

'Elsa,' Yann said suddenly. 'Her name was Elsa.'

'Sorry?' Briony said.

'The American woman was called Elsa. Can't remember her surname though.'

38

Late on Easter Sunday night, Adam and Lucy had looked up at the cloudless sky and gone to bed fearing the worse. Easter Monday and they were both up early and Adam groaned as he looked out of the window. 'It's not a heavy frost, but there's definitely been one. Come on, let's get down to the vines and see what the damage is.'

Walking down through the rows of vines in the south-facing field, Adam began to breathe a little easier. Every row appeared to be virtually untouched by the frost. Until the last two rows at the bottom of the slope. Lucy took out her phone to film the damage on those rows, comparing it to the others that had escaped the damaging frost for her next video.

Bruno was already there assessing the damage and muttering.

'We seem to have got off lightly,' Lucy said. 'Have you heard how other vineyards have fared?' She knew that Bruno had an active network of wine-makers both in the south and further upcountry.

'We've been lucky,' Bruno said. 'The truly hard frost reached as far down as the Languedoc department.'

'What do we do now?'

'We wait and we watch for secondary budding on these two rows and hope for a good summer and they catch up with the rest.'

'What about the frosted shoots and leaves?'

'They'll turn brown in the sun and drop off eventually,' Bruno answered.

'We'd better go and check the avocados,' Adam said. 'You want to come up to the farm for breakfast in about half an hour?'

'Thanks. I'll see you then.' And Bruno turned his attention back to the vines.

Adam and Lucy walked quickly across to the avocado plants and both heaved sighs of relief as they moved between the rows and saw they too had thankfully survived the frost.

'I'll add a short video of these onto the vine one,

showing how well the avocados have survived,' Lucy said.

* * *

Briony woke early on Easter Monday and lay in bed half listening to the dawn chorus, cocooned with her own thoughts under the duvet. Yesterday morning with Elliot before and after he'd hugged the tree was uppermost in her mind. Had she done the right thing in not hugging him? She pushed her doubts away and consoled herself with the thought that Elliot actually asking her for a hug was a sign that their friendship was becoming stronger.

As the birds' chorus became quieter Briony got up and made for the bathroom. After breakfast, she was going to do some research on her laptop and then start to formulate a proper plan for setting up the brocante.

Jeannie was already downstairs with the coffee set up and bread sliced ready for the toaster.

Sitting out on the terrace after breakfast, Briony opened her laptop. 'I'm going to see if I can find out who this EM is; she was clearly important to Great-granny. Not got a lot of information to go on but...' she shrugged. 'It's worth a try.'

Briony typed the name Elsa plus several of the names Marie-Louise had mentioned in her journal. But Google kept showing 'no results'. After half a dozen failed attempts, Briony gave a frustrated sigh.

'No luck?' Jeannie said.

Briony shook her head. Her hands hovered over the keyboard trying to remember how Yann had described the woman. As they came back to her she typed them in.

Elsa + 20th century celebrity + American + arranged parties + French Riviera + the nineteen thirties.

Anticipating the 'no results' answer again, she pressed enter for one last try.

But a second later she had a result. There was a name and photos of a woman called Elsa Maxwell, with several links to information about her on the screen. Briony sat back and looked at the pictures. Was this her great-granny Marie-Louise's friend Elsa?

When she clicked on one of the links and read that Elsa Maxwell had lived with a friend in a small Provençal farmhouse in the village of Auribeau-sur-Siagne in the countryside behind Cannes, Briony felt her excitement rising. That village was just a kilometre or two away. This had to be the woman with the initials EM that Marie-Louise had been friends with. Even if this unprepossessing woman looked nothing like the image of her Briony had visualised in her mind.

Most sites she clicked on the links to, described Elsa Maxwell as an 'American gossip columnist, author, radio personality and a professional hostess famed for lavish parties for royalty and high-society figures of the time'. 'Hostess with the mostess' was a frequent description. Together with the much-used old-fashioned phrase 'closet lesbian'.

So was that the reason Albert had been so adamant that Elsa wasn't a respectable woman and Marie-Louise was not to be seen with her? Attitudes amongst the people he knew and lived amongst were so different in those days. Elsa might mix with, and be accepted by, the wealthy, royalty and well-known figures of the twentieth century, but Albert, from all accounts, was a parochial product of the nineteenth century and would have found it hard to accept the new morales of a world changed by the Great War.

Briony saved the original page with all its links as Jeannie put a cup of coffee in front of her. 'Mum, I think I've found our mysterious EM,' and she pushed the laptop across to Jeannie.

After Jeannie had looked at several of the links, she agreed with Briony. 'Poor Marie-Louise.'

Briony nodded. 'At least we know now why Great-granddad Albert was so anti her friendship with Elsa, but we still do not know why Great-granny stopped painting. And that's one mystery I don't think we'll ever solve.'

Briony closed the page down and opened a new file.

'Right. Time to start planning my new business. Which basically involves setting the unit up with some stock, creating a stock list, doing an advert, painting the parrot cage, planting up the handcart, deciding on a name and finding a signwriter. All in just a few weeks.'

'Yann is taking me out for dinner this evening. He's booked a table at the Auberge in Cannes. Honestly I seem to have done nothing but eat since I got back, but I'm all yours for the day,' Jeannie said.

'I was hoping you would say that. Fancy working up at the unit with me today? I know it's a holiday, but I also know time from now until the day I open will fly past. We can put up the trestle tables from the garage and see where they fit best. Need to find some cloths to cover them. And then maybe start going through the boxes I took up from the garage and decide what to sell, what to keep and what to throw.'

* * *

The day passed in a flash as, between the two of them, they decided on the best position for tables, where the parrot cage would go when ready and lamented the lack of shelves. They opened several boxes and made a note of the items they were going to put on display, and Briony made a stock list spreadsheet on her laptop. One of the boxes contained some vintage tablecloths that would cover the trestle tables beautifully.

Briony's phone pinged with a text message from Elliot as they were starting to wind up and get ready to go back to the cottage.

> Fancy a small picnic down by the lake at eight o'clock?

Briony immediately text back.

> Yes please. Can I bring anything?

> Just yourself and Meg.

'You're not the only one with a date tonight,' Briony said, turning to smile at Jeannie. 'I'm having a picnic with Elliot.'

* * *

Jeannie and Yann had left for their dinner date in Cannes before Briony locked the cottage doors behind her and walked with Meg down to the lake. It was a perfect late-spring evening, the temperature from the day still lingered in the air as a half-moon started to show in the sky.

Elliot was already there standing near the shoreline watching Luna swimming. A shallow wicker basket with a cloth over the contents was on the bench and a bottle of Prosecco was half buried and chilling in the water at the edge of the lake. He turned and smiled as soon as Meg alerted him to Briony's arrival. He greeted her with a kiss on the cheek before stooping to pull the bottle out of its impromptu cold place.

'Now, where shall we have our picnic?' he asked. 'On the bench or shall we wander out onto the jetty?'

'I quite fancy sitting and dangling my legs over the water, but what about the dogs if we sit on the jetty?'

'I predict Luna will follow us and lay down on the jetty hoping for tidbits and Meg always follows her so...' Elliot shrugged.

'The jetty it is then,' Briony said. 'I'll carry the basket while you take care of the bottle.'

A few minutes later and they were both sat at the end of the jetty, legs dangling over the edge and the picnic basket between them.

'Am I allowed to peek in the basket?' Briony asked.

'In a moment,' Elliot said as he reached in and pulled out two wine flutes, which he handed to Briony, before starting to carefully release the cork from the bottle with a satisfactory pop and then pouring them each a drink. '*Santé*,' he said and Briony smiled and clicked her glass against his. 'Before we eat, I want to thank you for yesterday. You listened and responded with such kindness. Kindness that I really appreciated.'

'You're not down and out still from Robyn's unkind knockout blow then?' Briony said quietly.

Elliot shook his head. 'No. You helped me stand back up again. I've pushed the pain of that final revelation into the far corner of my mind, where I've buried all the other detritus of my marriage.' Elliot took a sip of his drink. 'I am not going to allow Robyn to disrupt my life ever again. My working life as a vet is back on track...' He paused and looked directly at Briony, before taking a deep breath. 'My personal life on the other hand needs a lot of help. I really like you and I sense that you possibly like me a bit too, so will you please help sort me out?'

Briony smiled. 'Yes, I can admit I like you too and I will be delighted to help you, but right now...' She stopped.

'What?'

'Can we please eat; I'm starving. What's in the basket?'

* * *

Half an hour later, the basket was empty. Elliot had made salmon, cucumber and mayonnaise sand- wiches, there were slices of melon with Parma ham wrapped around them, and one large dish of straw- berries and cream that had been shared between them – all washed down with the Prosecco.

'That was an absolutely perfect picnic, thank you,' Briony murmured. 'I hereby appoint you chief picnic maker for all future picnics.'

Elliot smiled and nodded. 'I reckon I can handle

that. Right now I think it's time we moved off the jetty and sat on the bench. It's getting a bit cold out here on the water.'

Sitting on the bench, the two dogs at their feet, Elliot's arm around her shoulders, Briony looked up at the moon shining in a darkening sky and gave a happy sigh.

'I forgot to tell you earlier,' Elliot said, breaking into her thoughts. 'I had a phone call this afternoon from Jill, the daughter of Meg's old owner, asking how Meg was and hoping she'd settled in well. She would also like to accept your offer of taking Meg in to see her father before it is too late, if you're still happy to do that. Her father is not in a good way.'

'Oh, that's sad. Did she say when she would like us to visit?'

'Wednesday afternoon. I'm off then and I could come with you.'

'Yes, I'd like that,' Briony said, giving an involuntarily shiver.

'Time to leave, I think,' Elliot said. 'The walk back will warm us up.'

Back at the cottage garden gate, Briony turned to Elliot. 'Thank you for a lovely evening.'

'Can I have a hug tonight?'

'Definitely,' Briony said, moving into his arms and holding him tight.

The kiss Elliot gave her seconds later was an unexpected welcome delight.

39

Tuesday morning and Briony went up to the farm ready to start the bed-changing and cleaning of the Cider House. The wedding photograph of Yann's grandparents was in her bag, in the hope that she could use the scanner in Lucy's office to make one or two copies.

Adam and Lucy were in the kitchen when she arrived talking about the weekend. Lucy jumped up when Briony walked into the kitchen, immediately pouring her a coffee and pushing the biscuit tin towards her. 'I know you're here to start on the Cider House, but first I'm hoping you can do some admin. We've had quite a few enquiries over the weekend and I'd rather get them out of the way before doing the domestic stuff.'

'That's fine.' Briony took the photograph out of her bag. 'May I use the scanner to make a copy of this please?' And she showed the photograph to Lucy. 'It's Yann's grandparents' wedding and my great-grandparents are there in the group.'

'Wow,' Lucy said. 'How amazing. Where did you find this?'

Briony quickly explained about the boxes and said she'd promised Yann a copy.

'Of course you can use the scanner – there's some photographic paper in one of the drawers.'

'Thanks. I'll take my coffee into the office and get on.'

It took Briony an hour to deal with the various enquiries and also to finalise some bookings for May and June. Once everything for the gîte business was up to date, she found the glossy photographic paper and scanned and made two copies of the wedding photograph.

As she closed the scanner down, Lucy appeared. 'Everything is up to date and entered on the spreadsheet, and the new confirmed bookings are in the wall calendar as well,' Briony said. 'I was just coming down to fetch the cleaning stuff and go over to the Cider House.'

'Great. I can edit my video on the computer now and get it live. I'll come and give you a hand then.'

Briony collected the basket of cleaning stuff from the utility room and made her way across to the Cider House. She daydreamed her way through the routine cleaning of the kitchen and bathroom as thoughts of the picnic the night before filled her head and she smiled happily, remembering how good it had felt to share a hug and a kiss with Elliot.

Lucy arrived in time to give her a hand with changing the beds. 'I'll take the bedding back to the farm to wash and dry,' she said as they remade all the beds.

'I was wondering whether I could change to another day for admin work?' Briony said as they strolled back up to the farm. 'Mum is going to man the brocante on Saturdays while I'm helping you with changeover day and the guests, but Thursdays might be a problem if I decide to open an extra day.'

'Shall we change Thursday to Monday for the admin and see how that goes,' Lucy said.

'Thanks.'

As she walked back down to the cottage, Briony thought about the things still to do on her list. The weeks were sure to fly by if she wanted to be ready by late May for the beginning of the summer season.

Jeannie was busy in the garden when she got home and after lunch the two of them sat on the terrace and went through the to-do list on Briony's laptop.

'There is still so much to do,' Briony said. 'So far on the list I've got: photograph the artisan units for the newspaper advertisement and get in touch with *Nice Matin*; order some business cards; find a shelf unit or two; finish upcycling the parrot cage; buy some plants and plant the handcart and probably the bicycle basket.'

'I can take over buying the plants,' Jeannie said. 'Geraniums, petunias and maybe some pansies? We'll need some compost too. Lots as the garden pots here need a top-up. I'll ask Yann to take me to the nearest garden centre because the *pépinière* won't have them, but they do have some agapanthus that I intend to buy.'

'Thanks. Pascal will be good for that journey,' Briony said, smiling.

Briony sprayed the parrot cage that afternoon, leaving it to dry in the sunshine as she and Jeannie went up to the unit to do some more sorting out. Both Holly and Calvin were there, the doors to their units open, and Briony quickly took a photograph of the three with their open doors.

'What does everybody think about the name "Briony's Belle Brocante" for my business? Has anyone got any better suggestions?'

'Sounds good,' Holly said. 'I like the alliteration with all the B's.'

Jeannie nodded. 'Yes, sounds good.'

'Briony's Belle Brocante it is,' Briony said.

While Jeannie started unpacking a few more boxes, Briony used her phone to type an advertisement, attached the photo, signed into the *Nice Matin* site, paid and sent it.

'That's something to tick off the list,' she said. 'Need to find a signwriter now to do a sign.'

'I can do that for you,' Holly offered. 'If you find a piece of wood and prepare it, I'll happily decorate it with the name.'

'Really? Thank you so much,' Briony said.

'How many days are you going to open?' Holly asked.

'I'm going to take it slowly, build the business up. I've got a lot to learn about how things work down here. In the beginning, I'm planning to be open from ten till five. Two full days a week, Friday and Saturdays,' Briony said. 'And Sundays two till five. I'll see how it goes and I might add a Thursday opening in the height of summer.'

'There's lots of red, white and blue bunting in this box,' Jeannie said. 'Shall we keep it for opening day?'

'Why not,' Briony said. 'Put it in a corner somewhere so we don't lose it. I'm going to drive Pascal up soon and bring a ladder, the handcart, the parrot cage and probably a few more boxes from the garage. Just to keep us busy and out of mischief.'

40

Wednesday afternoon and Elliot drove them both down to Antibes to see Meg's old owner. 'I feel I should know his name,' Briony said.

'It's Doug. Jill has said she'll meet us there.'

When Elliot drove into the care home car park, they found a subdued Jill waiting for them anxiously by the main entrance.

'Briony, it's lovely to meet you and thank you so much for taking on Meg. She looks extremely happy – and a little less fat,' Jill said, bending down to stroke Meg, who clearly remembered her. 'Dad isn't too good this afternoon, I'm afraid, but his favourite carer, a lovely Indian lady called Afareen, is with him at the moment. Shall we go in?'

Doug was in a private room on the ground floor with a window overlooking the extensive grounds.

Briony stopped at the entrance to the room and looked at Jill. 'Your father doesn't know me, I think it would be better if you take Meg in, so I'll wait here.'

Jill glanced at her father lying in the bed with his eyes closed and nodded. 'I think you're right,' and taking Meg's lead she walked into the room, while Briony and Elliot stayed outside and watched.

Afareen, the carer, smiled as she saw Jill and Meg approach the bed.

'Dad, I've brought someone special to see you.' Meg moved closer to the bed and Jill went to place her father's hand on the dog's head. But Meg had a different idea. She stood on her hind legs and gently placed both of her front paws on the bed and sniffed Doug's hand. Doug's hand twitched and Meg gave it a lick before placing her head on the bed between her paws. Jill, seeing her dad's hand twitch, gently placed it on Meg's head. Meg stayed still for thirty seconds or so, before carefully placing her front feet back on the floor and looking up at Jill.

Jill was brushing away tears when she handed Meg back to Briony. 'I'm certain he registered Meg was in the room. There was a soft smile on his face as we left. Thank you so much for bringing her. Afareen has told me he hasn't got long now. The rest of the family are coming soon.'

Elliot took Jill in his arms and hugged her gently. 'Let us know if we can help in any way again.'

'Thank you, I will.'

Both Elliot and Briony were silent as they walked back to the car.

'Shall we walk the dogs in Cap d'Antibes woods?' Elliot said, as he opened the car door, where Luna was waiting patiently and Meg jumped up to join her. 'Have you ever been to the chapel at the foot of the lighthouse?'

Briony shook her head. 'No.'

The ten-minute drive to Cap d'Antibes woods was quiet as both Elliot and Briony were lost in their own thoughts.

'We'll walk the dogs first. They can stay in the car then whilst we have a look at the chapel,' Elliot said as he parked the car.

It was cool in the woods and the two dogs were happy on their long leads sniffing their way along the footpath as Briony and Elliot strolled slowly along. The tranquility of the woods was soothing and all-encompassing, whilst the silence between the two of them felt companionable rather than uncomfortable. Briony, although sadden by the visit to the care home, breathed deeply and realised how happy she was at that moment.

Elliot had chosen a path that circled back to the car park. After giving the dogs a drink of water, they were happy to jump back in and lay down in the back of the car.

Making their way into the medieval Notre-Dame de la Garoupe chapel, Briony gazed around the walls with their seafaring decorations.

'Fishermen since the Middle Ages have come up here and prayed for safety at sea,' Elliot whispered in her ear. 'And to offer thanks and gifts for safe sailing after storms.'

'I feel I'd like to light a candle for Doug and also one for Granny,' Briony said, making her way over to the candles. Elliot joined her and together they lit candles and placed them carefully side by side on the table, before turning and leaving the chapel hand in hand.

* * *

Yann was more than happy to be Jeannie's driver and helper in the hunt for finding suitable plants for both the brocante and Owls Nest garden. 'We take a day out and go to the large garden centre the other side of Nice,' he said.

It was mid-afternoon before they arrived back and, after stopping briefly at Owls Nest to unload two buddleia plants, a white rose and a large bougainvillaea, they carried on up to the farm. Yann parked the Kangoo in front of the unit and began to unload the rest of their purchases: half a dozen bags of compost, pots of geraniums, cosmos, petunias, pansies.

Adam appeared not long after they'd started and gave them a hand to empty the car. 'You have an awful lot of plants here,' he said. 'Where on earth are they all going to go.'

'Mostly into the handcart or the bicycle basket and some of the geraniums will go down to the cottage,' Jeannie replied. 'Which reminds me. Those agapanthus you have, I'd like to buy those too. You need to do something about the *pèpiniére* by the way and we have an idea.'

'Okay. I think you'd better come up to the farm and tell me your idea for the *pèpiniére* over a cup of tea,' Adam said.

41

On the morning of 1 May, Briony took Meg for her usual morning walk down to the lake and found a bunch of muguets lying on the bench. She smiled as she picked them up and inhaled their sweet smell. There had been a small bed of these lily of the valley flowers in the garden in England, planted, her mum had always said, to remind her of the first time she'd been gifted a bunch. 'I'd never heard of the tradition of giving them as a token of love and appreciation before.' Briefly, Briony found herself wondering – was this traditional gift saying anything about the way Elliot felt about her?

There was a card with the flowers and Briony smiled as she read the message.

Have supper with me tonight? Eight
o'clock. Xx

Walking back to the cottage, Briony's thoughts
were filled with Elliot and the way she felt about him.

Jeannie glanced at the flowers in Briony's hand
when she walked into the kitchen. 'Elliot?' she said.

Briony nodded.

Jeannie smiled as she pointed to the vase on the
kitchen table filled with the small white bell-like
flowers.

'Yann?' Briony asked.

'Yes, they were by the front door this morning.'
Jeannie looked at her daughter. 'He was the first
person to ever give me these flowers years ago,' she
said quietly.

Briony, putting her own bunch in a vase, stopped
and looked at her mum. 'I always thought it was Dad
who gave you the first bunch, but it wasn't was it? You
planted that patch of lily of the valley at home to remind you of Yann – how he felt about you all those
years ago.'

Jeannie nodded. 'I've always been very fond of
Yann, but I didn't realise just how fond of me he was
when we were young – until it was too late to do anything about it.'

Briony was thoughtful as she placed her vase of muguets next to her mum's on the kitchen table. Were they both being given a second chance for love here in France? Her mum with Yann, years after they first met and herself with Elliot. Elliot, the new man in her life who was so lovely and so different to her ex-husband.

* * *

Jeannie had invited Yann to have supper with her that evening and he arrived as Briony left to walk up to Elliot's. 'See you later,' she called out. 'Enjoy your evening.'

Luna gave an excited bark as Briony knocked on the door and Elliot called out, 'Come on in. I'm out in the courtyard.'

'This is lovely,' Briony said, looking around the yard with its palm tree in a pot and a pale pink bougainvillea spreading itself out along the back wall of the cottage. 'Love your aftershave,' she said as Elliot leant in to give her a welcoming kiss. 'Dinner smelt delicious as I came through the kitchen.'

Elliot looked guilty. 'It's confession time. I bribed Lucy to make one of her wonderful fish pies. I could have made you cheese on toast, but I thought Lucy would get a kick out of knowing you were dining here tonight.'

'Thanks a bunch,' Briony said, laughing. 'Lucy will be asking lots of questions next time I see her, I already know what she's like as far as you're concerned.'

'She just wants me to be happy,' Elliot said in a silly voice. 'And right now,' he added in his normal voice, 'I am.'

'Thank you for the muguets this morning,' Briony said. 'I'm afraid I left it too late to find a bunch for you.'

'You know the tradition of why the French give them on the first of May?'

'Yes,' Briony said.

'Good,' Elliot said, giving her an intense look before turning away. 'Fish pie needs to come out of the oven,' and he disappeared back to the kitchen.

Sitting out in the courtyard eating the delicious fish pie that Lucy had made and enjoying a cool glass of white wine, Briony, like Elliot, knew that right now she was extremely happy. The picnic on the lake had been wonderful and romantic, but somehow sitting here in the tiny courtyard, a candle flickering on the table, French café music playing softly in the background, it was romantic and intimate, making Briony wonder where the evening might end.

Dessert was a meringue nest filled with raspberries and cream. 'I didn't make the nests, but I did fill them and put the cream on,' Elliot said, laughing as he placed them on the table.

After the desserts were eaten, Elliot suggested coffee indoors and Briony cleared the table whilst he organised the coffee. It was all very normal, friendly activity until Elliot caught Briony by the hand as she closed the door of the dishwasher and gently pulled her into his arms.

'I can't wait any longer to kiss you.'

Coffee was forgotten for several minutes as Briony responded to Elliot's kisses.

It was the quacking noise coming from Elliot's mobile on the work surface next to them that drew them apart. 'I have to answer it, that's the alert for the practice. I'm not on call tonight, but something may have come up.'

Elliot reached out and picked up the phone.

'Hi, Julian. Is there a problem?'

As he listened, his facial expression changed and he gave a sigh. 'It was expected but still sad. Thanks for letting me know. See you in the morning.'

Elliot put his arms around Briony again.

'Julian wanted to let us know that Doug passed away an hour or so ago.'

42

May began to go by in a whirl for Briony. As the days lengthened and the sun shone, the temperature started to rise and her life settled into a routine of being Lucy's Girl Friday two days every week and organising everything she needed to get done for the brocante on the other five days. Amongst other things, she did remember to find a suitable piece of wood and prepared it for Holly to signwrite the brocante name across it. One Tuesday morning when she went up to do some gîte admin, she took the wood with her and left it with Holly.

She'd been working in the office for sometime before a quieter-than-normal Lucy joined her.

'Are you okay?' Briony asked.

'The summer season is about to kick off and there is so much to do. Menopausal brain fog seems to have taken me over. And for some reason I'm also missing the girls more than usual. Easter seems such a long time ago and I'm not sure when they'll be home again. I should be used to them living away by now, we've been empty nesters for so long, but...' Lucy shrugged.

'Maybe it's something to do with being in a different country to your children? Rather than just empty nest syndrome?' Briony said.

Lucy looked at her. 'You could be right. I hadn't thought of that. I can't just pop into town to see them, meet up for a coffee. It all has to be booked, put in the diary.'

'Would you like me to do more of the admin? Take some of the pressure off you, maybe even give you time to fly over and surprise them?' Briony asked. 'Or maybe I could give you a hand in the house on another day?'

'That's sweet of you, but no. You've got enough on your Girl Friday plate, plus setting up the brocante. I'll do some baking; that always cheers me up.' Lucy smiled at Briony. 'How are you? Looking happier than when I first met you, that's for sure. I wonder if that's down to the French air or someone in particular? My brother-in-law is a changed man too, which I suspect is down to you.' She looked at Briony with a questioning look.

Briony felt herself blush. 'I am much happier than when I first arrived, it has to be said. I confess Elliot has a lot to do with that.'

'Good. Right, I'll leave you to the spreadsheets and go bake a cake. Tea and a slice before you leave later, okay?'

* * *

It was another two hours before Briony went down to the kitchen for the promised cup of tea. Adam was there enjoying a mug of tea and a large slice of lemon drizzle cake. He looked up at her with a smile.

'Has your mum told you that she has made me a very happy man? No? I helped her and Yann unpack the car after their garden-visit spree. Jeannie took the opportunity to tell me I'm losing money by not having the *pépinière* open at regular times and not having someone there to help customers. Gave me a proper telling-off.'

'That's Mum,' Briony said, waiting to hear what else Jeannie had said.

'But if I like the idea and want them to, both she

and Yann are happy to man the *pépinière* on the days the brocante is open. It's so close to the artisan units, they can do the two between them.' Adam paused. 'I accepted immediately of course. I couldn't possibly say no, thank you.'

Briony laughed. 'She's a force to be reckoned with is my mum.'

'She's cleaned the *pépinière* out of agapanthus too. Said they needed more attention than they were getting and they were perfect for Owls Nest as well as the brocante'.

'Agapanthus are one of Mum's favourite flowers, after roses and daffodils and sunflowers. She can never decide which is her absolute favourite,' Briony said, laughing.

* * *

When Jeannie learnt that Yann hadn't been down to the lake for years, she determined he had to see the changes down there. The perfect opportunity arose when he came for supper one evening. Briony and Elliot were sorting out more boxes up at the brocante prior to opening day, before having supper together at Elliot's.

'Come on, let's walk Meg down to the lake before

we have a glass of wine with supper,' Jeannie said. 'You have to see how Adam has improved the area. So many birds now and the trees have space to breathe and grow. The yellow irises on the edge of the water have been so beautiful this spring.'

Walking along the track with Yann holding her hand and Meg running ahead, Jeannie took deep breaths of the summery evening air that was punctuated with the noise of cicadas. She sent up a silent prayer of thanks to the universe for bringing her back to live in her favourite place in the world and for re-uniting her with the love of her life. Reaching the bench by the lake the two of them sat down. Yann caught his breath as he looked around. 'Adam, he makes an already lovely place into a beautiful paradise.' The pair of them sat contentedly both deep in their own thoughts for several moments before Yann stood up. 'I would like to walk the jetty.' And gently he pulled Jeannie to her feet.

Together they walked along the wooden jetty and stood watching as Meg took the opportunity to jump into the water for a swim. Yann shook his head as he looked out over the lake. 'Jeromé and me, we spent so many *vacances* down here as young boys, teenagers, before life took over.' He sighed. 'It is a good job we have no knowledge when we are young of what lies before us.' He turned and took Jeannie in his arms. 'I cannot deny my life has been good, I adore my daughter Pauline, and Evette and I, we were happy in our own way but my biggest regret has always been you weren't in my life. But now you are and life has never looked better. I love you, Jeannie Aubert.'

As he bent his head to kiss her, Jeannie whispered, 'I love you too. Always have. Always will.'

43

The evening before opening day of the brocante, Briony and Jeannie sat out on the terrace together enjoying a glass of rosé. Jeannie was reading a paperback and Briony took the opportunity to start looking through the diary-cum-journal again. The last few weeks had been so busy she hadn't had a chance to even pick it up. She turned a couple of pages on from the last entry about expecting a baby that she'd read all those weeks ago, hoping to read some happier entries by her great-grandmother Marie-Louise.

But there was no further mention of any mid-twentieth-century celebrities as Briony slowly turned the pages. Lots of the pages were blank until several pages from the end there was an entry:

EM has been in America for weeks now. I miss her and wish I could talk to her, ask her advice. Tell her about the baby. But even when she returns, I know I am unlikely to see her. I have heard all the dark rumours that are circulating about her and her friend Dorothy Fellowes-Gordon since they returned to America. And Albert refuses to let me mention her name in the house. Certain people, both men and women, are like red flags to Albert.

The other thing that provokes Albert to be cruel to me is finding me painting. He dislikes my paintings, which he calls wishy-washy rubbish. I have tried to explain how much I love the Impressionist paintings of Matisse which are really popular at the moment, but he never listens.

Briony turned to the last page. And there it was, the very last entry in the journal that told her why Marie-Louise had stopped painting at such a young age.

EM never spoke a truer word than when she told me how hard it is for a woman to be accepted as other than merely a wife or a mother. I am not brave like she is, I do not have it in me to fight the old-fashioned prejudices of men so publicly. I have decided that I will be content with my life as a mother and hope for better for my child should I give birth to a baby girl, rather than the son Albert wants. I have decided too, that I will stop painting. Not because of the baby, but life is easier when I do not antagonise Albert. I have placed everything from EM and all my paintings into boxes. I shall ask Thomas the cowman to place them in the attic one day when Albert is away at market. I miss painting already.

Briony sighed as she wiped a tear away and placed the diary on the table.

'Why the tears?' Jeannie asked quietly, looking up from her paperback.

'I've discovered why Great-granny stopped painting,' Briony said and carefully pushed the diary across the table towards her mum. 'Read the last two entries. So sad.' Briony picked up her wine and sipped it as she watched Jeannie read.

An emotional Jeannie wiped her own tears away as she looked at Briony. 'It's beyond sad. We can only be grateful that we live now. A time that is not perfect, but,' she shrugged, 'it's still better than then.'

Briony nodded in agreement. If only she could time-travel back and tell Marie-Louise that she'd discovered her paintings in the attic and loved them so much. Tell her that people in the twenty-first century were going to see and admire the ones she'd framed and hung in the brocante as a permanent exhibition of her work.

* * *

'It's a big day tomorrow for Briony,' Lucy said as she and Adam walked up through the farmyard after their evening dog walk with Django. Stopping in front of the brocante they looked at the bunting, the 'Briony's Belle Brocante' sign and the colourful array of flowers. 'I do hope it is a success. She's worked so hard for it to be up and running for the summer.'

'I'm sure it will be,' Adam said, glancing at Lucy. 'It's lovely to see all three of the artisan units finally occupied.'

Lucy nodded. 'Having the brocante here will surely bring more people up for the other two businesses and the *pépinère* so it's a win-win all round. We're invited to a barbeque at Owls Nest tomorrow evening, by the way. Briony wants to say thank you for all the help and to celebrate the opening. I'm sad that Giselle died but so happy that Briony and Jeannie have moved into the cottage,' Lucy said. 'Briony and I are starting to become real friends.'

'Elliot seems happier these days too,' Adam said with a questioning look. 'Not that I see much of him now he's working.'

Lucy smiled. 'That's down to Briony, who is also happier than when we first met her.'

'Come on. Let's get back to the farm and have a nightcap on the terrace,' Adam said, 'and you can tell me more about my brother's new relationship.'

'I don't know anything other than they are both happier than they were – and if I did know more, you know I wouldn't tell you anyway,' Lucy said.

44

Friday morning and Briony was up extra early to take Meg for a walk to the lake. Sitting on the bench watching Meg swim in the water, her thoughts drifted to that last entry in the diary. She felt so sad for her great-grandmother. Briony could hardly imagine how different and difficult life had been in those days, living in a patriarchal society where black was black, white was white and there could be no grey in between.

There were birds flitting to and fro in the early-morning sunlight and unexpectedly Briony saw a flash of blue land on a small branch overhanging the lake. She held her breath as the kingfisher sat there for a moment before suddenly taking off, diving to expertly catch a small fish and flying away. Briony smiled. It had to be a good omen to finally see a king-fisher on today of all days.

Elliot stopped by on his way to the practice with flowers, a good luck card and gave her a tight hug and a quick kiss. 'Good luck. I'll try to pop back at mid-day; if not, I'll see you tonight.'

Briony, with Meg on the lead, and Jeannie walked up together to the brocante. The bunting pinned around the entrance was fluttering in the morning breeze. Yann had fixed the newly painted sign de-claring the unit to be 'Briony's Belle Brocante' above the door. The handcart, now filled to capacity with tumbling geraniums, petunias and yellow pansies, had been positioned to one side of the door, the bi-cycle with its overflowing basket of mixed flowers was leant against the side wall. Everything about the brocante brought a smile to Briony's face.

She opened the door and stood for a moment just taking in the scene before her. The parrot cage was hung in the far corner with a huge green fern inside it. There were two of Marie-Louise's paintings, now framed, hung on the wall behind the worktable with its card machine, notebook and pen for writing sales in, and a pile of business cards. Three or four tables had been placed strategically to create a sense of space and room to walk around. Everything for sale had a price tag attached to it. She hoped that people would realise that if there was no price on an item it wasn't for sale. The framed Cannes Film Festival programmes hung on the far wall came into that category, as did Great-granny Marie-Louise's paintings. If the right collector came along, she might be persuaded to sell the Festival programmes, but the paintings would never be sold.

By 10.30 when nobody had appeared, Briony was struggling to stay positive. Jeannie and Holly tried to cheer her up saying it would happen. People would come. And they did.

Between eleven o'clock and twelve thirty, they had fifteen cars appear on the yard. From comments Briony overheard, people were pleased to discover both the artisan workshops as well as the brocante. She smiled as she saw Holly wrapping pottery carefully, several times during the morning. There weren't many sales in the brocante, but people said they would be regular visitors. And Calvin found himself monopolised by a woman in jodhpurs and wax jacket, thrilled that she had found someone local to mend the leather tack for her five horses.

Everyone who came was offered a welcome glass of rosé and Briony handed out her business cards.

Meg spent most of her time under the table nearest the door watching everyone.

Lunchtime was quiet, as expected, and Jeannie handed around salad baguettes and, as everyone had a coffee from her large flask, Lucy appeared with a basket containing cake. She apologised as she handed Briony a large good luck card. 'I'm sorry I didn't make it down earlier, but I hope the morning went well.'

Elliot appeared briefly and snaffled a piece of cake, kissed Briony and was gone again.

The village clock could be heard striking two o'clock as the first of the afternoon customers appeared in the yard. The afternoon was even busier than the morning had been, with people constantly arriving and leaving.

As she closed the doors at five o'clock, Briony reminded Holly and Calvin that they were invited for a barbeque supper at Owls Nest to celebrate opening day and to thank them for their help.

* * *

By seven o'clock, Yann had sausages and pork chops on the barbeque and people were standing or sitting around chatting. The table was full of salads, crisps, cheese, pastries, the champagne was being poured and everyone was relaxed.

Briony looked around and smiled. All her favourite people were in the garden. Jeannie looking happy with Yann at her side. Lucy and Adam were talking to Holly and Calvin, while Carla was playing with Meg, Luna and Django.

Elliot appeared at her side with two glasses of champagne and handed her one. 'Happy?'

Briony nodded. 'There's just one person missing tonight who I wish could be here...' She sighed. 'But if she were, none of this would be happening.' She held out her glass to Elliot and they clinked glasses and Briony said quietly, 'Granny Giselle.'

After everyone had left and Briony and Jeannie had cleared up, they shared a small nightcap together before bed, sitting out on the terrace as dusk fell.

'Granny Giselle would be so proud of you,' Jeannie said quietly. 'You've started to live the life she hoped you'd find in France.'

'I missed her tonight,' Briony said. 'But I think she was here in spirit.' Briony was quiet for a moment as she stared down the garden towards the trees. 'Are you okay about working the brocante tomorrow on your own? I'll pop down in between guests arriving, but I'm not sure how long I'll be able to stay.'

'Yann is coming to keep me company, so don't worry; between us, we will manage. I doubt we will be as busy as we were today.'

'Okay. Oh, Mum, look,' Briony uttered a gasp and held her breath as she saw the head of a tawny owl appear in the hole of the broken branch, pause briefly before launching itself into the air and gliding across the garden. 'Finally, proof that Owls Nest does still have an owl. What a perfect end to the day.'

* * *

Briony and Jeannie walked up to the brocante together with Meg on Saturday morning. They tidied the tables and the shelves, making sure everything looked neat and tidy and putting out some extra stock.

'What time is Yann coming to join you?' Briony asked as she prepared to leave and go to the farm.

'Any time now,' Jeannie said. 'He's going to take Meg for a walk when he gets here.'

'I think there's only one set of guests arriving to-day, so hopefully I'll be able to pop down and check on you mid-morning. I'll see you later.' And Briony made her way up to the farm, hoping it wasn't all going to be too much for her mother.

'The guests in No.2 the Stables left early this morning,' Lucy said. 'No guests in either No.1 or No.2 this current week, sadly. So just one welcome basket to go in the Cider House, plus a quick check around in there as usual, and then if you could do the domestics in No.2. and set it up ready for the next guests.'

'What time are today's guests due?'

'About two o'clock,' Lucy said.

'I'll do the necessary in the Cider House, and then go and have a quick check on Mum in the brocante and then do the Stables. Is that okay with you?' Briony asked.

'Yep, sounds good.'

There were three or four people browsing in the brocante when Briony went down before eleven o'clock. 'Everything all right, Mum?'

Jeannie nodded. 'Yann's gone to the *pèpiniére* with a customer, he'll be back in a moment.'

'I'm on my way to the Stables, so if you need help urgently, maybe give a toot on Yann's car and I'll come straight over.'

As she made her way over to the stables, another car drew up outside the brocante.

Letting herself into the Stables, Briony began to wonder if Saturdays were going to be a problem when all three gîtes were busy. Fingers crossed that she hadn't made a mistake believing that she could open a brocante as well as be Lucy's Girl Friday for the summer.

45

Jeannie's first reaction when Yann told her he'd booked a table at the five-star restaurant in the Carlton Hotel, Cannes, for Sunday lunch was to say no.

'Can't we go on a weekday instead? I worry about leaving Briony on her own in the brocante for the last afternoon of the first weekend.'

'I checked with Elliot and he's not on call so will be around to help. I want us both to have a special memory of the beginning of this special time in our lives,' Yann said, giving her a hug. 'I promise we'll spend the rest of the summer helping Briony whenever she needs it.'

Briony was equally adamant that she should go.

'Ideal opportunity to wear one of Giselle's posh frocks we kept. You haven't had the chance to dress up for ages. Let Yann spoil you and don't worry about me. I doubt that Sunday afternoon will be busy.'

In the end, Jeannie stopped protesting and took the smart black Ralph Lauren frock out of its protective cover. Tying the Hermès scarf around her neck, she was pleased with the result.

'You look beautiful,' Yann said when he arrived to collect her.

'The pair of you make a great-looking couple,' Briony said, agreeing with Yann about her mum and thinking that he looked incredibly smart in his navy suit. 'Enjoy lunch.'

Walking into the Carlton on Yann's arm, Jeannie felt a little apprehensive. It was years since she'd been anywhere half as posh as this place, but Yann was clearly quite at home. Shown to a table out on the terrace, Jeannie slowly relaxed. 'This place is something else, isn't it,' she said quietly, looking around. They were alone for the moment, but Jeannie knew the place would be humming in no time.

'It will be our place for celebrations from now on,' Yann said. 'Jeannie darling, there is something I need to tell you and when I've done that, there is something I want to ask.' He glanced up as a waiter approached. '*S'il vous plaît* – ten minutes?'

The waiter nodded and walked away.

'The other evening on the jetty when I told you I loved you, there was something I forgot to say. I want you to know that I've always wished I'd met you before Jeromé did. Because from the day you and I met, I've loved you from a distance. But...' he shrugged. 'My best friend had already told me you and he were engaged and that you were getting married soon. The unwritten code of our friendship meant that I had to step back. Even though at times I suspected you had feelings for me.'

Jeannie gave a rueful smile. 'I did. And you know now I still do.'

'Do you remember the joke I made about being Jeromé's "best man"?'

'Never forgotten it,' Jeannie said quietly.

'I know you'd hate me to make a fuss and embarrass you here,' Yann said softly. 'Would you give me your left hand, please?'

Jeannie stared at him wide-eyed as she held out her hand.

'Jeannie, will you marry me?'

'Yes,' she answered instantly, with no need to think about it.

Yann slipped a vintage aquamarine and diamond ring onto her finger. 'This belonged to my maman. I was instructed to give it to the woman I truly loved. It was never Evette's. You are the only woman I could ever give it to.' He gave a deep sigh of relief. 'So, it all comes good in the end. This "best man" is finally the one you will marry. And he plans on being at your side for the rest of our lives.'

46

Briony ate her salade niçoise sitting out at the table on the terrace before making her way up with Meg to the brocante ready to open for the first Sunday afternoon. Once there, she left the door ajar and got busy straightening out items and filling gaps where things had sold with replacement items from the box under the table. She wrote reminders in the notebook about sourcing some similar stock of the more popular pieces. Whilst she was busy, Meg made herself at home under the table as usual.

Elliot surprised her turning up just before two o'clock with Luna. 'I thought I'd come and be your assistant this afternoon,' he said, hugging her.

'Thank you. I'm not expecting to be too busy, I

think the weather is so nice people will be making for the beach,' Briony said.

'Then we get to enjoy each other's company,' Elliot said.

The afternoon, as Briony had predicted, was the quietest day of the opening weekend, with no more than ten customers making their way up to the brocante. A couple turned up for the *pépinière* and Elliot dealt with them.

As she locked the door at five o'clock, Elliot glanced at her. 'Fancy celebrating the success of the first weekend of the brocante being open with a huge ice-cream and a stroll along Cannes harbour?'

'I think that's a brilliant idea,' Briony said. 'Some sea air.'

A quarter of an hour later, Elliot had squeezed the Toyota into a small parking space near the harbour and they were strolling along the quay with the dogs on their leads, enjoying a large ice-cream each – pistachio for Elliot and caramel cream for Briony. One of the Îles de Lérins tourist boats had unloaded passengers back from a visit to the islands and the quay was crowded, separating Briony and Elliot for several moments.

Briony knew that the crowd would soon disperse back into Cannes and Elliot would be at her side again in minutes, so she slowed her pace before stopping to look across the harbour at the large luxury yachts moored there, and waited. She'd taken the last bite of her ice-cream cone when her body went rigid with shock at the sound of a loud familiar voice as its owner made their way along the quay. Briony held her breath and stayed perfectly still, hoping that she wouldn't be noticed.

'Thought I'd lost you for a moment with that crowd,' Elliot said, touching her arm, making her jump. 'What's the matter? You're trembling and you're very pale. Do you feel ill from the ice cream?'

She shook her head. 'No. I just heard a voice I never wanted to hear again. I'll be fine in a moment.'

Elliot put his arm around her and turned as the shout of 'Briony, it is you. Fancy seeing you here.' And the owner of the voice bore down on them.

'You down here visiting Granny again in that godforsaken village somewhere up in the hills?' Marcus had clearly been enjoying a boozy lunch and was well on the way to being drunk.

'Marcus.' Briony stared at him, willing him to go away, hating the inquisitive looks passers-by were giving the three of them, wishing that she was safely back at the cottage.

Marcus suddenly registered that she wasn't alone

and that a man had his arm around her shoulders. 'Are you with him now?' he demanded, jerking his head in Elliot's direction. When she didn't answer, he turned to Elliot. 'Always did think she was better than she is. I was married to this woman and now she ignores me, won't deign to talk to me.'

'I wonder why that is,' Elliot said, an edge to his voice. Silently, he held out Luna's lead to Briony, which she took after a quick anxious glance at him.

'Oh, been filling your head with nonsense about her ex-husband, has she? Well, let me tell you, matey, it was me that divorced her, not the other way round – couldn't take any more of her whinging. You're welcome to her, mate, that is all I can say.'

Elliot leant in to Marcus and swiftly grabbed a fistful of his shirt and blazer and pulled him close. Holding him firmly, he looked Marcus in the eyes and spoke slowly and deliberately. 'I am not your mate. I am your sworn enemy from this day. If you ever come near Briony again, I promise you, you will regret it. You are a despicable drunken man and I have a mind to inform the two gendarmes who are walking this way that you've been drunkenly disturbing the peace. Here in Cannes they don't like that kind of behaviour and you might find yourself in a cell for a few hours to sober up. So I suggest you scarper when I let you go. Or perhaps I'll keep you here and let them deal with you?' Elliot said thoughtfully.

Marcus glared at Elliot before wrenching himself free. He was lost in the crowd before the gendarmes reached Briony and Elliot.

'Did we have a problem here?' one of the gendarmes asked.

'No, officer. Just a man who can't hold his drink.'

Elliot took Luna's lead from Briony and, holding her by the hand, said, 'Come on, let's get you home.'

Sitting in the car as Elliot drove them home, Briony sighed. 'I feel such a fool for just standing there, but I simply blanked out when he appeared. I didn't know what to do. I am so glad I wasn't alone. Thank you.'

Owls Nest was empty when Elliot dropped her and Meg off. He didn't want to leave her, but she insisted she was fine, kissed him goodbye and told him she'd see him tomorrow evening down by the lake.

Briony sat out in the garden, Meg at her feet, after Elliot had reluctantly left her, determined to push all thoughts of Marcus out of her mind once and for all. She'd come a long way in the last few weeks and now had so much to look forward to. Her own business, good friends and best of all she and Elliot were at the beginning of a relationship that she knew was based on true love. Seeing a drunken Marcus so unexpectedly had been a massive shock. After she'd left him and started divorce proceedings, for months she'd dreaded the possibility of bumping into him everywhere she went in Bristol, but not once had that happened. Strangely it had never occurred to her it could be down here that he would appear in her life again.

But she was determined that it was now a life that Marcus would never again be allowed to influence or to be a part of.

47

When Briony stumbled out of bed the next morning and made her way to the kitchen after a fitful night's sleep, Jeannie was humming to herself as she made coffee and toast.

'Someone sounds happy,' Briony said.

'That's because I am,' Jeannie said, holding out her hand to show Briony her ring. 'Yann asked me to marry him yesterday – and I said yes.'

'Oh Mum, that's such a beautiful ring. Congratulations. I'm so happy for you and Yann.'

Jeannie looked at her curiously. 'Thank you. You look terrible. Didn't you sleep?'

'Not very well. I had a nasty shock in Cannes yesterday.'

Jeannie poured two coffees and handed one to Briony. 'Tell me.'

'Elliot and I went down for a celebratory ice cream and Marcus put in a drunken appearance. But it was so unexpected and horrible I just went to pieces.'

'What did Elliot say or do?'

'Grabbed him by his shirt and jacket and threatened him if he ever came near me again he'd be sorry. Then let him go before the patrolling gendarmes could arrest him for drunken behaviour.'

'Good for Elliot. Does Marcus know you live down here now?'

'I don't think so because he muttered about visiting Granny and was rude about the cottage and down here.'

'At least Elliot has got the measure of him now, so I should just put it out of your mind. Forget you ever knew the horrible man. You're building a good new start here and you've got Elliot in your life now. And he's a good man.'

'That's another thing. What kind of woman must he think I am having got involved with someone like Marcus?'

'The woman he was involved with wasn't exactly

a good woman from what we hear,' Jeannie said. 'So he will know exactly how easy it is to get involved with the wrong person. He's not going to judge you for a bad marriage, he's going to have empathy for you because he's been there.'

Listening to her mum, Briony began to feel better. She knew Elliot had been through a public hell with Robyn, that's why he had been so hesitant about getting to know her in the beginning. He'd been wary of being hurt again. Her own broken marriage had been a private hell, but it had made her equally cautious about starting another relationship. Something special was developing between her and Elliot and she knew she'd never forgive herself if she didn't nurture it and allow them both to love again. But before that could happen, she had to talk to Elliot and tell him the truth.

* * *

Monday evening, Briony, Jeannie and Yann were sitting out in the garden enjoying a glass of champagne which Briony had insisted on opening to toast their engagement when Elliot and Luna turned up at the garden gate.

'Luna wants to know if Meg can come out and play early tonight?' he said, laughing.

Briony smiled. 'Of course she can. But first come and join us for a glass of champagne. We're celebrating.'

'We haven't had the chance to tell anyone yet,' Jeannie said. 'But yesterday Yann asked me to marry him and I accepted.'

'Congratulations to you both,' Elliot said. 'I wish you every happiness.'

When Briony and Elliot eventually set off for the lake, they let both dogs off the lead and they bounded away along the path. Elliot reached for her hand as they walked and Briony willingly hooked her fingers around his.

'Jeannie and Yann look so happy,' Elliot said.

'I'm really pleased for them both,' Briony said. 'They've known each other for years. I'm not sure if you know, but Yann was my dad's childhood friend and is actually my godfather. Mum is really happy to have a special person in her life again.'

The dogs were already splashing around in the lake when Briony and Elliot reached the bench and sat down.

'How about you, are you all right after yesterday's

incident?' Elliot asked, sitting back and putting his arm around Briony's shoulders, pulling her close.

'Yes,' Briony said, leaning into him. 'I've talked it through with Mum and she insists I have to put it and Marcus behind me. And she is right, I do. But I also need to talk to you about why I have somewhat barbaric thoughts about Marcus. We both need to know the truth about each other's past relationships. You've already confided in me and I want to tell you about my marriage.'

Elliot squeezed her shoulders gently. 'I'm listening.'

'My mum is under the impression that I left Marcus and divorced him because of our "irreconcilable differences". They were part of the reason my marriage failed but not the whole truth. And, by the way, I divorced him, not the other way round, like he told you yesterday. I don't want Mum to ever hear about the main reasons, okay?'

Elliot nodded.

'I've always wanted a family. When Marcus and I married, I thought that was what he wanted too. Turns out that was the first lie. He doesn't like children. Didn't intend to ever have any. But he didn't say any of this in the beginning. We agreed to wait for a couple of years before trying for a family, which I was fine with at the time. When I finally said we'd waited long enough and I wanted to try for a baby, he laughed in my face. Because at sometime during those years, he'd had a vasectomy without my knowledge.'

Briony was silent for several seconds.

'I was devastated on several counts, the fact that he'd lied, the fact that he'd gone behind my back for the operation and the fact that if I stayed with him, I would never have the child – children – I wanted. I hadn't been particularly happy in the marriage before all this blew up, Marcus was a bit of a verbal bully and difficult to live with. So I finally plucked up the courage and left him. I probably won't be able to have the children I wanted as I'm getting on a bit – a geriatric in the maternal world.' Briony gave a short laugh. 'But at least I'm not living with false hope eating away at me any more.'

'Briony, come here,' and Elliot pulled her into his arms and held her tight. 'I'm so sorry for what you've gone through, but I promise you I'll never lie to you about anything, nor ever treat you so horribly. I know it's early days, but I've fallen in love with you.' He kept her in his arms, before tilting his face towards her and kissing her.

It was only the arrival of two soaking wet dogs they didn't see or hear coming minutes later who showered them both with cold water that drew them apart. 'That will teach us to mind the dogs,' Briony muttered, leaning in again for one last kiss.

48

CHRISTMAS EVE, SIX MONTHS LATER

'Hannah. Debs. Hurry up. Briony and Elliot are expecting us at seven o'clock and it's already quarter-to. You know how I hate being late.'

'Two minutes, Mum,' Hannah called out. 'Debs is having a mini crisis with her hair. You can always go on down without us – we know the way.'

'Shall we do that?' Lucy said, turning to Adam, who was in his usual place at the kitchen table looking at his laptop.

He shook his head. 'No. We'll walk down *en famille* with Django.' He glanced at Lucy. 'I've just been looking through the accounts for the year. It's been a good one all round. The grape harvest was good and the reports from the co-op indicate that our wine is going to be the best we have produced.'

'Brilliant news. *La vendage* was hard work, but that makes it all worthwhile.'

Adam nodded. 'I think we'll bite the bullet next year and start to invest in all things necessary to produce the wine on the farm. And then in another year we'll have our own wine label.'

'That will please Bruno,' Lucy said. 'How about the avocados? I know we unexpectedly harvested some this year but not enough to sell.'

'Next year will be better,' Adam said. 'Have you looked at your accounts for the gîtes yet for the year?'

Lucy laughed. 'I don't have to. I know we've had a brilliant year. Briony and her spreadsheets give me a monthly update, profit and loss, and a marketing assessment. Those advertorials in the glossy magazines really paid their way. Briony's been brilliant. Not sure how I'm going to manage without her next year.'

Adam gave her a horrified look. 'Why? I thought the arrangement worked well for both of you.'

'She told me this week that she's resigning after Christmas because she wants to concentrate on the brocante and other things. I can't complain because she was only supposed to be my Girl Friday for the summer and now it's the end of the year.'

'Can't you tempt her to do another summer?'

Lucy shook her head. 'No. And it wouldn't be fair to her. She's got a new life to live with Elliot now as well as running the brocante.'

* * *

Yann's house in the village sold at the end of summer. Currently, he and Jeannie were renting the nineteenth-century 'maison de maître' in the village, which Jeannie absolutely adored. Jeannie had persuaded Yann that an apartment in Cannes, whilst lovely, wouldn't have a garden and as they both loved gardening it would be rather silly to buy something like that. She was rather hoping that he would like the news she heard in the village today.

As she gave her wrists and neck a quick squirt of her favourite perfume, Joy, she smiled at Yann, who was looking at her with the loving expression she saw on his face every day. 'I am so lucky,' he said. 'Sometimes I pinch myself to make sure my life now isn't a dream.'

'We are both lucky,' Jeannie said, giving him a quick kiss. 'Both our lives are so different, so much better than this time last year.'

'And to think, in seven days we're finally getting married,' Yann said.

'I can't wait,' Jeannie said.

Now as they both got ready to go up to Owls Nest for Christmas Eve aperitifs and stay over and spend Christmas Day itself with Briony and Elliot, Jeannie asked, 'Do you know what I was told in the village today?'

Yann shook his head. 'No. Will I like it? Tell me.'

'We can buy this house if we want to in the New Year.'

She waited for his reaction.

'I'm guessing that is what we want, *n'est pas*?' Yann asked with a huge smile. 'The next step. A home we create together.'

'Oh, I do want it so much,' Jeannie said.

'Then it is decided. We buy it.'

'Thank you,' Jeannie said reaching up to give him a lingering kiss.

* * *

Briony pulled the last batch of mince pies out of the oven and left them on the side to cool. Taking her apron off, she hung it on the back of the kitchen door out of the way. Time for one last look around the cottage to make sure everything was ready before everyone arrived.

She and Elliot had decorated Owls Nest with all the decorations she remembered from her childhood, as well as some new ones from the big Christmas market down on Cannes quay. There was a large tree in the sitting room, again decorated with things she remembered from her childhood. Christmas carols were playing in the background.

Standing by one of the French doors looking out over the garden, she saw Elliot busy winding Christmas lights around some of the trees. Not the owl tree though in case the lights disturbed the owls who had shown themselves several times over the summer and Briony loved watching them.

Elliot saw her watching and gave a wave before disappearing into another part of the garden.

Briony's thoughts turned to how her life had changed during the last year. Life had slipped into a happy routine – working at the brocante three full days and two days up at the farm. She and Lucy had formed a firm friendship and she knew Lucy was sad that next year wouldn't be the same.

The summer season had been busy, but there had been a good life/work balance – she and Elliot had made time for getting to know each other properly and she had no doubt that they loved each other. At the end of the summer season when Jeannie had moved in with Yann, Briony had asked Elliot if he'd like to move into Owls Nest. To her joy, Elliot had been more than happy to accept.

'Everything ready for our first Christmas party?' Elliot asked as he walked into the sitting room and put his arms around her.

'Hope so, everyone will be here soon.'

'Julian wanted to talk to me today,' Elliot said quietly.

Briony glanced at him. 'Nothing serious?'

'It was actually,' Elliot said. 'He wanted to know if I would be interested in becoming a partner in the practice.'

'What did you say?' Briony was fairly certain she knew what his answer would have been.

'I said yes of course. Best Christmas present ever.'

'Um, I shouldn't be too sure about that,' Briony said, wondering whether now would be a good time to tell him the secret she'd been hugging to herself until she'd been one hundred per cent certain. She had planned to tell him tonight after midnight mass in the village church, but maybe now would be better. It was a secret which she knew he would be as happy about as she was.

She leant in and whispered in his ear and knew she would never forget the look on Elliot's face as he heard the two words 'I'm pregnant'. With a whoop of joy, he pulled her into his arms and held her tight.

This time next year they would be a family. And secretly, if it was a girl, Briony hoped Elliot would like the name Marie-Louise.

* * *

MORE FROM JENNIFER BOHNET

Another book from Jennifer Bohnet, *Secrets Beneath a Riviera Sky*, is available to order now here: https://mybook.to/SecretsBeneathBackAd

AUTHOR'S NOTE

All the characters in this book are from my imagination with the exception of one, Elsa Maxwell. She was quite a high-profile figure in the first half of the twentieth century, both in America, England and France. She was a mixture of journalist, pianist, party arranger, composer, author and many other things, and did indeed mix with the rich and famous, including royalty. She was a fascinating character, if little known now in the twenty-first century. A fun fact about her: she is credited with organising the first treasure hunt by car in London. If you're interested in reading more about her:

The Celebrity Circus. Elsa Maxwell. W.H. Allen. 1964

Inventing Elsa Maxwell. Sam Staggs. St. Martin's Press. 2012

ACKNOWLEDGEMENTS

Huge thanks as always to the Boldwood Team for all their hard work. Caroline Ridding, my editor, Jade the copy editor and Rachel Sargeant the proofreader, in particular for their patience with this technology-challenged writer. Thanks to all the bloggers and to Rachel Gilbey, blog tour organiser extraordinaire. Big thanks go to Sue Baker of Riveting Reads and Vintage Vibes who held a launch day party for me which was great fun.

Thanks to Richard, my husband, who picks up the slack in the kitchen and the housework I repeatedly fail to do because 'I'm on a deadline' and lets me use him as a sounding board when I hit a plot block!

And thanks of course to all my readers who make it all worthwhile. Thank you, one and all.

Love, Jennie x

ABOUT THE AUTHOR

Jennifer Bohnet is the bestselling author of over 14 women's fiction titles, including *Villa of Sun and Secrets* and *A Riviera Retreat*. She is originally from the West Country but now lives in the wilds of rural Brittany, France.

Sign up to Jennifer Bohnet's mailing list here for news, competitions and updates on future books.

Visit Jennifer's website: www.jenniferbohnet.com

Follow Jennifer on social media:

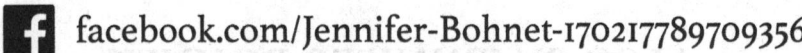

ALSO BY JENNIFER BOHNET

Villa of Sun and Secrets

A Riviera Retreat

Rendez-Vous in Cannes

A French Affair

One Summer in Monte Carlo

Summer at the Château

Falling for a French Dream

Villa of Second Chances

Christmas on the Riviera

Making Waves at River View Cottage

Summer on the French Riviera

High Tides and Summer Skies

A French Adventure

A French Country Escape

Secrets Beneath a Riviera Sky

A French Inheritance

Boldwood

Boldwood Books is an award-winning fiction publishing company seeking out the best stories from around the world.

Find out more at www.boldwoodbooks.com

Join our reader community for brilliant books, competitions and offers!

Follow us
@BoldwoodBooks
@TheBoldBookClub

Sign up to our weekly deals newsletter

https://bit.ly/BoldwoodBNewsletter

www.ingramcontent.com/pod-product-compliance
Lightning Source LLC
Chambersburg PA
CBHW010856130726
47900CB00017B/2739